"Who the hell
Sister Bridget. "How did you get in here?" He reeked of body odor, urine, and sour alcohol.

Devil, we meet. Sister Bridget stood, bat in hand, determined to hold her ground. Jesus gave his disciples power to cast out demons, and though she was certain that this man was evil incarnate, she was not confident she could cast it out. She felt emboldened by the Holy Spirit though. "Alejandro, I know you had a difficult childhood. The horrible things that happened to you were not fair. Those abuses were not your fault, and it's not too late to turn your life around."

El Gigante threw the two girls to the ground, smirked, and relished bringing his big boot down, crushing Araceli's leg. The girl screamed and sobbed. Leticia scrambled to her friend's side. The giant then turned to Sister Bridget. He laughed, taking pleasure in his cruelty.

"I have come to get these girls. Give them to me without any trouble!" Sister Bridget imagined Jesus' disciples standing with her, shouting with her.

Bring the Light

by

Annette Montez Kolda

Bring the Light

Cover Art by *Diana Carlile*

The Wild Rose Press, Inc.
PO Box 708
Adams Basin, NY 14410-0708
Visit us at www.thewildrosepress.com

Publishing History
First Edition, 2022
Trade Paperback ISBN 978-1-5092-4217-7
Digital ISBN 978-1-5092-4218-4

Published in the United States of America

Dedication

For Meredith

Acknowledgments

Much gratitude to The Wild Rose Press for believing in *Bring the Light*. Thanks especially to my editor, Ally Robertson, whose insights about point-of-view transformed my narrative.

Thank you to my wonderful beta readers: Maryjane Kennedy, Melissa Gravett, Meredith Anglin, Christopher Chapa, and Willie Montez. And thanks most of all to my super beta reader, my husband, Dr. Tim Kolda.

In medical matters, my two friends, Dr. Anna Lozano and Dr. Michael Breen, were invaluable.

My lawyer friends, Rosanne Easton and Rita Morales Naranjo, provided great insights and information in legal matters.

I'm thankful for the opportunity to write a story of love that derives from the human interaction of crossing barriers.

Chapter 1

Sister Bridget prayed each morning as she jogged the dark streets of East Austin. And upon returning to the grounds of Our Lady of Guadalupe Church, she concluded with a plea. One that had been etched upon her heart thirty-eight years ago. *God bless the victims of crime and violence in this world.* Clutching her rosary beads with sweaty fingers, she touched its tiny crucifix to her forehead, then the center, left and right of her chest, tracing the sign of the cross. She kissed the miniature corpus that clung upon the silver cross and tucked the rosary into the pocket of her damp sweatshirt. The sun had not yet risen, but the July morning was already getting hot. Her companion, a wiry terrier named Milagro, ran off into the darkness, his nose to the ground.

Sister Bridget whistled, but when the little dog didn't return, she followed the rocky steps down the bushy garden path. For a sizable, middle-aged woman who was almost six feet tall, the descent was ponderous. The trail led to the Mary grotto, a rocky, cave-like structure with an open front. Dozens of candles in colorful glass holders flickered there, casting soft shadows upon a statue of the Virgin Mary cloaked in green and gold. Milagro paced excitedly in the dancing candlelight. He whimpered and sniffed at a lumpy thing on the ground. Perhaps a cat or a squirrel?

Whatever it was didn't move. The poor creature was probably injured…or worse.

"Milagro! Shush…quiet boy." The thing on the ground twitched as Sister Bridget bent near. *Blessed Mother Mary.* It was a baby. She knelt and leaned in for a closer look, and the baby let out a sharp cry. Sister Bridget flinched. The infant's slick skin glistened in the candlelight, completely exposed. She pulled her sweatshirt off and wrapped the baby in it. Taking the child, she hurried across the church lawn. "Shh." She cooed and patted the baby's back, her heart pounding against the child's body. "Oh dear, dear, dear." Fretting, she fumbled for her key, grateful for the light that she kept on at her little house. She lived alone on the edge of the parish grounds.

She rushed through the door, flipped on the light, and took a good look at the child. The baby fidgeted and wailed. Its sharp peal buzzed and vibrated Sister Bridget's eardrum.

"Jesus, Mary and Joseph. This baby is tiny. Just born." Sister Bridget was a midwife. She knew a newborn when she saw one.

She held the baby snug against her shoulder, grabbed a quilt off her bed, and folded it over a few times on the couch. She set the squalling infant on the blanket and removed the damp sweatshirt. A girl. Her plump umbilical cord had been raggedly cut or bitten. Still covered in smeary clots of blood and the white, waxy vernix of birth, the baby flailed and bawled, her face red and swollen, her thick, black hair damp from birth. Sister Bridget wrapped the child in the huge blanket and thought of the Virgin Mary who once wrapped baby Jesus in swaddling clothes.

Cradling the infant, Sister Bridget gazed at the child's tiny face. The baby quieted and probed Sister Bridget with dark, animated eyes. Cooing with perfect pink lips, the infant fluttered her arms gently. *Oh God, how wondrous.* Sister Bridget held the newborn to her bosom. No matter how many babies she'd delivered, each was a miracle to her. The child's mother *must* be close. Maybe watching to see if the baby was safe. Sister Bridget imagined a scared mother out in the dark somewhere.

She called 911, and then she called MaryAnn Solis, a young mother who lived on the other block. MaryAnn arrived before the police.

"Sister Bridget?" MaryAnn looked sleepy and stunned. "What's...I mean..." She shook her head and ran her fingers through her long, tangled hair. "I came as fast as I could. Did Daniel hear you right? He said you *found a baby?*" The petite young woman had come straight from bed wearing a Dallas Cowboys t-shirt that reached to her knees and pink flip-flops. She pushed her thick hair behind her ear, and a large, overflowing diaper bag slipped off her shoulder.

"Your husband heard me correctly, *mija.*" Sister Bridget lightly swayed the infant. "Milagro found the baby in the grotto."

"Oh, my G...what? Milagro *found* it?" She stared at the bundle in Sister Bridget's arms. "*Milagro*? Your little dog?" She glanced at the dog, who sat perfectly still, only shifting his glance. "Whose baby *is* this?" The young woman looked to the door through which she had entered. She lifted and peeked under the blanket. "Wow. Just born. This poor little...uh..." She lifted the blanket again. "Girl."

"Did you bring diapers, dear?"

MaryAnn stared mutely at the newfound infant.

"MaryAnn. *Mija*, did you bring diapers?"

The young woman blinked and nodded. "Yeah. Oh yeah. Yeah. I got diapers, and formula…I think…" She set her bag of supplies on the floor, took the baby, and placed her onto the couch.

Sister Bridget rummaged through her kitchen drawer for a flashlight. "I telephoned the police. They'll arrive shortly."

MaryAnn nestled the baby's bottom onto a disposable diaper and was about to wipe its torso with a soft cloth.

"Don't clean the baby off, dear. Let EMS do that. They'll need to collect evidence in order to identify the child and determine when she was born." Sister Bridget had learned a bit about pathology in medical school.

MaryAnn swaddled the newborn in a receiving blanket from her own child's supplies. "Well, hi, sweet pumpkin." The young mother smiled and cooed. The baby fussed; MaryAnn gently bounced and swayed her.

"The police and paramedics should be here in…" Sister Bridget looked at her watch. "…one and a half minutes, if I calculate correctly."

With the child in MaryAnn's care, and with flashlight in hand, Sister Bridget set off to find the baby's mother.

The infant wailed. "But…so…wait. Should I…" MaryAnn stammered, raking through her diaper bag. "I can't find the formu—"

Sister Bridget couldn't wait. With Milagro at her heels, she glanced back at MaryAnn who was settling onto the sofa to breastfeed the screaming child. *Good mama*, Sister Bridget thought as she closed the door behind her.

Outside, jarring police sirens pierced the darkness, and then quit. Silent APD cruisers and EMS vehicles cast blue and red beams upon the slumbering neighborhood. Sister Bridget kept her flashlight off so the officers wouldn't question her. That would slow her down. Behind the church, out of sight of the emergency responders, she followed the garden path to the candlelit grotto.

Who could have left that child all alone? She shined the flashlight upon the statue of the Virgin Mary whose hands were folded in prayer, eyes downcast. Milagro sniffed the spot where the baby had lain.

Hearing faint moans, she ventured into the darkness at the side and back of the rock grotto. Stopping to listen, she cast her light about, following the sound through the overgrown hedges. A chain-linked fence separated the grotto's gardens from the parish school's practice field.

"Is someone there?" She squinted into the darkness. As she cast her light beyond the chain-linked fence to the left side of the field, movement caught her attention on the right, and she swung her flashlight in that direction.

"Hello! Who's there?"

Tossing the flashlight over the fence, she gained footing on the chain links and clambered over. She landed crouching on both feet and ran toward the noise, slipping on the dewy grass, the fence clanging behind her. Milagro ran the periphery of the fence to the open gate on the other side.

Her flashlight cast a shaky glow, and she caught a

glimpse of someone beyond the soccer field. Whoever it was disappeared around the back of the wooden playscape. She could hear the crunch of the playground's pea gravel. Sister Bridget ran faster to catch up, but there was no one there. Only Milagro. The little dog jumped, chased his tail, and barked.

"Shush. Quiet boy." She held a finger to her lips and stood still to listen, but heard only the crackle of a police radio, car doors, and voices coming from the direction of her little house. She turned to go back. But there it was again, a soft lamentation. She turned and called out, "Who's there? Wait. Stay where you are. I'm coming to you." She followed the sound and caught sight of a trail of blood that led to the little chapel that was attached to the parish offices.

The recessed area at the entrance to the chapel was dark, but the door was ajar, propped open with a backpack. Candlelight shone through.

Sister Bridget called upon the Holy Spirit and entered the small worship space. Milagro knew to wait outside. She flipped a switch. Stark florescent lighting flooded the small space.

And there, on the tiled floor, before the stone altar, lay a woman in a pool of blood.

Sister Bridget knelt by her side. There was no possible way this woman could have been the same person she'd been chasing. There was too much blood. The woman lay in a fetal position, her thick, black hair veiling her face. Careful not to move her head and neck, Sister Bridget lifted thick strands of sweaty hair to reveal the face of a young girl, possibly a teenager. The girl's mouth hung open slightly; her eyes were closed.

"Dear. Wake up." Sister Bridget smoothed the

girl's hair. "Sweetheart." *Oh, my Jesus.* Sister Bridget looked to the tabernacle behind the altar and pleaded, *help.* The girl's lower half looked like a body-shaped sponge soaked in blood. She wore jeans, sneakers, and a t-shirt. Sister Bridget lifted the girl's bloody wrist and felt for a pulse. But she'd lost so much blood, Sister Bridget couldn't even detect a heartbeat.

She placed two fingers, which were now covered in blood, on the girl's carotid artery, and there, she felt a weak beat. *Thank you, Jesus.* She went to the doorway and shouted for the police. Then, she turned to the girl. "I'll return shortly. I'm going for help."

But as Sister Bridget passed through the door, she heard footsteps in the gravel again. Someone was running in the play yard. Shouts rang out and a blinding light shone. Milagro barked angrily.

A male voice rang out in the darkness. "Hold it! Stop right there. Put it down." Sister Bridget looked down at the flashlight she held in her bloody hand.

"Drop it! I said drop it! Put your hands up where I can see them!" The commands were those of a police officer. Shushing Milagro, Sister Bridget dropped her flashlight to the ground, raised her hands, and squinted into the intense light.

"There's a girl needing hel—"

The gruff voice cut her off. "Keep your hands up. Don't move." Three police officers approached with guns drawn. They stared at her bloody hands and clothing.

Chapter 2

"Oh, this is…um, not what you might think." Sister Bridget, looked down at her bloody clothing, illuminated by the police flashlights. "There's a young girl in the chapel. The baby's mother. Hemorrhage. Probably caused by a retained placenta. She'll die if she doesn't get treatment immediately."

"Hold it. Keep your hands where we can see them. Wait here." The officer gestured to the other two. "Keep her here." He entered the chapel. "Holy moly…" Hearing this worried Sister Bridget even more. The officer emerged, speaking into his shoulder mic. "This is Officer in Charge, Sergeant Rios. We need EMS over here *now*. The little church on the other side of the playground. Not the main church. We got the baby's mother. She's bleeding pretty bad." Then he addressed a female officer. "Show EMS where we're at." He let out a breath. "Who's the girl? What's she doing in there?"

"I don't know *who* she is." Sister Bridget lowered her hands and took a step toward the chapel.

"Hold it. I said hold it." The officer pointed his gun at her. "Keep your hands up."

She raised her hands again. *I must be a sight,* she thought.

"Officers, I'm Sister Bridget Ann Rincón-Keller. I'm a religious sister."

"A religious *sister*? You mean like a nun?" Sergeant Rios cast his flashlight to her bloody clothing again. Milagro barked angrily. "Whose blood is that? Is it yours? Are you all right?"

"The blood is from the girl. I was checking for a pulse. And I saw someone running on the playground." Sister Bridget wanted to mention it while that person might still be close by.

"You saw someone? Who? What did they look like? Was it a man or a woman?" Rios took out a notebook.

"I don't know. It's too dark. I couldn't tell."

"Oh. I know who you are," said a young officer. "You're Sister Bridget." She was known as a bit of a crime solver in East Austin's Latino neighborhood. "I remember you found that missing girl." The red-headed officer spoke with enthusiasm. "The one that ran off with her high school coach."

Sister Bridget had an ear to the ground. If people or items went missing, or vandalism occurred, she was known to yank an ear or two. In the case of the missing teenager, Sister Bridget had followed clues and tracked the girl and her coach to a little-used motel on the interstate.

"Indeed. May I go to the girl now?" Sister Bridget worried about the girl in the chapel.

"Wait. What about this person you say you saw? Where'd you see him? Or her? Which way did he go? What was he wearing?" Sergeant Rios asked.

"Like I said, I don't know if it was a male or female. He *or she* was running on the playground toward the parish office." She stopped and thought about it. "No, I couldn't tell you what the person was wearing. I followed, and when I got to the office, there was no one there." Had she imagined seeing someone running? There was no possibility it could have been the girl, judging by the shape in which she'd found her. "Then I heard the girl and saw that the chapel door was open." It was as if someone had led her to the girl, but she didn't express that thought. It was just a feeling she had.

Sergeant Rios addressed the young officer. "Check out the church grounds. I'll call in back-up and get a cruiser to patrol the area. Whoever it was might still be hanging around."

He allowed Sister Bridget to go to the girl. She hurried in and stroked the young woman's hair. "Help is coming. Hold on, dear. Your little girl needs you. Hold on." She looked at her watch, tempted to manually remove the girl's placenta herself. Such a procedure might cause infection, but infections were treatable. Death was not.

Then paramedics entered the little chapel followed by Father Bartosh, Our Lady of Guadalupe's plump, little pastor. The priest was dressed in black clerics, his collar sticking out, his shirt half tucked. Sister Bridget stood back with the old Polish priest to make room for the emergency workers. The paramedics stabilized the girl's neck and turned her onto her back.

"I suspect she has a retained placenta. She is in hemorrhagic shock." Sister Bridget clasped her hands nervously. The paramedics glanced at her without pausing. One giving the girl oxygen, another preparing an I.V., and the third cutting away the girl's bloody jeans.

"This poor girl gave birth and left her baby at the

grotto," Sister Bridget told Father Bartosh.

The little priest looked up at Sister Bridget. He squinted his blue eyes. "What's hemorrhagic shock?"

"Loss of consciousness due to loss of blood." She spoke in a low voice, trying not to distract the paramedics.

"Oh, sweet Jesus." Father Bartosh sighed and rubbed his bald head, looking about. "Where's the baby? Is it alive? Did it die?"

"The baby is alive. She's at my residence, in MaryAnn Solis's charge."

"Come with me, Sister." Father Bartosh tugged at Sister Bridget's arm. "Let's let the paramedics do their job."

She resisted.

"Let's get some air. Let the professionals do their job." Father Bartosh placed his arm around her waist and took her hand. His head reached to her shoulder. Sister Bridget relented and walked out into the fresh, new morning. The sun cast scant, pink rays, enough to turn the world gray.

A wren's high-pitched melody pierced the morning like a canticle. Her little dog, Milagro, barked, leapt, and sniffed at Sister Bridget's bloodstained clothing.

The parish was abuzz. Police gathered information and took pictures. Neighbors congregated at the curb with MaryAnn, as she wiped her eyes and watched the ambulance go. MaryAnn's husband, Daniel, dressed in workman's clothes, passed their young son to MaryAnn. She buried her face on Daniel's shoulder, their toddler snug between them.

As the ambulance pulled away, another arrived.

Sergeant Rios joined Sister Bridget and Father

Bartosh by the chapel. "They're taking the baby to the hospital. Crying at the top of her lungs. What I know about babies, that seems normal."

Sister Bridget introduced the sergeant to the priest. Rios waved a blue-gloved hand. In his other hand, he carried the backpack that had propped open the chapel door.

"Is the girl's identification in there?" Sister Bridget inclined her head toward the backpack.

"We'll see." Rios held up the backpack, turning it side to side, inspecting it. "We'll hand it over to Evidence. They'll give it a good look. Fingerprints and such." He placed the backpack in a large plastic bag. "We'll need to talk to the girl when she recovers."

If she recovers, Sister Bridget thought.

She certainly knew the severity of a retained placenta. After college, she'd graduated from medical school, but her path diverged, and she became a religious sister instead of a medical doctor. And though she had only been a midwife for a year now, she had delivered plenty of babies.

****

Sister Bridget dropped her bloody garments onto the floor of the steamy shower and scrubbed her hands and knees. Red suds circled the drain and disappeared.

She made haste, wanting to get to the hospital to check on the girl and the baby. But accounting for all the items of her black and white habit proved arduous, as usual.

Impatiently, she struggled with the numerous items of her religious habit. First her undergarments, then the white, ankle-length tunic with which she had continually grappled. "Why on earth do they make tunics for religious sisters with zippers on the back?" Milagro lay in a sunbeam on Sister Bridget's bedroom floor, his head resting on his paws. She reached behind her back, grasped for, and missed the elusive slider. "For a woman with no earthly spouse...how do they expect..." Twisting her arm behind her back, she finally gripped the zipper, and tugged hard.

She paused to catch her breath. Looking into the mirror, she saw vestiges of her mother and father. They had been physicians in Mexico City. Her height and fair skin, she'd inherited from her German mother, an imposing figure who carried her doctor's bag to palaces and slums. Her brown eyes and curly, black hair matched that of her Mexican father. Though now her hair was flecked with gray.

After rubbing her hair with a towel and brushing it, she placed a black, two-sided, apron-like scapular over her white tunic. On her belt, she hung her silver and black rosary beads. She placed her white cowl over her neck and shoulders, securing it with snaps. Lastly, she positioned her white coif onto her damp curls and neatly attached her black veil.

Grabbing her bible, she hurried out the door, heading for the little chapel where she liked to worship, but it was cordoned off with yellow police tape. She tried the wrought iron bench at the Mary grotto, but it too was blocked off. She prayed there anyway. She sat crossed legged on the grass, outside the police tape, while officers conducted their tasks. She gazed upon the spot where Milagro had found the baby. Then sighing, she gave her full attention to her beloved, her divine spouse. Opening her prayer book, she read of Elijah's encounter with God. Elijah heard God's voice not in the forceful wind, nor the powerful earthquake, nor the blazing fire. Rather, the prophet Elijah encountered God in a tiny, whispering sound. Then he hid his face in wonder and awe. Sister Bridget closed her eyes and thought of the words of the psalmist, *be still and know that I am God.* Enveloped by that *knowing*, like a sea creature in its life-giving ocean, her heart swelled.

She reflected on the tiny baby's perfectly formed fingers, her toes, her little round face, and sentient eyes. What a joy to behold. Like the whisper that Elijah heard. She too felt a desire to hide her face in awe.

Next, Sister Bridget called the clinic and asked the volunteer there to move her patients to the afternoon.

First, she would check on the young mother and her newborn. How could she not? She grabbed her satchel, swung it over her head and across her bosom. As usual, the June day was bright and hot, but her dark, wayfarer sunglasses cut the glare. The glasses had been in lost-and-found long enough. She appropriated them as her own. Waving to neighbors, she made her way to the bus stop on Comal Street where she joined a young mother and an elderly lady with a lopsided walker and a shopping bag. Two male laborers stood leaning against the fence behind them.

"*Buenos días.*" Sister Bridget gave a little bow. The group returned the greeting. The mother and elderly woman tried to give up their seats for her. "*No, no. No te preocúpen.*" Sister Bridget coaxed the ladies back onto the bench, but they insisted on at least sliding closer together to make room for her. To be treated with such deference was embarrassing, but she was grateful for kind gestures.

As the little group chatted, a black and white police cruiser pulled up. The young officer in the passenger seat lowered his window. "Good morning."

After a beat, only Sister Bridget returned the greeting. Then she recognized him. He was the young officer she had met that morning.

"Can I help you, Officer…?" Sister Bridget didn't think they'd been introduced.

"Adams. Patrick Adams. Pat." He smiled brightly. The sun glinted off his short-cropped, strawberry blond hair. "Um…yes. We were on our way to the church when we saw you."

"Kind of hard to miss." The driver laughed; he was a heavyset man with a buzz haircut. Officer Adams gave him a *cut it out* look.

"Anyway, we were heading to the church—" He looked over his shoulder. The other officer, his eye on the rearview mirror, was motioning the drivers to go around. "Would you mind coming with us, Sister? Detective Estevez has some information he wants to go over with you." Morning traffic started to back up. A timeworn Sentra noisily spewed exhaust. Someone laid on their horn.

"Detective Estevez?" Sister Bridget asked.

"Wait. Do you have a warrant or what?" The young mom stood and rolled her baby's stroller forward and back.

The laborers looked down, trying to go unnoticed. The elderly lady looked up, just then noticing the police car.

Officer Adams got out of the car. The young woman went quiet and sat back down.

Ignoring the mom, the officer addressed Sister

Bridget. "Detective Estevez is in charge of the case. He tried to call, but he couldn't find you, so he sent us over. Can you come with us? You're not under arrest, ma'am."

"I was in route to check on the young lady and her baby. I assume the detective has information about them?"

"Can't really say. But it's probably a safe bet."

Sister Bridget liked Officer Adams. "In that case, yes, I'm happy to come with you, my son."

She turned and kissed the cheeks of the young mother and the elderly woman, wished the laborers a good day, and climbed into the backseat of the police vehicle, gathering in her tunic before the officer slammed the door.

"Oh, excuse me? Officer Adams? The individual that I saw running on the parish grounds? Did you ever locate that person?"

"I was wondering about that. Are you sure you saw someone? We looked around, covered a lot of blocks. Whoever if was must've been pretty slick. Never found a trace of anybody."

Yes, she was sure she had seen someone. *Pretty slick, indeed.*

****

Detective Estevez was a tall Black man. He wore gray pants, a starched, white shirt, and a light, shimmery blue tie. His short-cropped hair and neat facial stubble lent to his sleek, handsome appearance. He rose and put his suit coat on when Sister Bridget entered. Other officers stared, but he ignored them. She ignored them too; she was used to it.

"Sister Bridget." Estevez extended his hand,

smiling. He was slightly taller than she. "Nice to meet you. Here, have a seat." He spoke with a Spanish accent; Puerto Rican, she guessed.

The large room, partitioned with low walls, was divided into multiple workstations. As she glanced around, the officers, some seated at desks, others standing in small groups, turned their attention back to their tasks.

Detective Estevez's workspace contained a row of four short, black file cabinets, a chrome and wood desk, and three chrome, cushioned chairs. On his desk were two computers—one had a large screen displaying a detailed map of South Texas, Mexico, Honduras, and Guatemala. The other was a laptop. Its screen was black. Leaning against the wall, mounted on tack board, was a marked-up terrain map of Texas and Mexico. But what caught Sister Bridget's eye was a board laid-out with photos mounted on an easel-like stand. Five even rows of pictures. The images were of young girls, adolescent and younger. Six brown-skinned, dark-haired girls per row. They had been photographed in various environs: at school, at home, on the street. They seemed to strain at their photo paper, eager to be set free.

Estevez placed a chair close to his desk, across from his own. Sister Bridget didn't sit though. She couldn't turn her back on the photos. She felt obligated to pay the youngsters their due, though only their photographs were present.

"In which department do you work, Detective?"

"I'm part of APD's Human Trafficking unit."

"I see." She kept her eyes on the girls' pictures. "Who are they?" She looked closer.

"Missing girls." Estevez rubbed his cheek, studying Sister Bridget. "Probably human trafficking." He paused, turning his gaze to the pictures too. "Mostly from Guatemala and Honduras. Some from Mexico."

Oh, dear Jesus.

Peering into the girls' faces one by one, Sister Bridget stopped abruptly. She recognized one. It was a picture that was set off to the side a bit, paired with another. Though she hadn't seen the girl with her eyes open before, she recognized the cheekbones, the forehead, the shape of the face. It was the girl who had lay in a pool of blood on the chapel floor. In the photo, the girl's almond-colored eyes sparked with life, long, dark hair shone, and clear skin glowed. Skin the color of sun-bleached adobe. A pretty girl to be sure.

"How is she?"

"She's hanging in there. The doc put her into a—what do you call it—a man-made coma."

"An induced coma? Did they say how long she'd be in the coma?"

"About six days."

Good idea indeed. Sister Bridget had seen for herself the girl had lost a great deal of blood. She would need time to heal.

"Where was this photo taken?" It was different from the others. Behind the girl was a backdrop that said *Immigration and Customs Enforcement.*

"South Texas Detention Center. In Pearsall."

"The ICE detention center? It's near San Antonio, correct? How on Earth did she get from there to here?" She looked back at the photo. The teenager's bright eyes sought the camera lens. "What's her name?" Sister Bridget gazed into clear, earnest eyes. "Who is she?

Where's she from?" She straightened and turned to Estevez.

"Her name is Isabel Ortiz. Age fifteen. She was fourteen when she disappeared from her home. She's from a rough place. A town outside Mexico City." He opened a file folder and read, "Ecatepec. Border Patrol picked her up trying to cross into Texas." He rose and walked over to the easel. "Caught her crossing in Granjeno, ten miles from McAllen. All alone and pregnant. She slipped away from Pearsall while being transported to the hospital to get checked. ICE is plenty hot about it. Let me tell you, Ms.—er—*Sister*..." He glanced at his notes. "Rincón-Keller, *nobody* escapes immigration custody. I mean *no one*.

"And this girl, here." He pointed to the photo that was paired with Isabel's. "This is Juana San Miguel. Also, from Ecatepec. The two girls disappeared together back in January."

Sister Bridget scrutinized the other snapshot, a school picture of a merry girl with apple cheeks and curly, frizzy hair. No, she didn't recognize the second girl. But she knew the place from which the two girls had come. She herself had grown up in Mexico City and had always been taught to avoid the crime-plagued suburb of Ecatepec. The place had gotten that way as more and more impoverished people from all over Mexico sought work in Mexico City, building shacks on hillsides adjacent to the metropolis though no electricity nor running water existed in those outer areas. Over the decades, some utilities were added, but unfortunately, violent crime moved in too.

"Juana San Miguel's family provided this photo." Estevez removed both photos from the easel—Isabel and Juana—and placed them on his desk. Juana's face was freckled, open, full...and happy, her eyes were filled with mischief. Her thick, light brown curls were pulled back in a ponytail. Isabel's face was smooth, sweet, and heart-shaped, with a widow's peak hairline.

"We were glad to see the pregnant girl, Isabel, show up. We had already informed her mother and were in the process of deporting her when she disappeared from the detention center."

"How can I help?" Sister Bridget said.

"Please sit, Sister." Estevez indicated the chair across from his desk. "I want to show you something. Something that will be of interest to you."

She sat, and he handed her a clear, zippered bag. "Don't open it. It's evidence."

She knew how to handle evidence. Through the plastic, Sister Bridget saw a sheet of lined paper marked with fading pencil, worn smooth, and barely legible. It was creased from being repeatedly folded and unfolded. She turned it toward the light and looked closely. Written in stiff print was her own name, misspelled, SISTER BRIGET ANN RINKON KELOR. Underneath her name were printed OUR LADY OF GUADALUPE CHURCH and the address.

"I'm sure you know about *human trafficking*," Estevez said.

"Of course, Detective." She glanced at the photos, and her blood rose. "I most certainly do know of the inhumane practice of exploiting people for profit." In her heart, she said a wordless prayer for the girls. Goose bumps rose on her forearms. "Where did you get this paper?"

"It was in the girl's backpack." He paused. "Are

you *sure* you don't know her? Why would she have your name in her backpack?"

Sister Bridget took another look at the girl's photo. Was there something she was missing?

"I don't know this girl. What's going on here?" And then it dawned on her. "Are you accusing me of human trafficking?"

Estevez took a deep breath and leaned back in his chair, his fingers steepled under his chin. "Ms. uh, I mean *Sister*." He glanced at his notes again. "Rincón-Keller. I can only go by the information I have. Here's this paper." He extended an open hand toward the evidence. "Some kind of clue, wouldn't you say?" He held up his hand to stop her reply. "A clue to what, I don't know. But somebody gave this girl your name and address. Maybe to bring immigrants across the border illegally. Maybe to dupe them."

She thought of the unscrupulous human traffickers, that plagued her beloved Mexico.

"Money. It's always about money. Drugs for money. Weapons sometimes, and humans." Estevez leaned back, once again steepling his fingers. He waited for some reply. "Nuns take a vow of poverty, is that right?"

"That's right, Detective." Sister Bridget knew where this was leading. *Her money.*

"Well, as you may know, we do routine background checks on witnesses and suspects—"

"Suspects? Do you suspect me of a crime?"

"Why do you have a million dollars in your bank account?"

"You mean my *trust*." Sister Bridget's brother was its trustee. And it wasn't quite a million.

"Still, the money is yours."

Sister Bridget had wished to donate the money to charity long ago when she first inherited it from her parents, but her brother, her only sibling, talked her into keeping it in a trust. "In case the nun thing doesn't work out," he had said.

"I get it. You inherited the money. I know, I know, your parents were well-to-do physicians. Well-regarded, sure. Just odd. I don't know. Vow of poverty and all." She detected a glint of amusement in his eyes. He enjoyed making her uncomfortable.

"Not to worry, Detective. I do not break my vow of poverty." She didn't fear scrutiny. Her order, the Sisters of St. Paul, required a vow of poverty, but she was not obligated to give away her wealth.

"Yes, I get it. Your situation. Inheriting money, not touching it really, just a few withdrawals…" *Chiefly for the care of my little dog,* Sister Bridget thought, "…no deposits…ever…only interest payments."

"Thank you for that update on the state of my own trust. Now can we get back to that note?" She pointed to the plastic bag. The note with her name and address on it.

"Okay, sorry, sorry. Didn't mean to offend." He waved his hands, palms outward. "Just odd for a nun to be sitting on a million dollars." His eyes sparkled and he smiled. She didn't. "That's all I'll say about it."

"Thank you." That darn money was embarrassing.

"Okay, as far as the note goes, since you say you don't know anything about it…" He raised an eyebrow at her. She stared at him. "I'd say the only person that can explain it is that girl in a coma. We'll have to wait for her to wake up. Since she was looking for you, certainly she'll talk to you."

If she wakes up. Sister Bridget looked at her watch. "I must go, Detective, I want to visit the girl and the baby this morning. I assume they're at Children's Hospital?"

"The baby, yes. They took Isabel to University Hospital."

She rose to go. "Detective, did you really think I was a human trafficker?"

He tried and failed to suppress a smile. His deep-pitched laughter rolled happily across his face, lighting up his eyes. "No, I just wanted to tease you about being rich and poor at the same time."

"Glad I could amuse you." She nodded curtly.

"You're a very interesting person." He offered a handshake.

"You're an interesting person, too." She shook his hand and departed his cubicle.

Chapter 3

Sister Bridget stepped off the bus by the massive stone and steel Children's Hospital. A stream of vehicles crept by, reflecting sunrays, and agitating the heat. The mass of concrete skirting the hospital pulsed like a welt under the tenacious noon sun.

A thin breeze fluttered her garments, offering minimal relief as she followed red signs to the emergency entrance. Glass doors whizzed open and cold air drew her into a crowded, tan-walled waiting room.

Sister Bridget waited for the receptionist to slide open the window. "Good morning, dear. Was a newborn, a girl, brought in this morning?"

The receptionist, a young, smooth-faced Latina, barely glanced at Sister Bridget as she scrutinized her computer monitor and tapped at the keyboard. "Are you a family member?" The woman maintained a neutral demeanor.

Sister Bridget sat in one of the two chairs that faced the receptionist's window. "No, I'm not family, but you see..." She lowered her voice. "A baby was born this morning at Our Lady of Guadalupe Church."

The receptionist acted as if she'd heard those words every day. "Take a seat in the waiting area." She closed the window and picked up her phone.

Sister Bridget did just that, and it wasn't long

before one of her waiting-room companions approached.

A squat, elderly woman in a thin housedress and sneakers lumbered over and sat next to her. She asked Sister Bridget to pray for her great-grandson. The boy was sick, and the doctors didn't know what was wrong with him. Sister Bridget was used to strangers asking for prayers. Some must have thought she had an exclusive line to heaven. "Of course, my dear. What's your great-grandson's name?" She took the woman's hand in both of hers.

"*Se llama Francisco*, but we call him Frankie." The old woman wiped her eyes and blew her nose into a balled-up tissue. Her crinkly, gray hair sagged, escaping from its hairpins. Sister Bridget handed the woman a fresh tissue from her pocket.

Sister Bridget closed her eyes and made the sign of the cross. "Heavenly Father, we ask for your mercy and love. Please heal Frankie. We ask this through Jesus Christ, our Lord. Blessed Mother, please pray with us for little Frankie." Then the two ladies whispered the *Our Father* and the *Hail Mary* prayers in Spanish.

Sister Bridget felt God's presence. The *Knowing* permeated. *Be still and know that I am God.* It filled her with light and warmth, trust, and security, as if being cradled by a mother. She harbored the cares and anxieties of a content child, which were to say, *none*. She sat that way with her eyes closed, communing with creation, and holding the lady's hand.

Someone coughed and said, "Excuse me."

Sister Bridget opened her eyes. Before her stood a middle-aged blonde woman, her hands folded. The petite lady's navy-blue pumps matched her skirt. Her blouse was creamy silk.

"Sister Bridget? Pardon me for interrupting."

"Yes, hello." Sister Bridget turned to the elderly lady, smiled, and patted her hand. "I'll be praying for your great-grandson." She kissed the old woman's cheek.

She stood and extended her hand to the petite blonde. "I'm Bridget Ann Rincón-Keller." Sister Bridget towered over her.

"Yes, yes." The petite woman smiled. "We've actually met before. I'm Rose Phelps. I'm a social worker here at the hospital. We met…oh…years ago." She gave Sister Bridget a meaningful look. "The little boy," she lowered her voice, "sad case."

"Oh yes, Rose, my dear." Sister Bridget kissed her on both cheeks. Indeed, she had met the social worker when she had had to contact Child Protective Services a few years ago. She pictured the poor malnourished boy. But he was older now and well cared for by his grandparents. Sister Bridget had kept an eye on the child.

She waved to the old woman and followed Rose through the secure double doors into the hushed emergency treatment area.

"Do you know anything about the baby that was brought in this morning?" Sister Bridget followed Rose into her office.

"Have a seat, Sister. Yes, yes, the baby is fine. In fact, I'm amazed at how well that sweet girl is doing."

"May I see her?"

"Of course, yes, but I have some news to tell you." Rose closed the door and sat behind her desk. "There's a radiology tech. She was on shift this morning when the baby came in. Susan's her name, the nicest, sweetest girl you could ever meet. She and her husband…childless, you know. Fine people."

Sister Bridget fidgeted with her rosary beads. She nodded at Rose's words, eager to go to the child. Somehow, she already missed the baby that she had only held for a few minutes.

"Well, Susan has just *fallen in love* with Baby Doe." Rose smiled. "She and her husband had already decided to adopt and have gone through foster training and everything. I mean, they started the process some time ago, and…well…" She paused and looked away with a smile. "And, well, when that little angel was brought in this morning…" Rose had tears in her eyes. "Susan took one look at that little girl, and she feels as if the baby is a…a gift from God."

Was the baby a gift from God to the radiology tech? What about the young woman, the mother? Sister Bridget pictured the girl in a pool of blood on the chapel floor. On the one hand, Sister Bridget recognized the sense in what Rose was saying, but deep in her heart, she hoped that the baby and mother would be reunited. "Yes, I see, and how is the baby's health?"

Rose's smile faded. Certainly, Sister Bridget's response wasn't what the social worker had expected. Rose probably expected her to be pleased for the radiology tech and the baby.

"Oh, she's healthy…and strong." Rose resurrected her smile and enthusiasm. "Only a little over five pounds, but her APGAR score is good."

Sister Bridget knew the test wasn't a true APGAR since it must be administered during the first five minutes of life, but she was pleased to know that all the

APGAR measurements, the newborn's skin color, heart rate, reflexes, muscle tone and breathing, were good.

"Susan has gone off shift, but she couldn't bear to leave that precious baby. She's with her now."

Sister Bridget hoped the tech wasn't unduly getting her hopes up. The baby already had a mother, and Sister Bridget wasn't giving up on her. The girl had lost a lot of blood, yes. But she was getting good care. The induced coma along with blood transfusions would aid in the girl's recovery. Sister Bridget prayed that the girl *would* recover. "Rose, my dear, may I see the baby?"

"Yes, of course. Come, come." Rose gestured excitedly.

They left the emergency room and crossed through the waiting room to another corridor.

"The baby was transferred to the PICU for the time being." Rose's heels clicked on the hospital tile. After several more corridors and double doors, the two ladies entered a patient room that was quiet but for the gentle creak of a rocking chair. The pink sheets on the hospital bed and bassinette were crisp and unwrinkled. The room smelled of malty, vitaminy baby formula and lavender. The slats of the window shade filtered the noonday sun, and muted rays of light shone upon Susan and the swaddled baby on the rocking chair.

It was a serene environment, and after what the baby girl, Jane Doe as they called her, had been through, Sister Bridget was grateful to find the child fast asleep in safe hands.

"Susan, this is Sister Bridget," Rose whispered. "This is Susan Johnson." The social worker barely contained her excitement. Susan, slender, her shiny brown hair twisted and pinned, looked to be in her thirties. Still clad in blue hospital scrubs, she rose and placed the infant in the bassinette, tucking the receiving blanket snug. Susan kept her eyes on the baby as if witnessing a miracle. Baby Doe hiccupped, smiled, and settled back down to doze, her black, fuzzy hair soft on the crib sheet. The three ladies looked on, smiling too.

"Is she jaundiced?" Sister Bridget noticed a yellow tinge to the baby's skin.

"Oh. The doctor didn't say anything. I'm pretty sure the blood test didn't show a high bilirubin." Susan drew her brows together. She flipped the wall switch and the room lit up. "Hmm…doc just checked her…" she looked at her watch, "two hours ago. Baby was fine." Susan removed the infant's blanket and lifted her pink onesie to expose her belly. Sure enough, yellow.

"It's mild though, right?" the social worker said. "My first baby was jaundiced, and it wasn't serious. It cleared up on its own."

"Yes, but—" Susan began.

"She was just born this morning." Sister Bridget understood the various implications of jaundice.

Susan wrapped the blanket back onto the baby. "I'll go get the nurse."

"Don't a lot of newborns get jaundice?" Rose asked after Susan had left the room. "It's nothing serious, right?"

"It's usually not serious if the jaundice begins twenty-four hours *after* being born," Sister Bridget explained. "This baby was born this morning. When jaundice occurs *within* the first twenty-four hours, it can be a sign of a different, more serious problem."

"Oh, I didn't know that," Rose said.

Sister Bridget had seen jaundiced babies during her

obstetrics rotation in medical school. A mother had brought a jaundiced newborn to the hospital, but by the time the baby got treatment, permanent brain damage had occurred. Sister Bridget kept that story to herself.

Susan returned followed by a nurse who checked the baby. Then a tech arrived to draw blood.

The doctor arrived and looked over the data on the baby's chart. He didn't introduce himself. "Blood culture came back positive." The grey-haired, hunched-over doctor was tired. Impatiently, he scribbled on the chart and handed it to the nurse. "Let's start an I.V. and move her to the NICU. Ampicillin Gentamycin." He turned to go.

"Wait...what...doctor?" The words caught in Susan's throat. She struggled to speak. Tears welled up. Rose put her arm around Susan's shoulders.

"Not to worry, my dear." Sister Bridget said the words the doctor hadn't spoken. "Ampicillin is an antibiotic that should clear up the infection in six days."

The doctor turned back. "Yes, that's right." He glanced over the top of his reading glasses at Sister Bridget and seemed surprised by the presence of the three ladies. Sister Bridget surmised he had probably been up all night. "Did you have other questions?" he asked.

Sister Bridget felt it best to let the poor man get some rest. "We're fine, Doctor. Thank you."

He walked out of the room with a wave.

The baby was transferred to the neonatal intensive care unit. The way Susan stuck by the baby's side, wringing her hands, was exactly what an anxious mother would do, Sister Bridget thought.

"Praise be to God. The baby is in excellent hands,"

Sister Bridget said to Rose, as she prepared to go. What would have happened to the baby if Milagro hadn't found her when he did? *Well, no need to fret about that,* she told herself. "I'm off to see the baby's mother at the University Hospital now."

"The poor thing," Rose said. "Too bad she and the baby couldn't be in the same hospital."

"Oh, well, the baby is better off here in the Children's Hospital, and the girl will get the care she needs at University Hospital."

Sister Bridget kissed Rose's cheek and took her leave.

"Oh, and by the way, don't worry about Maria," Rose said.

"Maria?"

"It's the name Susan has decided to use for the baby while she's in foster care. Susan has taken leave from her job to care for her."

"Oh." It was a good development, of course, but the distance between the baby's world and that of her mother was widening. Already. And in six days, after the course of antibiotics, the baby would be released from the hospital. But released to whom?

Chapter 4

On the sixth day, Isabel Ortiz emerged from the induced coma and thought she'd encountered an angel. In flowing robes of black and white, the celestial guardian hovered and whispered incantations.

The drugs used to induce a coma caused hallucinations. She thought she saw imposing chrome blocks besetting her from all sides, regarding her with flashing blue eyes. Silvery, green snakes slithered into her body, delivering dark secrets. Helpless to resist or run, Isabel closed her eyes and retreated to the darkness.

Light pressed into her cave, but darkness trapped and extinguished the beams.

Later, haltingly, Isabel approached the cave's opening and emerged into the alien world. But this time, the place was not wholly unworkable. Her surroundings seemed familiar, like she almost belonged there.

Nauseating pain wracked her whole body. Metal rails lined the sides of the bed in which she lay. Machinery whirred and beeped. Clear liquid flowed into her arm from puffy bags that hung from poles. She watched the fluid flow through a clear tube into a bandaged area on her forearm. She tried to focus on just that little bit of pain, like a pinch, where the tube entered her arm instead of the agony that tormented her everywhere else.

The room smelled like the alcohol her mother used to clean her brother's scrapes and cuts. And a little like pee too. Where were her mother and brother? They should be here to see this. She reached with her other arm, the one that wasn't bandaged and tried to grab hold of the side rail to pull herself up, but instead, knocked something to the floor. It crashed and sounded like it broke into a billion pieces.

The hospital room door opened, and the black and white angel appeared. The angel said, "Oh!" She smiled a friendly, happy smile and rushed to collect the fallen item—a TV remote control. So, the angel was real—she was a big nun, tall with wispy black and gray curls escaping from underneath her veil. Isabel's head throbbed, so she closed her eyes, but then her head swam, and she felt like she would throw up. So, she opened her eyes again.

"Praise God and good morning," Sister Bridget said in Spanish, the only language Isabel could understand. "How are you feeling?"

Isabel felt sick, but she didn't feel like saying so. Her mouth was dry and gummy.

"I'm Sister Bridget." That name sounded familiar. Isabel didn't know why she was in a hospital or how she had gotten there. "Excuse me, one moment." The nun held up a finger. "I must let your nurse know that you're awake." The nun left the room and returned with two nurses in blue hospital scrubs.

"Well would you look who's up," the male nurse said upon entering the room.

To Isabel, the nurse was a living nightmare. The tall, dark-haired man with a deep voice triggered terror.

She screamed and tried to rise from the bed to run. In her mind, she saw another man, a giant with devil eyes, long, greasy hair, a face filled with hate. A monster.

She struggled to break free, screaming nonstop, her body forcing her brain to remember. Telling her she must run. El Gigante was coming for her!

"Oh, my sweet Jesus." Sister Bridget held firm, blocking Isabel from climbing out of the bed.

Both nurses reached for her too, as she attempted to climb over the bedrail. The male nurse's touch sent Isabel into a blind frenzy of screaming and shaking and scrabbling over the railing. She tried to shove Sister Bridget. She needed to get away from the nurse, but she couldn't get past the nun.

"My son, it's okay. It's okay. We can handle this," Sister Bridget said to the nurse as she struggled with Isabel.

"Yeah, Richard, go please." The female nurse had to shout above Isabel's screams. "I think she's afraid of you."

Isabel couldn't stop the torment. She relived the memory of El Gigante grasping her neck and yelling in her face. His breath like sewage, his skin thick and pitted, the color of cigarette ashes.

She could hear his words. "Your mother doesn't want you! She hates you!" His disgusting spittle in her face. "*Basura!* Nobody needs you anymore."

She remembered El Gigante grabbing her from the car. Then his hands around her neck, lifting her high off the ground. When she was on the verge of blacking out, he flung her to the ground like trash. She recalled clasping her knees over her pregnant belly, as she landed on rocks and spiny foliage, gasping for air.

Isabel remembered these things, and now she felt the same sensations all over again. El Gigante's grip cutting off her blood flow and her breathing. Her eyesight slowly going dark, reduced to tunnel vision. In her mind, only one thought—protect her unborn baby.

Now in the hospital, she clutched her belly to protect her baby once more, but there was nothing there. "He killed my baby." She screamed at Sister Bridget through tears. It was gone. The baby was gone.

"*Mija*, nobody killed your baby." Sister Bridget shushed and reassured her.

But Isabel's mind was chaos, and she couldn't comprehend. Dazed and entangled in the bedding, railing, and I.V. tubing, she gave up. She'd lost everything. Everything she fought so hard to keep—the most important thing—her baby. The nurse lowered the bed rail, and Isabel allowed Sister Bridget to help her from the bed and brace her around her waist as the nurse smoothed the bed sheets and sorted the tubing.

Isabel's leg muscles wouldn't work. Her body sagged toward the floor, but the nun held her up.

All the while, Sister Bridget kept up a flow of calm, gentle words.

Isabel hung her head. She was limp and empty.

Sister Bridget and the nurse settled her back onto her bed. Isabel closed her eyes. The nurse tucked her in and left the room. Isabel drifted into a light sleep with a sensation of sinking through the bed and falling through the earth.

She heard the nun sliding a chair across the room, moving it close to her bed. "Do you mind if I sit with you?"

Isabel opened her eyes, glanced at Sister Bridget,

and turned away.

"Isabel?" Sister Bridget cajoled, reaching for her hand. Isabel pulled away.

"Isabel, *mija*, you said, 'he killed my baby.'" Sister Bridget spoke softly. "Isabel, nobody killed your baby. Your baby is fine."

Isabel remembered the horror of El Gigante throwing her and her baby to the ground. She could see the result for herself—the rise in her belly was gone. There was no baby. How could her baby be fine?

"Go away." Isabel wished the nun would just leave her alone. She closed her eyes and turned away.

The IV pump made small, heaving noises.

"I'll be here when you want to talk about your baby." Sister Bridget settled in and reached in her pocket for her rosary.

Isabel didn't speak for a long while. Finally, she turned to Sister Bridget. "Why don't you leave me alone? I hate you."

Sister Bridget sat quietly.

Finally, Isabel spoke again. "*Que pendeja soy.*" The words caught in her throat. "I was going to name my baby Lucas or Gabriela." Tears slipped onto her cheeks.

Sister Bridget looked into Isabelle's eyes. "Don't say that about yourself, *mija*. You are a strong girl. Look at everything you've been through. And now you are better. Gabriela is a beautiful name for your baby. Your baby is just fine."

"But El Gigante killed my baby. Didn't he? Did he?" What was going on? *Could* her baby be okay? Was her baby alive? What was going on?

"No, my darling, nobody killed your baby. Your

baby is just fine. You have been through a great trauma. You just can't remember right now, but your baby is fine."

She looked at her belly. How could her baby be alive if it was gone? There was nothing there. The pain of losing her baby hurt even more than the pain throughout her body. "If my baby didn't die, then where is it?" She showed the nun her belly. "See, it's gone."

"You gave birth to your baby. She is also in the hospital. A different hospital."

"What? *She*?" Did the nun call the baby *she*? Isabel felt the blood drain from her face. She swallowed, shook her head, looked down at her belly again. "I didn't have my baby. I *couldn't* have. I would know if I had my baby."

"*Mija*, I would never lie to you. Your baby is alive and healthy. It is a little girl."

"No…that can't…why can't I remember? How can that be?"

"You lost a lot of blood. You've been sleeping for six days. You have suffered a lot. That's why you can't remember."

"I can't believe it. Let me see my baby." *Six* days?

"Your baby is with a lady named Susan." Sister Bridget explained that Susan and her husband were foster parents. "Your baby is ready to be released from the hospital, and Susan will take her to her home to take care of her."

"I'm ready to get out of the hospital, too. I'll just go get my baby now." Isabel threw off her covers and attempted to lower the rail.

"*Mija*, no. You must wait for the doctor to say it's

okay. And when she does, you will go home with me."

"No, I don't want to go with you. I'll just go get my baby and go to *my* home."

"I need to talk to you about that," Sister Bridget said.

"But can I see my baby now? Do I really have a baby?" She sniffed and swiped the back of her hand at her nose. She couldn't believe her luck. One minute she thought her baby was dead, but the next minute, she was not. *If* it was true.

"Yes, of course, dear. *Mija*, do you remember anything about giving birth? Do you remember where you left your baby?"

"But you said she's okay, right? I didn't leave her anywhere. She's okay, isn't she?" Fear crept into Isabel's body like a burn to the skin, its pain spreading. She only remembered the gigantic man, the monster, and she didn't even know if *he* was real. She was afraid to ask. She didn't want to talk about him. That was the only thing she remembered—the man throwing her and her baby. Other than that, her memory was like a solid black block. She couldn't get around it. She remembered her mother and her brother. She remembered walking to school with her girlfriends, and her *best* friend, Juana, but if she tried to go forward in her mind, there was nothing there, just the black void through which no memories could pass. All she remembered was the big man, the monster, El Gigante. She couldn't even remember how she got to the hospital.

"*Mija*, your baby is fine. She's in good health," Sister Bridget said.

"When can I get her?" Isabel rubbed her eyes.

Sister Bridget handed her a tissue. She blew her nose and shifted her feet under the covers. A nurse came in and took her blood pressure, pulse, and temperature. "Is my baby real?" She asked the nurse, but the nurse didn't understand Spanish. Her voice was hoarse and scratchy. She struggled to modulate it. She coughed and cleared her throat. "This is not a mistake, right?"

Sister Bridget dampened a washcloth and wiped Isabel's face as she translated for the nurse.

"Of course, your baby's real." The nurse smiled. Sister Bridget translated.

"When can I see her? When?"

"I must explain something to you," Sister Bridget said. "I know you don't remember, but you left your baby at the church where I live. Because of that, you must have a hearing in court. A judge will decide if you can have your baby back."

"What? No, I didn't leave my baby anywhere. I couldn't have. It's not true." How could the nun's words be true? They couldn't be. She would never have left her baby anywhere.

"I know, *mija*. I know you would never do anything to harm your baby on purpose." Sister Bridget's voice was soothing. "I found you in the little chapel at the church. You had lost a lot of blood. That's why you are here. It has taken six days for you to get better."

Isabel didn't remember any of that.

"No. I *can* have my baby back. I have to have my baby. I need her." Isabel covered her face and collapsed into tears, exhausted. "I didn't leave my baby anywhere. I need to get my baby. *Please*."

"Isabel, *mija*, you've been through a horrible

experience. There is much you don't remember, and that's okay. It's understandable. It will take time to get your memories back.

"I believe you didn't mean to do anything wrong, but now you must go to court to get your baby back. It's the law." Sister Bridget lightly stroked Isabel's shoulder. "But Immigration has given me permission to be your sponsor until then. You'll come stay with me for a while. Everything will be fine." Sister Bridget patted her hand. "You'll see. It's hard to be patient, but everything will be fine." Sister Bridget hoped her words would prove to be true.

The nurse left and a hospital worker came in with a tray of food.

"Now you just eat your breakfast, and you'll feel much better. You'll see. I bet your baby is having her breakfast right now too." Sister Bridget smiled and removed the cover from the plate of food. Isabel wasn't hungry. The smell made her nauseous.

"From a bottle, right?" Isabel said.

"Yes, that's right, your baby will have her breakfast from a bottle."

"I can name her whatever I want, right? I can name her Gabriela, right?"

"Oh yes, *mijita*, you can give her any name you please. I think Gabriela is a beautiful name."

Chapter 5

Early the next morning, Sister Bridget prayed the rosary by Isabel's hospital bed while the girl slept. Then she worked quietly on her computer. She looked over her caseload of expectant mothers, took notes, ordered supplies, and communicated with staff. She also rearranged her midwife appointments and informed her colleagues that she wouldn't be taking new patients for the time being. Next, she looked into Aeromexico prices, and emailed her brother. She would need money for the airline ticket, and he was the trustee of the money she'd inherited. But she'd wait before actually purchasing the ticket.

These chores were reason enough to love her laptop, which she carried in a black neoprene bag wherever she went. Her computer was the world at her fingertips. She also used it for research. And she live-streamed Mass from all over the world. She even FaceTimed her sisters in Mexico City, the headquarters for the Sisters of St. Paul. And Zoom united her religious community from wherever they were scattered.

At daybreak, faint light slowly brightened the hospital room. Detective Estevez knocked lightly, and Sister Bridget let him in, pressing a finger to her lips, and whispering, "She's sleeping."

"I'm awake," Isabel said in a singsong tone, as if

yielding to the inevitable.

"This is Arco Iris." Estevez spoke in Spanish. He offered a white, plush unicorn to Isabel. Its horn was rainbow colored. "For you." He pronounced *arco iris*, rainbow, with an endearing Puerto Rican accent, the *r's* as *d's*, the *s* just a breath. Sister Bridget couldn't help but notice. She loved languages.

Isabel wordlessly accepted the small stuffed animal, her brows pinched. "Thanks." She looked away.

"What a nice gift. Isabel, this is Detective Estevez." It occurred to Sister Bridget that Isabel may have feared the detective like she feared the nurse the previous day.

"Hi." Isabel looked down at the unicorn in her hands.

"Good to meet you." Estevez smiled and sought eye contact, but Isabel avoided his gaze.

Sister Bridget helped the girl to the bathroom while Estevez waited in the hallway. When Isabel was settled back in her bed, Sister Bridget called the detective back in.

"Well, aren't you making good progress. Up and walking around and everything. Very good." Estevez's demeanor was cheerful.

"Yes, her doctor will be sending her home tomorrow." Sister Bridget sat close to Isabel, protectively patting her hand. The poor girl must have been through a nightmare.

"Home?" Isabel said, wide-eyed. "They'll give me my baby first though, right?"

"Oh, not home to Mexico. Not yet, *mija.* Remember, you will live at my house until you have your hearing. It will be so nice to have a young guest." Sister Bridget lived alone, and of course, had never had a child of her own.

"Do you feel up to answering a few questions, young lady?" Estevez asked.

"No." Isabel looked down at the stuffed animal.

"I spoke to your mother." His tone was cajoling.

Isabel's face turned red. Her eyes teared up. "What did Mamá say?"

"She is relieved beyond belief that you're okay," Estevez said. "She was frightened that she'd never see you again, so you can understand, she is a very happy mama."

"She is?" Isabel's voice was trembly. A big tear spilled onto her cheek.

"Of course she is, *mija*," Sister Bridget said. "Why do you think she wouldn't be?"

"I thought my *mamá* hated me."

"Why would you say that?" Sister Bridget asked.

"Because El Gigante said…" She shook her head and looked away. "I don't know. I don't want to talk about it."

Sister Bridget exchanged glances with Estevez.

She took Isabel's hand. "It must have been very frightening for you, a horror." She smoothed Isabel's hair away from her face and gave her a fresh tissue.

"What did *El Gigante,* as you call him, what did he tell you?" Estevez asked.

"He told me my mother didn't want me because she wasn't sending him money." Isabel looked at her belly. "Does my mother hate me because…because…I had a baby?" She tipped her chin up bravely, but then lost that little bit of resolve and covered her face with her hands, crying.

"No, no, *mi amor*." Sister Bridget placed her arm around the girl's shoulders. "Your mother doesn't hate you. She loves you. Having a baby is not the end of the world. Your mother loves you. It will all work out. God finds a way. You'll see."

"And she said she *did* send money." Estevez took a notepad from his coat pocket and flipped through the pages. "It was on January 13, the day you and your friend, Juana San Miguel, went missing from school."

"Me and Juana were missing from school?" Isabel drew her brows together, eyes wide. She looked to Sister Bridget.

Sister Bridget wasn't familiar with current studies, but it occurred to her that Isabel's memory loss could be attributed to anoxic brain injury. Certainly, the girl had lost much blood; perhaps the lack of oxygen to her brain caused her memory loss. Or the strong coma inducing drugs could cause it. Even the trauma she had endured could result in subconsciously blocking out memories. She hadn't even remembered that she'd given birth to a healthy baby, for heaven's sake.

"My mother sent money?" Isabel scrunched up her face, confused.

"I have spoken to your mother. She told me that she sent almost five thousand pesos to the Western Union office in…" Estevez looked at his notes again. "Guanajuato, León."

Isabel looked at him blankly. "My mother doesn't have money."

"She borrowed it from her employer and other people."

Isabel nodded. It seemed to Sister Bridget that the

girl was taking in information and piecing it together like a puzzle of someone else's life.

"Why were you in Guanajuato?" Estevez asked. "How did you get there?"

Isabel shook her head, lips stretched downward. She shrugged, but then began to tremble. Sister Bridget held her tight, but it seemed like the girl couldn't stop shaking.

"Oh, my God. I remember Juana. Where's Juana?" Isabel's words became a sob, her eyes wide. She looked terrorized. "Does El Gigante have her? Did he kill her?" Screaming, she sat up in the bed and pulled the catheter from her arm. Blood spewed crimson onto her arm, the bedding, and the floor.

"No, *mija*, leave it in." Sister Bridget reached for the tubing, but it was too late. The bloody catheter dangled alongside the bed rail, dripping blood and clear liquid.

"I have to go. I have to find Juana." Isabel pushed Sister Bridget away and shook the bed rail, attempting to lower it.

"No, you don't have to find her." Estevez brought a chair from the other side of the room and sat close by Isabel's bed. "Listen to me."

Isabel stopped struggling and gave Sister Bridget a desperate look.

Sister Bridget brought gauze and tape from the nurse's supplies. She put pressure on Isabel's catheter site, and taped gauze into place to stop the bleeding. She clamped the tubing. "It's only saline you were getting. It's fine.

"Detective Estevez wants to find Juana too. He won't hurt you." Sister Bridget handed Isabel a tissue and used a wet cloth to wipe blood from her arm.

"Other people are looking for your friend," Estevez said. "Listen, sweetie, your friend is still alive. Her father, her uncle and the police are looking for her."

Isabel dared to look into the detective's eyes. "She's alive? Where is she?"

"That, we don't know." He went quiet, and he and Isabel watched Sister Bridget wipe blood from the bed railing and the floor. "Think, honey. Can you remember? Where was the last place you saw Juana?"

Isabel bit her lip and cried. "I don't know. I don't know."

"*Mija,* shh, it's okay." Sister Bridget poured water from a foam pitcher and handed the cup to the girl. Isabel set the cup on the side table without drinking.

"Do you remember going to Mexico City with Juana?" Estevez asked.

"No," Isabel cried.

"Do you remember being in Guanajuato?"

Weeping, Isabel shook her head, the word *no* catching in her throat.

"Torreon?"

"No, I can't remember any of that." Isabel covered her face with her hands. "All I remember is me and Juana were in El Gigante's car. That's all I remember."

"She said she can't remember, Detective." Sister Bridget gave him a reproachful look. "There, there, now, now. The important thing is that Juana is alive, and we know this because, why, Detective?" Sister Bridget straightened the bed linens and looked sideways at Estevez.

"She called her father from Torreon." Estevez rose.

"See? Hear that? Juana called her father from

Torreon." Sister Bridget smoothed the girl's hair. "You rest now, *mija*."

"Yeah, get some rest, sweetie." Estevez headed to the door.

****

"Just a word, please, Detective." Sister Bridget exited the room just as Isabel's breakfast was brought in. She found him waiting in the hallway.

"Detective."

"Yes, Sister." He looked at the floor and rubbed the back of his neck. He probably expected a scolding.

"You asked Isabel about Mexico City, Guanajuato, and Torreon. I assume these are the places Juana has been traced to? And this *El Gigante,* he must be the kidnapper, no?"

"Both families, Juana's and Isabel's, were extorted by the same guy. Difference is Juana's family kept sending money. Her dad owns a *tienda*, a little grocery in Ecatepec."

"This El Gigante that Isabel mentioned? Who is he?"

Estevez looked down the hallway. "Here, come with me." He took Sister Bridget's elbow and found a waiting area. They sat on a vinyl sofa.

"This guy—El Gigante—is a monster by the name of Alejandro Maldonado. A real strange bird. A strange, *horrible* bird." Estevez shook his head. "It's rare for a criminal to work in isolation. Most get absorbed into a drug cartel, or they at the very least have to be associated with a cartel and pay them in order to operate. It looks like this guy acts on his own. And he never stays in one place."

Sister Bridget felt nauseous. She resisted

flashbacks to an incident that had occurred when she was a child growing up in Mexico. She couldn't let her mind dwell there though. Not now.

"And the stories. You wouldn't believe. Scary stuff. This guy likes to beat up kids. Injure them, you know, so the kids show visible injuries, then he takes pictures and sends the pictures to the kids' families. Demands money. Of course, the families send the money, but then he sends more pictures. He wants more money, and again and again, but not one family, not one that we could tell, ever got their child back. This guy's a—" The detective glanced up at Sister Bridget and stopped.

Preying on a family's love. Sister Bridget felt an ache in her stomach. The detective looked at her with sympathy, softness in his eyes.

"And you think this man has Isabel's friend, Juana?"

"Sorry to say, yes. But our girl, Isabel Ortiz..." Estevez nodded toward Isabel's room. "She seems to have escaped him by some miracle." *Yes, thank you, Jesus,* Sister Bridget thought.

"We know what Maldonado looks like." Estevez took out his phone and showed Sister Bridget a newspaper article. "You can see why she refers to him as *El Gigante*."

Sister Bridget took her reading glasses from the pocket of her tunic. In the photo, a tall, hefty man in handcuffs struggled and snarled at the Mexican police officers that held him. Thick, sweaty locks of black hair dropped down over one eye. Sister Bridget understood why the kids would refer to the man as *El Gigante*, the giant. The man towered over the officers.

Early in life, Sister Bridget loved to study the indigenous peoples of Mexico. El Gigante was most definitely a descendant of the fierce Karankawa peoples that hundreds of years ago resided in Chihuahua and what is now the state of Texas. The newspaper image showed a colossal man, well over six feet tall. Yes, his height, bone structure, and thick hair surely marked him as Karankawa.

Sister Bridget enlarged the article and read a bit. She got the sickening gist of the story and handed the phone back to Estevez. "Can you kindly send that article to my email?" She would try to learn as much as she could about El Gigante. That article would be a good start.

"Sure thing, Sister. The son-of-a...I mean...the guy wasn't in police custody for long though. Managed to kill two officers." Sister Bridget went cold. "Went back and killed a third one at the guy's home, if you can believe it." Oh yes, Sister Bridget could believe it. The lives of Mexican *policía* were precarious. They either cooperated with the criminals or faced horrible retribution.

"Maybe you can talk to Isabel. She managed to escape the devil. Maybe she'll remember more. Maybe she can tell us something that can help find her friend, Juana. And better still, the whereabouts of that piece of sh—er, I mean, that man, Alejandro Maldonado, El Gigante, as she calls him."

"I wasn't aware that American law enforcement had such an overt interest in Mexican crime. I know about clandestine operations to infiltrate the drug cartels, but human trafficking and kidnapping of Mexican citizens? It's hardly an American problem."

"It becomes our problem though. I'm sure you agree."

Sister Bridget pictured the unattended baby and Isabel bleeding on the floor of the little chapel. "Agreed."

"ICE has field offices in Mexico. Believe me, finding this guy is high priority. But the problem is—"

"Getting Mexican law enforcement to cooperate." Sister Bridget finished his sentence. She sighed. "My country has a problem with corrupt institutions and inept police. I know."

"Exactly. But still, we have an opportunity here to catch this guy, maybe extradite him to the U.S. Put him away."

Sister Bridget's interest was piqued.

"I was thinking maybe you could get some information out of Isabel," he said. "I could try to talk to her—"

"You *do* speak Spanish."

"Only the best," he quipped. "My family's from—"

"Puerto Rico," Sister Bridget guessed.

"How'd you know? Most people peg me as African American."

"What? African American? With *that* accent?"

Detective Estevez laughed, hearty and boisterous. He caught himself and lowered his voice. "You got me."

"Your Spanish pronunciation is clearly Puerto Rican. Dropping your consonants, replacing soft r's with l's, dropping your—"

"Okay, okay, I get it, I get it." He cut her off, still laughing. "You know your Spanish dialects."

"Detective, you do realize…"

"That the giant is making a beeline for the U.S. border? I'm not a detective for nothing, Sister." He chuckled softly.

"If we follow his path, perhaps we can locate Juana." Sister Bridget mapped El Gigante's route in her mind.

"We?"

She ignored the question. "Detective, since you *are* a detective not for nothing, why do you think El Gigante is taking a conspicuous path to the border?"

Estevez rubbed the back of his neck again and grimaced. "He's running away."

"Running away from whom? From what?"

He stared at her for a moment. Those eyes. "A small drug cartel in Mexico City. They produce a sought-after commodity."

"Yes? What is it?"

"Crystal methamphetamine. The good stuff, potent and pure. El Gigante helped himself to a kilo."

"What? He stole from a cartel and is bringing it here?"

Detective Estevez approximated an American accent. "Near as we can figure." In his normal tone, he said, "Worth about ten K on the U.S. market."

Sister Bridget placed her hand over her mouth and looked away. She turned back. "And what about Juana? Is she really still alive, or were you just saying that?"

"El Gigante is a criminal that multi-tasks." Estevez shrugged. "DEA thinks he still has her. Collecting money from Juana's father while he waits for the big pay-off from the meth."

Chapter 6

The following day, Isabel moved into Sister Bridget's little house on the edge of the parish grounds. She'd given birth on July 9. Now here it was, July 18, and she still hadn't seen her baby.

Sister Bridget welcomed Isabel into her small residence. Milagro met her at the door. He wasn't a pretty dog. He was little and skinny with spiky gray and black fur. To tell the truth, he was kind of ugly, but in a cute way. He sniffed at Isabel's leg and sat down, smiling and wagging his tail. A smiling dog that didn't jump or bark or anything? Isabel had never seen a dog like that.

"Is this your dog? I didn't know *monjitas* had dogs. What's its name? Is it a boy or a girl?" Isabel crouched to pet the terrier.

"This is Milagro. He's a very good boy. He found your baby by the Mary statue."

"It's not true!" Isabel glanced up at Sister Bridget, her eyes wide. She rubbed Milagro's head and scratched behind his ears. *This* little dog found her baby?

"Yes, it's true."

"Why can't I remember? I don't know why I would leave my baby by a statue." Isabel shook her head, refusing to believe it. "I would never do that."

"You see, you lost quite a bit of blood that night.

When things like that happen, sometimes people can't remember. There could be other reasons—the coma, the terrible things you went through."

"I just don't think I would leave my baby all alone by a statue."

"You weren't in your right mind, *mija*. I agree with you. I don't think you would ever do that on purpose."

"I wouldn't." Isabel ran her fingers through Milagro's streaky coat. She expected the dog's fur to be rough and prickly, but it was soft. Milagro rolled over onto his back. Isabel laughed, rubbed his belly, and gave him a tickle. After that, the little terrier followed her throughout the house.

Isabel wore shorts and a t-shirt. She carried a clear plastic bag that held pajamas, undergarments, and socks that Sister Bridget had given to her. Also crammed into the bag was the rainbow unicorn that Detective Estevez gave her.

Sister Bridget's home was nice. It had a wooden floor. Isabel's home just had dirt. It was her job to sprinkle water and sweep the ground to keep it smooth. Now at Sister Bridget's house, she caught a small, underlying scent of Mexico. It was a faint whiff of her country's adobe and dirt and plants, maybe? Homesickness took hold, and her eyes stung as she looked about the house. To the right of the entry was a tan sofa with colorful Mexican pillows, two wooden chairs and a low table. On the table, stood a little, stand-up clay cross, looped with colorful rosaries. A battered bible had been left open. Above the couch, on the wall, hung a painting of Our Lady of Guadalupe, Jesus' mother, dark-skinned and dressed in a green cloak with gold stars. The painting made her long for her own mother.

"Oh, that's the same as the picture in Ciudad Mexico." Isabel told Sister Bridget that almost her whole town made a mile-long procession to the Basilica to take flowers to Our lady of Guadalupe every year on December 12. Isabel pictured her mother looking so young and happy, folding colorful crepe paper into flowers for the Virgin. Mamá scrimped all year to buy that paper.

"Every year, Mamá tells me and my brother, Ramón—Ramón has Down syndrome—she tells us the story about the Virgen de Guadalupe." She nodded seriously at Milagro who listened intently. "La Virgen appeared to a poor *indio* named Juan Diego who asked La Virgen to show him a sign. So, La Virgen asked God for a miracle. So, God made roses grow in the snow. Juan Diego bundled the roses into his *tilma* to show the bishop, and when he opened his *tilma* to show the roses, there was a picture of Our Lady right there on his *tilma*." The *tilma* that now hung in the basilica. She pictured her little brother's broad face, his almond-shaped eyes filled with wonder. "Mamá says it was to show that God loves the poor people."

Isabel quietly regarded the painting. "I never really thought about it too much. We always just made the flowers and walked to the basilica with Mamá. Do you think it's true?"

"What's that, *mija*?"

"Does God love the poor people?"

"Oh yes, *mija*." Sister Bridget also gazed at the painting.

Isabel turned from the painting to the other side of the small house. To the left of the front door was a kitchen with brown cabinets and white appliances. A light-colored wood table and chairs took up space in the back left corner. On the wall behind the table hung a rustic cross.

Sister Bridget showed Isabel the bedroom where sunlight streamed through gauzy, white curtains. The shear drapery reminded Isabel of the see-through veil her mother wore to Sunday Mass. The bed was covered with a yellow bedspread embroidered with pink and red flowers. A braided yellow rug lay upon the floor.

"How long do I have to stay here?"

"This is where you'll sleep, *mija*." Sister Bridget patted the full-sized bed. Was the nun ignoring her question?

"Where will *you* sleep?"

"Oh, I'll be comfortable on the couch." Sister Bridget plumped up the bed pillow and smoothed the bedspread.

"I can sleep on the couch." Isabel couldn't imagine sleeping on Sister Bridget's big bed all alone. In her home in Mexico, she slept on the floor with her little brother. Her mother slept on a couch; her father had left long ago. "I won't be here very long anyway. How long do I have to stay here?"

"No, dear. You've been through a lot. You need to rest. You must sleep on the bed." Sister Bridget opened a drawer. "I emptied this for your things."

Why wasn't the nun answering her question?

"And you asked, 'how long will you be here?' The answer is, I don't know. It depends on what the immigration judge says tomorrow."

When Isabel heard *judge*, it felt like her heart dropped to her stomach.

"I don't need to put my things in there." She held her bag behind her back. "And I don't need to see no judge either. I just want my baby, so I can go home. Back to Mexico."

"I'm sorry, *mi amor*, but you must have a hearing before you can get your baby."

"But, before I see the judge, can I at least *see* my baby?"

There was knocking at the door. "I'm afraid not, *mija*." Sister Bridget rubbed Isabel's arm. "Let me just get the door...oh, there is a bathroom right here." She opened a door in the hallway and extended her arm. "*Mi casa es su casa.*"

Isabel placed her belongings on the bed and sat crossed legged on the floor to play with the little dog. She thought back to before the whole thing happened. She had been fourteen; Eduardo was nineteen. She attended school; he did not. She and Juana had been at the *tianguis*, the street market. Juana, always so mischievous and filled with fun, had said, "Eduardo likes you." Isabel hadn't even known who Eduardo was. Juana pointed and Isabel looked. He was staring at her with laughter in his eyes. And oh, how beautiful his eyes were. Now, Isabel caught her breath at the memory of that sudden flush. She'd never made a connection like that with a boy before. Eduardo was tall, with thick, neat, black curls, long eyelashes, his eyes the color of honey, lips plump and pouting.

Isabel had admonished Juana. "Why did you make me look at him?" After that, it was as if everything happened in slow motion. She remembered turning around, and there was Eduardo right next to her, almost touching. Her eyes at the level of his chest. So close, she could smell him—he smelled like candy, spicy *tamarindo* candy.

Now almost a year later, she thought back to when she realized she was pregnant. Juana had told her, "You guys will get married." But this spark of hope was squashed with Eduardo's final words to her—"*Pues no es mio*." How could he say that the baby wasn't his? Anyway, by then, he'd found another girlfriend.

She stepped into the bathroom at Sister Bridget's house. Milagro sat watching from the hallway. The walls were painted soft yellow like butterfly wings, and the same gauzy curtains veiled the small window. A wreath of white seashells hung above the toilet. It was a nice toilet. At her home, she and her family used a hole in the ground with a crate on top. They shared it with other families. She looked into the mirror. Her skin, which used to be smooth and brown, was now dry and yellowish. Her long, black hair, ashy and dull. Leaning in closer, she stared into her own eyes. They were the same color and everything, but they looked flat, like a mannequin in a store window. She searched her almond-colored irises and her pupils, looking for her home, her *mamá*, her little brother, her best friend, her school, and Eduardo before he stopped loving her, but she found none of those things.

It wasn't *nothing* though. Now, looking harder, she saw something. Something sad. Suddenly she felt like a stupid girl. She hadn't even known what boys did to girls until Eduardo took her to his brother's apartment. She was embarrassed to look at herself. She turned away from her reflection and rubbed her eyes hard. When she lowered her hands, there was Milagro, looking concerned, tipping his head to one side.

"*Hola,* Milagro." Isabel tried to smile. She covered her face again so the little dog wouldn't see her cry. *Where was Juana right then?* Her heart raced; was El Gigante hurting Juana at that very moment? She couldn't stand not knowing where her best friend was or even if she was alive.

Isabel heard a man's voice. She scooped up Milagro and peeked around the corner into the living room. It was Detective Estevez. He carried a grocery bag and was following Sister Bridget into the kitchen. He wore blue jeans and a white t-shirt with writing on it. The detective and the nun were speaking English. Were they talking about her?

Isabel retreated to the bedroom and cuddling Milagro, drifted off to sleep on the thick, soft rug next to Sister Bridget's bed.

She awoke with her heart pounding wildly and her baby kicking in her belly. A dark, menacing beast hulked nearby. Milagro licked Isabel's nose and whined as if to say, *it was just a dream. It wasn't real.* She hugged the little dog tighter and looked down at her belly. It was a dream.

The savory aroma of roasting meat and toasty *tortillas de maiz* hung in the air. And something spicy. The scents like home made her stomach growl.

Light from the window was dim, and she was getting hungry. Hopefully, the detective had gone.

Milagro followed her into the living room, and there sitting on the couch were Sister Bridget and Detective Estevez. They were laughing quietly. What could be funny? They both turned and smiled at her. The table was set for three.

"You're just in time for some supper. Come,

come." Sister Bridget ushered Isabel to the table. They ate tender roasted chicken and rice mixed with peas, kernels of corn, and bits of carrot. Isabel tore pieces of corn tortilla and used them to scoop up the saucy chicken and rice. She raised the small bundles of food to her mouth. The others laid down their forks and did the same.

Isabel's stomach ached in anticipation of more questions. Since leaving the hospital, she had remembered more. Things she didn't want to talk about. But there were no questions. The detective and the nun only talked about their own families. Detective Estevez told funny stories about the mischief he and his brother got into when he was little. He claimed that when he was a boy, he and his brother had climbed onto the roof of their house and spit watermelon seeds onto their aunt's head as she gardened in the yard. The detective said that for years, the old aunt told the story of the *wondrous watermelon seeds from heaven.* One seed had taken root in the garden and had produced a miraculous watermelon. The nun's laughter was deep and husky, and Isabel laughed too, she couldn't help herself, picturing the aunt being tormented by the boys. *Her* brother was a good boy. Ramón would never do such a thing. She missed him. She remembered the little game she used to play with Ramón. He was eleven and was catching up with her in height, but she held his hand nonetheless, for mentally, her brother was like a four-year-old. Walking on the sidewalk, swinging their arms, she would say, "*Yo te…*" and her brother would answer, "*amo!*" It was a fun game because her little brother hardly ever raised his voice above a whisper except when he shouted, "*amo!*" It was because *amo, I love you,* was easy to say.

After a while, their dinner plates were empty, and Sister Bridget rose to clear the table. Isabel and the detective followed, plates in hand.

"Isabel, *mija,* Detective Estevez has some questions he would like to ask you." Sister Bridget filled the kitchen sink with soapy water.

Isabel looked to the window. It was dark out. She felt trapped. The plate in her hand rattled. Sister Bridget reached for it and embraced her.

Estevez took the plate from Sister Bridget. "Look, sweetie, no one's going to hurt you. You're safe here." He tried to catch her eye, but she evaded him. "This is a safe place." The running water in the sink grew into a steamy pile of suds. Estevez shut off the faucet.

"*Mija.*" Sister Bridget led Isabel to the living room. "Detective Estevez only wants to help." They sat on the well-worn couch. Milagro leaped onto Isabel's lap and licked her chin. A wet giggle slipped through her tears. She hugged the dog and buried her face in his fur.

"Think of it this way, the bad memories are the darkness. Talking about them is the light. It's like turning on a light. The things that happened are not so scary anymore if you talk about them." Sister Bridget soothed Isabel's hair. "I promise."

Isabel heard Detective Estevez in the kitchen washing the dishes. *Raro.* She'd never known a man to wash dishes. That was a woman's job.

Isabel released Milagro and accepted a tissue from Sister Bridget.

She told herself she was a mother now, and she was strong enough to tell. "It all started in Mexico City. That's where the men stole us. Me and Juana." Isabel sniffed and blew her nose.

Sister Bridget stiffened and went white. Detective Estevez stopped rattling the dishes. He sat apart from them at the dinner table and took out his notebook.

"Detective Estevez traced you to Mexico City. You saw a doctor at the women's clinic, correct? What happened after that, *mija*?"

"Juana told me I could get an abortion at the clinic in Mexico City." Isabel remembered asking Juana what an abortion was. Juana said she didn't know, but her cousin had had one, and it made the baby go away. 'Go away where?' she had asked. But Juana didn't know either. So, without ever telling her mother she was pregnant, she and Juana set out on the subway to Mexico City. "We went to the clinic, but they said no, that I couldn't get an abortion because the baby was more than twelve weeks. So, we were going back home, but there was a man…outside the clinic." Isabel rubbed her nose with the back of her hand. Her voice caught and wavered. "He said he would show us another place where I could get an abortion." She pictured the small, unwashed, broken-faced man. The right side of his face was melted and falling, his eye caved in under folds of thick, scaly flesh. Isabel shuddered thinking about the vicious man.

Tears filled her eyes and she felt cold. There was something more about the broken-face man, but she told herself not to remember. She shivered, crossed her arms over her chest and tried to get warm. The nun took a yellow, knitted shawl from the arm of the sofa and placed it around Isabel's shoulders. The fabric's thick, plush threads smelled like Mexico.

Sister Bridget handed her another tissue and

hugged her. "Take your time, *mija*. Take a deep breath."

Wrapped in the shawl and with Milagro on her lap, Isabel pressed her lips into a mirthless smile. In her mind, she relived the moment in Mexico City. When the sun had dropped behind the mountain. It was like blinking, and the sun was gone. She and Juana hurried to the subway. But they didn't make it.

"That guy and another one, the giant one, followed us, I guess." Isabel feared the food she had eaten would surge up from her queasy stomach. She crossed her arms over her belly. "The man grabbed me when we crossed by an alleyway. The giant one was waiting in a car…they haven't found Juana, have they?"

"I'm afraid not. Not yet," Sister Bridget said.

Estevez came closer. He sat in one of the wooden chairs by the sofa. "Where was your friend the last time you saw her?" He was taking notes.

"It was when El Gigante, the giant one, took me out of the car and threw me on the ground. That was the last time I saw Juana. El Gigante left me there, and a Rarámuri boy found me."

"Where was this?" Estevez asked.

"Where the Rarámuri live. In Chihuahua by Urique." She thought about the Rarámuri, the people who lived in the canyons of the Sierra Madre. "I need to go back there to find Juana."

"No, *mija*, you must stay here and wait for your hearing." Sister Bridget smoothed Isabel's hair.

"I'll let Juana's father know. And the Mexican police." Estevez spoke on his phone in the kitchen.

"Sister? Do you think they'll find Juana?"

"They'll try their best." But the nun didn't look

very confident. Isabel didn't have much hope either. Most of the police in Mexico were on the side of the bad guys.

She could hear Detective Estevez talking into his phone in the other room. She heard him say Juana's name. He and Sister Bridget cared about her friend and were trying to help, but Isabel didn't dare to feel comforted. She couldn't feel better with Juana still out there. "Sister? Do you think Juana is alive?"

"That's what I'm praying for."

Milagro sighed. They smiled at the dog that had fallen asleep on Isabel's lap. "Tell me about Juana." Sister Bridget took Isabel's hand. "She must be a very special friend."

Isabel sniffed. "Juana's been my best friend my whole life. She would always come up with crazy ideas." She laughed a little and cried too. "Like once, when we were twelve, she tried to dye her hair blond." She giggled, thinking about Juana's hair. "It came out orange. Juana kept saying that she meant to dye it that way because she really wanted to be a *redhead*. Juana was all dancing around and singing 'Don't Cry for Me Argentina' all opera-like."

Sister Bridget smiled at that. "Juana sounds like a fun friend."

"She is. She cut it, but it grew back. Her hair." Isabel went quiet. "Juana could have gotten away, you know."

"What do you mean?" Sister Bridget asked.

"She wouldn't go without me. That's why El Gigante has her." Isabel felt like her eyes had run out of tears. She felt like it was her fault that her best friend had been captured by monsters.

"I remember now what Juana did. When they first stole us in Mexico City. The broken-faced man—"

"Broken-faced man?"

"That's what me and Juana called him. It was because half of his face was...I don't know." Isabel shuddered thinking of the man's half falling down face. "He...he got me in the car first, and Juana could have run, but she didn't. She tried to pull me out of the car."

"Oh, *mi amor*. Oh, what you've been through." Sister Bridget held her tight.

"That's when the giant man, El Gigante—he was in the driver's seat—he hit Juana with a piece of pipe. Hit her on the head, and she was bleeding so much and just slumped over on the seat of the car. She didn't move."

She remembered the devilish supplies El Gigante had kept in his foul-smelling car—knives, duct tape, metal pipe, razor-sharp wire, even some tools—pliers, a hammer, a saw. At first, she didn't know what the items were for, but she found out later.

Sister Bridget had her hand over her mouth, staring at Isabel with tearful eyes.

"They took us both in the car." Isabel's voice broke. "Juana didn't wake up for a long time. Blood on her face and head, in her hair and everything." She ran her fingers through her own clean hair and tried to picture where Juana could be at that moment. "When Juana woke up, that's when the broken-face man took a picture of me and her and sent it to Juana's father. And my mother."

Chapter 7

Isabel's new shoes squeaked on the shiny granite steps of the courthouse. Sister Bridget had given her a pair of black flats that pinched her feet. The nun had also given her a nice black and red plaid skirt and a white blouse with buttons. "I don't want to be here. I want to go home."

"*Mija*, why did you come to the United States then?" Sister Bridget spoke softly, not mad or anything.

Isabel wished she knew the answer. She looked away, embarrassed. She knew the nun didn't mean the words unkindly. It was just that she was ashamed to admit that she couldn't remember why she had come to the United States. She was starting to remember more and more though, and somewhere in her mind, she knew there was a reason.

"Nevertheless, *mija*, you must begin proceedings." Sister Bridget pushed open the heavy courthouse door. "You are a brave girl. You're a mother. Mothers must do a lot for their children." Isabel thought about her own mother who *had* done a lot for her children. That was true.

"There you are, Gidget," a tall, thin lady said in fluent Spanish. She had thick, blonde hair, cut like a man's, but thick and wavy on top and cheerful, brown eyes. And her big, happy smile made Isabel want to smile too.

Sister Bridget laughed and embraced the woman in the crowded courthouse hallway. "My dependable friend. I can always count on you."

Isabel wondered who Gidget was.

"Well, believe me, I was already here. Marty says I might as well bring my pillow and move in, I spend so much time here." She laughed and waved to a Latino man and woman who walked by. Removing his hat, the man paused and reached to shake her hand, bobbing his head, and apologizing for interrupting.

"Oh dear, I know you're very busy. Thank you for taking Isabel's case."

"Of course. I'm happy to help."

"And this young lady is Isabel Ortiz." Sister Bridget smiled at Isabel and extended her hand. "Isabel, this is your attorney, Amanda Jenkins."

"Very pleased to meet you, Isabel." Amanda shook her hand. "I understand you've been through a lot. Here, let's sit down and talk for a minute before we go in to see the judge."

Isabel looked around. There were important-looking men and women dressed in suits and skirts. They carried leather cases and computer bags. There were regular people too with serious expressions, whispering and talking nervously. She heard Spanish and English. *This was a mistake. Nothing good will come of it.* She should have run away.

"Now, now, *mi amor.* I know this is hard but try not to be afraid. I'll be here with you." Sister Bridget put her arm around Isabel's shoulders and led her to a bench against the wall where Amanda was removing documents from her briefcase.

Amanda looked up. "Sister Bridget, can you excuse

us for a moment?"

"Yes, of course." The nun took her leave.

Isabel kept an eye on Sister Bridget to make sure she didn't go far.

"Miss Ortiz," Amanda began. Isabel winced and stretched her face a bit to keep the tears from flowing. Amanda softened her voice. "Isabel, I want you to know there is something called attorney-client privilege. It means that I am *your* lawyer, and anything you say to me, I will keep it a secret. I'm not Sister Bridget's attorney; I'm *your* attorney. Understand?"

Isabel looked at the floor and nodded.

"Now, you must always tell me the truth. Okay?"

She nodded again.

"Okay, great. Sister Bridget emailed me your Notice to Appear. Here look." She held the document out so Isabel could see it. The document was in Spanish, but Isabel still couldn't understand it. "You must fully understand what you're being charged with."

"Charged?"

"Look here. Here is your name. See? You are called the *Respondent*." Amanda pointed to words on the document. "And here it says that you are being charged with entering the United States illegally."

How much trouble was she in? She felt sick; her chest felt tight like her heart was getting squeezed.

Amanda looked at her watch. "We only have a few minutes. Do you understand what the paper says?"

Isabel glanced at the exit door. She could pretend to go to the bathroom, slip out of the courthouse and hide. Then she could find her baby and steal her back. It wasn't really stealing. Gabriela was hers.

"Miss Ortiz...Isabel. Do you understand? Do you

have any questions?" Amanda looked at her watch.

"No questions." Isabel didn't *really* understand, but she didn't know what to ask.

"Okay, then." Amanda motioned for Sister Bridget to rejoin them.

"Dear, if you are serious about getting your baby back, you must cooperate." Was Sister Bridget reading her mind?

"Yes, I understand."

"Okay, good. Let's go." Amanda was already up and walking toward the courtroom. "Don't worry, dear. You won't be the only Respondent in the courtroom." They joined the many other immigrants that filed into the room. "They schedule a lot of cases for the same time. Others will go before you. You'll see; it's not that bad."

The courtroom was filling up. Amanda took a seat in the front.

"*Mija*, this thing that you must do is only the first step in the immigration process." Sister Bridget whispered as they took seats further back in the courtroom.

What was *the immigration process*?

Like the others, Isabel stood and then sat back down when the judge entered the courtroom. She'd expected a whiskery, old man, but he was kind of young.

People were called to stand before the judge, and she caught on to the process. A woman, who spoke Spanish, the translator, told the immigrants what the judge was saying. A few didn't need her to tell them because they spoke English. Each only took a few minutes. Amanda Jenkins stood next to many of them;

she was their lawyer too. A few who were called, didn't go forward.

"What happens if they call somebody, and they're not here?" Isabel whispered to Sister Bridget.

"They are arrested and deported."

It was good she hadn't run away.

One Respondent spoke a different language. Sister Bridget told her it was Hindi.

"Does nobody understand him?" Isabel asked.

"They will bring another interpreter for him," Sister Bridget explained. "The judge told him to come back on a different date."

The man bowed and nodded as if he understood.

"Is he Rarámuri?" Isabel whispered.

"I don't believe so, no. I think he is Indian."

"Yes. *Los Rarámuri, los indios*."

"No, *mija*, I mean the man is Indian from the country of India."

"Oh, yes, yes." Of course. She knew about the country of India. But it was funny how the Indian man's rich, reddish-brown skin and thick, black hair was just like that of the Rarámuri people who lived in the canyons of the Sierra Madre in Mexico.

Isabel's mind wandered to the gentle Rarámuri. It was good that these kind, helpful people existed in the world. The Rarámuri had saved her life after El Gigante had thrown her to the rocky ground and left her in Chihuahua. So, really, they had saved her baby's life too.

Isabel remembered El Gigante gripping her neck and lifting her off the ground. Juana had tried to help her, even jumping on El Gigante's back, yelling and crying, trying to make him release Isabel. And he did release her. But he forced Juana back into his car and sped off, leaving Isabel behind. Detective Estevez had said that Juana's father kept sending money. That was why El Gigante kept her.

Isabel recalled being all alone in the middle of nowhere. The white-hot sun smoldered, desiccating everything around her. She couldn't move her arm, and her ankle wouldn't hold her up. She must have blacked out from the pain. The next thing she knew, there was a soft whisper. "Are you alive?" Someone nudged her foot. She opened her eyes, but it was as if they were still closed. She couldn't see anything. It was pitch dark. And it had turned cold.

The guy didn't wait for her to answer. He rolled her onto her back. She winced even now, remembering the agony—her shoulder had been dislocated, her ankle was twisted and swollen. It had been too dark to see the guy's face. Without saying a word, the man picked her up and started walking. He walked a very long way. The sun had risen by the time the guy finally arrived at his destination and lay her down upon a blanket in his mother's hut among the Rarámuri. The mother took Isabel in and nursed her back to health. The guy's name was Marcelino, and later when Isabel got to know him, he admitted that he had carried her for twelve hours that night. He had happened upon her while journeying from Creel to his village of Urique with provisions for his family and neighbors. He had carried his purchases on his back and Isabel in his arms.

Now in the courtroom, Isabel's turn to go before the judge came too soon. When she heard her name, she felt as if her heart had stopped, then pounded too fast. Sister Bridget urged her to stand and go to Ms. Jenkins at the front of the courtroom.

Isabel stood halfway and noticed that Sister Bridget stayed seated. "Aren't you coming?"

"No, *mija*. Ms. Jenkins will be with you." She nodded toward the lawyer who stood at the front of the courtroom. Isabel sat back down.

"*Mija,* only your lawyer is allowed to be with you. I'll be right here. I won't go anywhere. Go on now." Sister Bridget pressed lightly on her back. Ms. Jenkins gestured to her. People turned and stared. The judge called her name again.

Numb, Isabel stood, walked forward, and took her place next to Ms. Jenkins.

Everything the judge said, the translator, a nicely dressed girl with a long ponytail, said in Spanish. The judge, an angular-faced man with black hair and glasses, asked her name, address, and native language. Isabel answered with a shaky voice, and then he asked if Amanda Jenkins was her lawyer.

Isabel looked to Ms. Jenkins, then turned back to the judge and nodded.

"Speak up, Miss Ortiz," the judge said.

She swallowed hard. Her throat felt dry. Amanda put her hand lightly on Isabel's back and kept it there.

"Yes," Isabel said.

The judge read from a file. "Isabel Ortiz is being charged with entering the United States illegally and escaping custody." He looked up at the two lawyers. "Okay, then. Who wants to start?"

The ICE lawyer stood and spoke first. The interpreter translated.

"Miss Isabel Ortiz, fifteen years old, a resident of Mexico, entered the United States illegally on May 2,

71

2018. Pregnant. Apprehended May 2, 2018. Detained in Pearsall." He took off his glasses and leveled a stare at Isabel's lawyer. "Your client, Ms. Jenkins, escaped custody on June 8, 2018. *That* just doesn't happen."

The judge banged his gavel on the sound block, and Isabel jumped.

"Mr. McNeal, direct your words to the court." The judge sounded angry.

"Yes, Your Honor." The ICE lawyer took his seat.

Amanda Jenkins stood and spoke next. "Your Honor, Miss Ortiz is fifteen. She was eight months pregnant when she was detained in Pearsall. She was terrified at the prospect of having her baby taken from her. Between the time she left detention and now, she has given birth to a healthy baby girl."

The ICE lawyer stood again. "Your Honor, the United States urges that Miss Ortiz be deported and the baby turned over to the state."

Amanda scolded him. "Mr. McNeal, you're not representing CPS. This isn't family court."

The judge banged his gavel again; the clamor reverberated throughout the courtroom.

"Ms. Jenkins, Mr. McNeal, direct your comments to the court, not to each other."

"Your Honor—" the ICE lawyer began.

The judge interrupted. "And, as you know, whether or not her baby is removed from her is not the business of this court."

When Isabel heard the interpreter say, "baby removed from her," she felt light-headed, and her knees buckled. Amanda put her arm around her and held tight. "Be strong, sweetie. For your baby."

Isabel tried to stand straight. *For Gabriela,* she

thought, struggling to keep her head high. She stared at the translator, waiting to divine the words that the ICE lawyer was saying.

"Miss Ortiz crossed the border alone. An unaccompanied minor." The ICE lawyer pointed his pen at Isabel without looking at her.

The judge removed his glasses, peered at Isabel, and shook his head. He looked tired. It was what it must feel like to disappoint a father. She lowered her gaze, repentant.

The judge put his glasses back on. "Unless Miss Ortiz requests relief, I order her immediate removal."

Good, Isabel thought. She wanted to go back to Mexico. She needed to go find her best friend, Juana.

"Tell him I'm not going back without my baby." Isabel hadn't thought to whisper.

"Your Honor, my client does request relief. She requests withholding of removal."

"Why is that, Ms. Jenkins?" The judge looked up from his notes.

"She is seeking custody of her child who is currently in foster care."

Chapter 8

It was still dark the next day when Sister Bridget completed her morning run. Austin was going on ten days of hundred-degree heat, so once again, she took her exercise before the sun rose. The darkness also served to hide her clothing: sweatpants and a t-shirt, not exactly the religious attire the Sisters of St. Paul were expected to wear. At least not in public. But she couldn't very well run three miles in an ankle-length habit, could she? Granted, *running* was not a term that could strictly be applied to her exercise. Her pace was somewhere between a saunter and a trot. Some might even call it a quick walk, but her speed matched that of her little dog. *Milagro* was the perfect name for the stray terrier, for indeed, since she had brought the dog into her home, his companionship was like a miracle. She was grateful for the joy Milagro had brought to her life.

As she got closer to her street, giant, ominous shadows loomed, warning of the Texas State Cemetery ahead. The haughty shapes weren't really shadows at all, but rather the huge oaks that lumbered over the resting places of prominent Texans. She didn't fear the graves. She quite enjoyed the grassy knolls and graceful oaks. *During the day*. In the dark though, she quickened her pace, and Milagro led the way past the menacing trees. How had she ever managed before Milagro? And now, by the grace of God, Isabel had come into her life. She'd only housed the girl for two weeks, but already she felt a protective bond and a special friendship with the teenager.

Once she passed the cemetery, Sister Bridget crossed over Fourteenth Street and spotted the illuminated cross atop the parish steeple. Turning onto Lydia Street, she stopped short. Something was wrong—an Immigration and Customs Enforcement vehicle was parked in front of the church. A white and green SUV with black lettering. Two other unmarked cars sat at the curb. A uniformed officer in a black bulletproof vest with ICE printed boldly on his back, stood casually looking at his phone by the Our Lady of Guadalupe fountain in front of the church's double doors. Did they have Isabel? Sister Bridget looked to the vehicles. They appeared to be empty. At least, so far.

How could this be? Had not the girl been released to Sister Bridget until the outcome of her immigration trial, not to mention, her family court trial? Why was ICE there?

Her little house was on the other end of the church property. She would have to pass the ICE officer to get there. She needed to get to Isabel before they did. The poor child had been through enough. The officers would surely give her a fright. Sister Bridget could at least prepare the girl for what was coming.

She scooped up Milagro and veered to the right into the yard of the Yañez family. She tripped over little Brandon Yañez's scooter, which he always left on the grass next to the walkway. Shielding Milagro in her arms, she landed on the grass and rolled onto her right side to protect the little dog. He let out a yelp, nonetheless. "There, there, no harm done." She cradled the dog like a baby and lumbered to her feet. She kissed him on the head, and he licked her nose. She should have known the scooter was there. It was always there.

Dear, dear, dear. Should she cut through the church playground to get to her house? No, she might be seen. It would be better to go around the block and approach her house from the other side. She would just have to add an extra block to her exercise. "Let's go." She set Milagro on the ground and doubled back the way she came. The dog followed. She elongated each stride, breathing hard and dripping sweat by the time she reached her house from the other direction. She cut across the neighbor's lawn so the officers wouldn't spot her, entered her dark carport, and carefully opened the squeaky screen door. She pulled the cord over her head on which she carried her house key, but the door was not locked. Had she left it unlocked? Not likely. She was meticulous about such things.

The house was dark. She didn't need a light to navigate her small, familiar dwelling. And she didn't want to draw attention.

Sister Bridget drew close to the bed where Isabel slept. "Isabel," she whispered. The room was pitch dark. There was no reply. Sister Bridget raised her voice. "Isabel, wake up, *mija*." She reached for the girl's shoulder, but there was only a pillow. "Isabel, wake up, dear." She reached further across the bed. There were only blankets, no Isabel. The girl was not in the bed. Had ICE already taken her?

She checked the bathroom, the living room, and the kitchen. "Isabel. Isabel, where are you?" Milagro hurried from room to room, sniffing furiously. The girl was not in the little house.

There was a faint knock at the door. Sister Bridget swung it open to find a disheveled Father Bartosh in robe and slippers.

"You really need to carry a cell phone." The little priest was bleary eyed and unshaven.

"Excuse me, Father?" She patted her pockets. Indeed, she had forgotten her cell phone.

He entered, but then turned around, stuck his head back out, and peered up and down the dark street. He came in and closed the door.

"Immigration and Customs came looking for Isabel." He wrung his hands. "They nearly knocked down the parish door."

"They arrested her?"

"No. God forgive me. I lied. I said no such girl lived here. I suspect they were unaware of your little house." He rubbed his grizzled chin.

"Where is she? Have they gone?" Sister Bridget said.

"She's not here?" They stared at each other.

"No," Sister Bridget said. "Has ICE gone?"

"Yes, yes, they've gone." He absently looked over Sister Bridget's shoulder and about the house. "The officers searched the rectory and the church. They even went into the sacristy. Turned over the altar linens in the closet…"

"Where is she, Father?" She switched on the overhead light.

"Have you looked all over?"

"Yes, yes. She's not here. I've looked everywhere." She was thankful her house looked like a regular home. And being at the edge of the church property, the officers wouldn't have known to check it. But where was Isabel?

"Maybe she's hiding." Father Bartosh checked the coat closet. "Maybe she saw the ICE officers and hid."

They called her name. Milagro sniffed at the bed comforter and the bathroom rug.

"If she were present in this house, Milagro would have found her." Sister Bridget held her hand to her mouth. *Blessed Mother, pray for Isabel.*

"Does she know anyone in Austin? Could she have gone to a friend?" Father Bartosh asked.

"No friends that I'm aware of."

Sister Bridget checked Isabel's drawer. "Her clothing is still here." Isabel's pajamas were strewn atop the bedcovers. "She took the time to change before she left."

"She didn't take her things, so I'm sure she'll be back." Father Bartosh's watery, blue eyes crinkled with concern. He closed his robe over his pajamas and tied the sash tighter.

"Of course, you're right, Father." Sister Bridget put her hand to her forehead and looked at the floor. She felt the anxiety she imagined a mother might feel.

"Once she sees the coast is clear, she'll be back. Don't worry, Sister." He patted her shoulder and took his leave.

Sister Bridget wasn't so sure about that. Isabel had expressed a desire to go back to look for her friend, Juana. But she had also made it clear that she wasn't leaving without her baby. She didn't know what to think.

She showered and dressed, then she prayed and

meditated.

With renewed confidence in God's help, Sister Bridget picked up the phone, and trapping the receiver between her ear and shoulder, she found Isabel's lawyer's number in the directory of her computer. While the phone rang on the other end, Sister Bridget gazed out the kitchen window as the darkness faded to muted gray. Somebody was looking back at her from behind the large mountain laurel next door. *Oh, for the love of Pete. Poor child. She must be very frightened.*

Amanda's receptionist answered the phone. "Good morning. Amanda Jenkin's office."

"Yes, hello, *mija*. Pardon me, I will call back later." Sister Bridget hung up the phone, distracted by whoever was hiding in the garden. *Was* it Isabel? There was only one way to find out.

"I'll be right back," she told Milagro.

She exited the house, crossed under the carport, and headed toward the neighbor's yard.

The person—*was* it Isabel?—rustled the laurel bush and dashed off, running fast and scattering leaves. She *or he* wore black pants and a black sweatshirt with the hood up. The clothing, the body type, something reminded Sister Bridget of that mysterious person she had seen on the school's playground that morning, the morning Milagro had found the baby. Was this the same person?

Sister Bridget knew Isabel's clothing. And the girl did not possess black pants and a hooded sweatshirt.

"Wait, dear, come back." Sister Bridget sighed, looking down at the fresh tunic that she had just put on. She shook her head. "Oh, for the love of—" She grabbed up the thick fabric and took off after whoever it was.

Across the street, Mr. Garcia dragged his trashcan, rumbling, to the curb. The slight carpenter wore his work uniform and boots. He pointed. "He ran between those two houses."

Sister Bridget didn't slow down. *He?*

Mr. Garcia raised his coarse voice. *"Necesitas ayuda?* You need help?"

Sister Bridget hollered and waved. "I'm fine. *Buenos días!"*

"You never going to catch him," he shouted. "I never seen nobody run that fast."

"We shall see about that." She huffed, flatfooted, her sensible shoes slapping the pavement. She picked up speed and turned onto the grass between the two houses. Her trail dead-ended at the wooden fence that separated two yards.

Whoever it was, seemed to have vanished. A resident German shepherd lunged behind the fence to her left, barking furiously and clawing the wood. A screen door squeaked, "Bruno! What's going on, boy?" It was Alma Westinghouse, mother of three teenage boys.

Sister Bridget opened the gate and looked in. Bruno jumped and licked her eyeball. "Alma, it's me." She rubbed her eye.

"Sister Bridget?" Alma, towel in hand, took hold of Bruno's collar, and using sign language, told the dog to sit and stay. Sister Bridget had learned a little sign language too in order to communicate with Alma's middle son. "What in the world? What are you doing?"

"Chasing someone."

"What? Again? Who are you chasing this time?"

"I don't know. Someone wearing black pants and a black sweatshirt with the hood up. Did you see anybody?"

Alma screwed up her face. "You don't know *who* you're chasing?"

"That's correct." Sister Bridget breathed hard, one eye shut tight.

She gave the dog's head a rub. "That's a good boy, Bruno. Good guard dog." The dog panted, tongue dripping. "Alma, did you see anyone?"

"No, but Bruno's been barking and barking. I had some bacon on the stove. I was wondering why he was making a ruckus."

"Which way did...uh, *he* go, Bruno?" Sister Bridget looked around, but of course, no one would have come into the yard, not with Bruno defending it. Alma gave Bruno a signal and the dog ran straight to the back fence that separated her yard from that of MaryAnn and Daniel. MaryAnn was the young mother that had looked after the newfound infant the morning Sister Bridget had found Isabel in the chapel. The running person must have climbed over the other neighbor's fence into MaryAnn and Daniel's yard.

Sister Bridget hadn't seen MaryAnn in several weeks, since the morning she, or rather Milagro, had found the baby. Now that she considered it, she hadn't seen MaryAnn nor Daniel at all lately, not even at Sunday Mass. Bruno let out a low *woof* at MaryAnn and Daniel's fence, not the furious clamor of before.

Sister Bridget tried to see between the wooden planks to the other yard, but the openings were too narrow.

"Here, try this." Alma carried a wicker lounge

chair. She set the chair lengthwise along the fence, and both ladies climbed up and looked over.

MaryAnn quickly snapped the window blind shut, but not before Sister Bridget spotted her.

She and Alma turned to one another.

"Now why would MaryAnn..." Sister Bridget began.

"Hide from us?" Alma finished.

"I know of one way to find out." Sister Bridget stepped off the chair.

"Where you off to?"

"I'm going around to the front door to pay MaryAnn a visit." Sister Bridget brushed downward, smoothing her tunic with both hands. She adjusted her belt, tucked stray hairs, and straightened her veil before marching, determined, past Bruno and out the gate.

Chapter 9

Amid shabby homes with peeling paint, MaryAnn and Daniel's old wooden bungalow stood out like a daisy among weeds. The house was freshly painted a soft yellow and featured a pretty blue door and shutters. Daniel, a painter, had done the work himself. Sister Bridget had watched his progress whenever she walked by. The color was called *Blue de France*, Daniel had said. *Ah, French, so it is,* she had thought to herself.

There were no ceramic pots, statues, showy flowers, nor other adornments like the rest of East Austin. Only short-cropped grass and two freshly planted cedar elms.

Sister Bridget stepped onto the clean-swept porch with its happy-face welcome mat and knocked at the French-colored door. There was no answer. She waited almost a minute before knocking again. She hated to wake MaryAnn's toddler. She tried the door handle. Locked. She went ahead and pressed the doorbell, but it didn't ring. If MaryAnn expected her to go away, well, then, she didn't know Sister Bridget at all, now did she?

"MaryAnn, dear. I know you're home." There was still no answer. "I saw you at the kitchen window." Sister Bridget rapped more forcefully on the wooden door; sharp pain pierced her knuckles. The door opened slowly, and MaryAnn peeked out, trying her best to act surprised, as if she had just then heard the knocking.

But Sister Bridget was good at catching a fibber.

"Sister Bridget...hi, um...sorry, I didn't hear—I mean..." MaryAnn looked to the side and gave up with a sheepish shrug. "Um, can I help you, Sister?"

Sister Bridget had no patience for lies. She bored into MaryAnn with her best intimidating stare.

"Um, well, thanks for coming by, but I'm trying to...uh...I'm busy right now. Sorry, can't visit." MaryAnn tried to shut the door.

Sister Bridget held the door and let herself in. She got stuck between the doorframe and the door as MaryAnn tried to shut it. "Oh, sorry, sorry, Sister, but thanks for coming by, but I don't have time..." MaryAnn was no match for Sister Bridget.

Sister Bridget pushed her way in, and there on the floor was Isabel stacking blocks with MaryAnn's toddler. Though the girl had been with Sister Bridget for two weeks, she hadn't noticed that the luster had returned to Isabel's straight, black hair. It spilled over her shoulder like a horse's mane. Her skin too, had regained a healthy glow; her eyes were bright and alert.

The living room was pretty, though disheveled. The appeal of MaryAnn and Daniel's sleek leather, L-shaped sofa and understated rugs on shiny wood floors was diminished by unfolded laundry, strewn-about blankets, and assorted baby items.

Seeing Isabel playing with MaryAnn's child brought home the irony. Sister Bridget saw two children, really. Isabel, still a child in many ways, yet biologically, she was old enough to give birth to a baby. *Oh, paradoxical life*, she thought.

She couldn't help but think that at that very moment, Isabel's own baby rested in the arms of a different mother, one more mature. Susan, the radiology tech foster mother, unable to have her own baby, was able to give Isabel's baby a home, love, and ample sustenance. Sister Bridget knew that Susan's heart overflowed with love for Gabriela—or *Maria*—the name Susan had chosen for the baby, but Isabel nurtured that baby throughout a dangerous journey and quite nearly died giving birth. She loved Gabriela too.

"*Buenos días, Hermana Bridget.*" Isabel looked up, smiling. She seemed…how did she seem? Different. *At home* with MaryAnn's child. *Happy?*

Sister Bridget fought the urge to scold Isabel for leaving the house. The girl probably wasn't even aware that doing such a thing would give Sister Bridget a fright.

"Look at this big boy." Isabel beamed. "His name is Benjamin. Isn't he cute?" The boy, almost ten months old now, squeaked and smiled.

"*Mija*, I am happy to find you safe. Yes, very cute." Sister Bridget spoke these words in Spanish, smiling at the child. Then switching to English, she looked at MaryAnn. "Could you not have phoned?" Though MaryAnn was Latina, she neither spoke nor understood the Spanish language.

"Sorry, Sister," MaryAnn said. "I did call."

Sister Bridget hadn't received a phone call.

"I only have one number for you. Is it a landline? It just kept ringing. There wasn't any voicemail or anything."

She must have missed MaryAnn's call while she was out for a jog. She had long resisted owning a cell phone, but now that she was a midwife, a mobile phone was essential. She was unused to carrying it with her though. She wrote her cell number on a post-it she found on MaryAnn's counter. "Here's my number." She handed the note to MaryAnn.

She let out a pent-up breath and reminded herself, *just be grateful that Isabel is safe. Thank you, Jesus.*

"I didn't know you were acquainted with Isabel." Sister Bridget said everything twice—once in English, and then in Spanish.

MaryAnn and Isabel exchanged glances.

"Well...I mean, there was that morning when the baby was born..." MaryAnn stammered. "I didn't exactly meet Isabel..."

"Marcelino brought me here." Isabel played pat-a-cake with Benjamin. Then she caught herself and gave MaryAnn a wide-eyed look. "I mean to say, I came here myself. Um...I know MaryAnn..." Her words trailed off, and she went silent. She gazed red-faced at the floor.

"Marcelino?" Sister Bridget looked from Isabel to MaryAnn. Neither would look her in the eye.

The house was silent except for an indiscriminate mechanical buzz emanating from the kitchen, the refrigerator probably.

Then a thin, young man entered from the hallway and pulled back the hood of his sweatshirt.

"*Soy Marcelino,*" he said, eyes cast downward. "Marcelino Quimare." The young man was lithe and muscular, slight of build. His smooth, suntanned skin, coppery. His black, coarse hair was buzzed on the sides, thick on top. His eyes, dark and soft looking. He had a youthful appearance, and yet, the term *old soul* came to mind.

MaryAnn's toddler fussed. The young mother

lifted him from Isabel's arms and spoke above the baby's cries. "Sit down, Sister Bridget." She swiped blankets and toys off the couch. "Sit. Sit. Let me just put the baby down. Marcelino, come, sit." When Marcelino didn't budge, because he didn't understand English, MaryAnn took him by the hand and led him to a chair.

"Here, let me help." Sister Bridget took the diapers and baby clothes off a gray, leather side chair and placed them on the side table. MaryAnn pointed to the chair and repeated to Marcelino, "Sit."

MaryAnn put the child down for his nap and brought glasses of water for Sister Bridget, Isabel, and Marcelino. Isabel and Marcelino politely declined.

"Marcelino, I am happy to finally meet you, my son." Sister Bridget paused to accept the water and thank MaryAnn. "I suspect you are the one whom I've been chasing this morning?" She took a handkerchief from her pocket and wiped her brow, then took a long drink of the cool water.

Marcelino's face grew red. "*Sí.*" He didn't look up.

"How do you know each other?" She turned from Marcelino to Isabel.

"I know Marcelino from Mexico," Isabel said.

"My son, what are you doing here? Why were you hiding? And why did you run away from me?"

The young man didn't look up.

"Marcelino was the one who told me that ICE was at the church." Isabel collected baby toys and put them in a plastic basket. "He told me I better come to MaryAnn and Daniel's house before they found me and took me away." She glanced up. "And I won't go back to Mexico without my baby." She lifted her chin defiantly and took a seat on the couch.

"What did she say?" MaryAnn moved more baby items and took a seat on the L-shaped couch. Sister Bridget interpreted Isabel's words.

"*Espérate*." Sister Bridget held up her hands. "Let's back up." She turned to Marcelino. "You were at the church the morning Isabel gave birth, were you not?"

He didn't answer. Isabel turned to Marcelino. "What? You were there when I had my baby?"

"*Sí.*" Marcelino's face burned crimson. He looked up and met Isabel's eyes. "You don't remember?" The way he looked at Isabel said a lot to Sister Bridget. The boy cared a great deal for the girl. That was clear.

"But why...how?" Isabel's shiny, black hair cascaded, slipping over her shoulder as she turned to Marcelino. "What happened? The nun found the baby by herself at the statue."

"The church was locked up." He held her gaze. "You were bleeding so much, so I carried you to the only place that was not locked—the little chapel with the altar. I was going back to get the baby, but the nun had already taken her to the little house. And then the police came."

Sister Bridget was happy to hear Marcelino's explanation. She knew Isabel hadn't abandoned her baby.

Isabel had told Sister Bridget that her last memory was of painful contractions after the lady had dropped her off in the darkness that morning. The girl couldn't remember much of anything after that. It must have been difficult for Isabel to accept information about herself when she had no memory of it.

Sister Bridget broke the silence. "I knew I had seen somebody. I told the police, but they couldn't find you."

When Marcelino didn't answer, Isabel piped up. "It's because he's a very fast runner. Marcelino is Rarámuri. The police never would have been able to catch him."

Marcelino's full lips twitched a bit, almost smiling.

Isabel sat forward and tuned to Marcelino. "Wait. You followed me all the way from the Copper Canyons? From Mexico?"

"*Sí.*"

"But why?"

"I just wanted to make sure you were okay." Marcelino looked at the floor. "There are a lot of *narcotraficantes.*"

Indeed, *narcotraficantes*, drug gangs, plagued the Rarámuri in recent years. The Sisters of St. Paul had a mission house and a women's clinic in the town of Creel by the Copper Canyons where the Rarámuri live. The Rarámuri people were known as the *running people,* a unique population with a remarkable love for running great distances, even hundreds of miles. They kept to themselves and were notoriously quiet, guarding their privacy by retreating farther and farther into the canyons of the Sierra Madre in the state of Chihuahua. The Rarámuri didn't trust people outside their tribe. To them, being questioned was rude and intrusive.

Indeed, Marcelino must care a great deal for Isabel. He left the canyons and followed her to a country filled with *chabochis*, the name his people assigned to anyone who was not Rarámuri. Their deep-seated reticence derived from generations of persecution.

"Well, my son, it's a very good thing you were there. I'm very happy to meet you, Marcelino." Sister Bridget smiled at him, though he didn't look at her. "I was beginning to think that Isabel's guardian angel had led me to her in the chapel that morning." She clasped her hands together. "And maybe he did."

"It was me." Rarámuri were a singularly shy people. Marcelino seemed to be in physical pain having to converse so much.

"Isabel, you didn't know that Marcelino followed you?" Sister Bridget tried to gain a clear picture.

"Yes—I mean no—I don't know. I only found out today that Marcelino was staying here at MaryAnn and Daniel's house."

For MaryAnn's benefit, Sister Bridget interpreted into English all that was said.

"And you've been here the entire time?" Sister Bridget pointed to the floor. "Since Isabel had her baby?"

Marcelino didn't answer. The hum from the refrigerator filled the silence.

"Okay, can I say something? I'd like to explain." MaryAnn paused, seeming to collect her thoughts. The others watched as she twisted and fastened her hair with an elastic that she wore on her wrist. "Okay, okay." She sucked in a breath. "Sister Bridget." She looked her in the eye, spread her hands out, then placed them both over her heart. "I am so, so sorry for lying to you." She hesitated. "Well, I mean strictly speaking, I didn't really lie to you. I mean, yes, it was a lie of omission, I guess you'd say…"

Sister Bridget looked at her watch. She didn't interpret to Spanish because MaryAnn really hadn't *explained* anything yet. Isabel and Marcelino listened, not reacting.

"MaryAnn, *mija*, what are you trying to say?"

"Marcelino's been living here with me and Daniel for the past three weeks, while Isabel was in the hospital and while she's been living with you." MaryAnn dropped her shoulders. "He's been sleeping on our couch."

Sister Bridget interpreted.

"Three weeks?" Isabel turned to Marcelino. "Why didn't you tell me?"

He didn't answer.

"What'd she say?" MaryAnn asked.

Sister Bridget interpreted, and again, no one said anything.

MaryAnn jumped in again. "It all started because Marcelino wanted to find out if Isabel and the baby were all right." She looked from Sister Bridget to Isabel to Marcelino. Isabel stared at her, uncomprehending. Marcelino looked to the floor. "He talked to Daniel that same day, the day the baby was born. When Daniel got home from work, he was getting out of his truck, and Marcelino came up to him and asked about Isabel and the baby. At first, we were kind of freaked out because Marcelino was like covered in blood, but he explained it was from when Isabel had her baby, and he carried her to the chapel."

Marcelino must have been watching MaryAnn, Sister Bridget thought. That's how he knew where to go.

"I'm sorry. I'm sorry. I'm really sorry." MaryAnn looked from Isabel to Sister Bridget. "I wanted to tell you. I promise I *wanted* to tell you and I was gonna, but then Daniel said—Daniel speaks Spanish really good— Daniel said that if we told you, and you're so honest and everything, that you would have to tell the border patrol or ICE or the police or something." When she stopped to take a breath, Sister Bridget interpreted her words for Isabel and Marcelino.

"Not because you're mean or anything. Sister, you're the sweetest person in the world, but Daniel said that Marcelino said that he knew Isabel from Mexico and they were friends. I mean, I feel like Marcelino is Isabel's true friend, right? I mean, he followed her all the way here from Mexico, right?" When Sister Bridget interpreted these words to Spanish, Marcelino looked like he would be sick, he was so embarrassed. Isabel blushed.

"You know, Marcelino was right to warn Isabel about ICE. If you think about it, if they had arrested her, then she would have gotten deported, then she would have to get separated from—Gabriela? *Gabriela*, right?" She looked to Isabel.

"Gabriela." Isabel nodded.

In her mind, Sister Bridget piled Marcelino's legal problems onto Isabel's. Now there were two undocumented immigrants to deal with. She forgot to interpret MaryAnn's words.

"Ahem." MaryAnn inclined her head toward Isabel.

"Oh, yes, sorry." Sister Bridget switched to Spanish. "MaryAnn said that Marcelino saved you from being taken away by ICE."

Nobody said anything.

Why *had* ICE shown up for Isabel? Hadn't Sister Bridget been granted sponsorship by the Immigration

Court? Hadn't the judge granted Isabel's appeal for relief from deportation? At least until it was decided whether she could have her baby back? What changed between yesterday and today?

"Sister…Sister." Isabel interrupted Sister Bridget's thoughts.

"Hmm, sorry, yes, *mija*?"

"Why did they come for me? Didn't the judge say I could stay and get my baby before they deport me?"

"I don't know the answer to that question. But I'll certainly call your lawyer and find out."

"Are they going to come for me again?"

"I don't know the answer to that question either. Your lawyer will have those answers." *She hoped.*

"Should I hide?"

Normally, Sister Bridget would have answered an emphatic *no*, but she wasn't so sure.

There was a knock at the door. Sister Bridget flinched, and her heart pounded.

MaryAnn peeked out the window. "I don't know who it is. He looks like a cop or something."

"What does he look like?" Sister Bridget asked.

"Tall, Black guy…good looking."

"Oh, yes, that's Detective Estevez. Let him in…" Sister Bridget looked to Isabel and Marcelino, who was on the edge of his seat, ready to bolt. "Hmm, I'll go outside and speak to him."

****

Estevez wore starched khakis, a blue plaid shirt, untucked with a navy suit coat. And he held Milagro in his arms. The little terrier yelped and wiggled at the sight of Sister Bridget.

"Detective? Milagro? What in heaven?"

"I looked for you at your house. Poor Milagro…" The dog woofed when he heard his name. "He was barking like crazy. Isn't that right, boy?" Estevez set Milagro on the ground, and the little terrier leapt, twirled, and skipped frantically about Sister Bridget's tunic as if he hadn't seen her in ages.

Estevez gave Sister Bridget an ironic look which she found…charming.

She raised an eyebrow, and they both laughed at Milagro's antics. "You were in my home?"

"Milagro really needed to…ahem…relieve himself, and you should really keep your doors locked. I went in through the carport."

I usually keep my doors locked, she thought. "And how did you know to come here to MaryAnn and Daniel's house?"

"I'm a detective." He smiled with his eyes. "Remember?"

She waited for further explanation.

"Your neighbor—*Alma?*—was watering her flowerpots. She told me you were here. I heard you had a little visit from ICE this morning." He smiled at Milagro's rollicking.

The dog started to slow down. Sister Bridget stooped to scratch the terrier behind his ears. "There, there, little one. Be calm."

Milagro took one more turn and lay at Sister Bridget's feet. He looked up, panting.

Sister Bridget stood and dusted dog hair from her hands. She took Estevez's arm and led him down the steps. "Let's go to my house. I'll make you a nice cup of coffee." She didn't want to take a chance. Maybe he was there to take Isabel too.

"Aren't you going to say good-bye to your friend?"

"No, no, it's fine. She's busy with her little boy. I'll phone her later." They walked around the block to Sister Bridget's house. Milagro followed.

"Where's Isabel?" he asked.

She waved the question away. "Oh, it's hard to say. You know how teenagers can be." It was a fib wrapped in a truth. She'd have to mention it at her next confession.

Chapter 10

Isabel waited nervously in MaryAnn's house for Sister Bridget to return. Had the *migra* come to get her? Should she run away?

She couldn't wait any longer. She went to the window, pulled back the curtain an inch, and peeked. But Sister Bridget wasn't there.

Isabel turned to MaryAnn who was standing close behind, also looking. "*Adónde fue la monjita?*" She asked though she knew MaryAnn didn't understand Spanish.

MaryAnn shrugged, shook her head, and said something. Without the nun translating, neither understood the other's words.

MaryAnn reached into her back pocket and took out her cell phone. She scrolled and swiped the screen till she got to an app called *Speak and Translate*. MaryAnn spoke into the phone, tapped an icon and the phone said in Spanish, "It was the detective guy. Tall, Black, good looking?"

"Oh, that's Detective Estevez. What did he want?" The app translated Isabel's words to English.

The baby whimpered in the other room.

"I don't know." MaryAnn shrugged. She stroked Isabel's back. "Hold on, let me get Benjamin. He probably needs a diaper change."

When MaryAnn disappeared into the baby's room,

Marcelino said, "We better go."

"Why?" Shouldn't she thank MaryAnn? And it was only polite to say goodbye.

"Come on." Marcelino looked her in the eye.

"Is it because you think Detective Estevez will come back and arrest me? Because he won't. He's nice."

"No." Marcelino almost touched Isabel's hand. He held back though. "It's just they will still be looking for you to deport you."

"How do you know that?"

"Just trust me."

One thing Isabel knew about the Rarámuri people was that they didn't like to talk, and Marcelino was saying a lot, so it must be important.

"Okay. Let's go." She started for the front door.

"Let's go out the back way." Marcelino quietly opened the door from the kitchen to the backyard.

"What if the police are there?" Isabel whispered as she followed him out.

"We aren't going to the nun's house. I think you're not safe there. They might come for you again." Bruno barked on the other side of the back fence. "Let's go this way. I want to show you something." He led the way through the side gate and out to the street, the opposite direction of Sister Bridget's house. They left the neighborhood and entered the business district.

"Where are we going?" Isabel glanced at a barbershop with a slow spinning barber pole—red, white, and blue. She told herself to remember it, so she could find her way back. A neatly combed middle-aged man with a newspaper tucked under his arm left the barbershop and entered the coffee shop across the street. She told herself to remember the coffee shop. "I need to go back to the nun. I don't want her to think I ran away or anything. I have to go to court to get my baby back."

"ICE will come for you again." Marcelino walked fast.

"They…the judge already gave the nun permission to let me stay with her." Isabel held back before crossing busy Cesar Chavez Street. "How do you know they will come back for me?"

There was a break in traffic, and Marcelino stepped onto the street. Isabel didn't follow; she turned and looked back toward Sister Bridget's house.

"Do you know why they came for you?" He stood in the middle of the street. "The police? The ICE?"

"I don't know."

He returned to the safety of the sidewalk, eyes downward. He took a deep breath, and then looked into her eyes. This time, he did touch her hand, but it was only his fingertips brushing against hers. Isabel remembered the Rarámuri way—the whisper of a greeting. It was like a butterfly fluttering on her fingertips.

The gesture was more than a regular handshake. Her whole body remembered with a fevered heartbeat, a flashback to Eduardo, her baby's father.

She tucked her hand behind her back. She didn't need Marcelino's fluttery touch. And she didn't need Eduardo either. She only needed to get her baby and go back to Mexico.

"I'm going back to the nun's house." Isabel turned to retrace her steps while she still wasn't too far. The nun held the path to the court and to her baby.

Marcelino caught up to her. "Just a little farther." He almost took her hand, but again held back. He was the shyest boy Isabel had ever known. He *had* helped her get away from ICE that morning. And he was the one that carried and walked with her for twelve hours after El Gigante had left her in Chihuahua. And if she believed what Marcelino told her, he was also there when Gabriela was born. She'd never asked him to do any of those things, but maybe she wouldn't have survived if he hadn't. Same with her baby. She'd go with him a little farther. But she kept track of how to get back to the nun's house.

They traversed another neighborhood. Spanish music hung in the air, and workers conversed in Isabel's native language, as they built up a pretty, modern home in between ancient, ramshackle cottages.

A dull roar of traffic emanated from a raised freeway beyond the rooftops of the small houses. Despite the distant crush of traffic, there before her was a quiet boulevard lined with hearty oaks. They crossed the street to an expanse of towering pecan trees beyond which beckoned a sleek, blue river.

Isabel and Marcelino crushed fallen leaves underfoot beneath the shade of the lofty pecan trees, their canopies like wide, luscious parasols. The Colorado River, wide and deep, made shushing noises and the breeze picked up the water's coolness and blew it onto Isabel's face. The refreshing breeze beckoned her, though the intense sun, still low, made her squint. They stopped at the water's edge and shielded their eyes from the sun's glint on the river's eddies.

"This is what I wanted to show you." Marcelino gestured toward the river. He kept glancing over his shoulder to the parking lot and the road. Was he waiting for somebody? Or was he checking for police?

Isabel watched the water's movement until she thought she might go blind. Looking away, she rubbed her eyes, but still light from the river danced before her eyes, so she turned her back to it and spotted a vacant picnic table. "Come on."

They both sat on the same side looking away from the river's reflections. Birds flitted branch to branch, twitting and chirping and full-on crooning. Isabel liked the way the air cooled her back. The river and the trees were pretty. The birds sounded nice.

She wasn't mad that Marcelino brought her there. "I'm getting hungry. What about you?"

Wordlessly, Marcelino pointed to a wild, bushy area to the south beyond the stand of pecan trees. A girl was reaching about the bushes here and there and placing something into a basket.

Marcelino gestured toward the girl. "Free food."

It was a community garden and like Marcelino said, the food was free. There were signs in English and Spanish. The Spanish one said, *Jardín Comunitario*. They picked juicy, ripe peaches, crooked carrots, and a handful of soft figs. They rinsed the dirt off in the river and ate their harvest at the river's edge.

Isabel knew Marcelino was holding back something he wanted to say.

Finally, he said it. "They are not going to give you back your baby." He looked sideways at her and actually caught her eye. "I'm sorry."

"What are you talking about?" Isabel wondered what had gotten into Marcelino. "The judge said...the lawyer said...you don't know anything about it. I'll go to court, and they'll give me my baby back. I know they will. They have to. It's only fair. Gabriela is mine."

He didn't say anything.

"Say something. It's because you don't know what you're talking about. Right?"

Someone walked up behind them. Marcelino looked up, and said, "*Buenos días, Daniel.*"

"Daniel? MaryAnn's husband? What's going on?" Isabel hadn't met Daniel before. He was medium height and muscular, like he lifted weights or something. He had short, thick hair and big, kind eyes with curly eyelashes. He wore paint-splattered jeans and work boots, a work shirt.

"Yeah, I'm MaryAnn's husband." Unlike his wife, he spoke perfect Spanish. "Listen, I asked Marcelino to bring you here so I could tell you something that I found out. I already told Marcelino." He looked to Marcelino for acknowledgement, but the young man didn't say a word.

"Tell me." Isabel just wanted to get back to Sister Bridget's house.

Daniel sat on the ground next to her, his legs bent awkwardly in unyielding blue jeans, not knowing what to do with his arms.

"Okay, listen, I work for a contractor." Daniel still fidgeted, trying to find a place to rest his arms. Finally, he stretched out and grasped his knees. Intricate green and blue tattoos covered his forearms. Isabel noticed that the underside of his right arm was bare but for a dainty blue "B" enclosed in a blue heart.

"A what?" Isabel looked back to his face.

"It's my work. I work for a contractor. My boss fixes houses, *remodels* they're called. I do the painting

101

part of the job."

"That's nice, but…"

Daniel took a deep breath. "You know that lady that's taking care of your baby?"

"Sister Bridget told me her name is…" Isabel couldn't remember. Then the name came to her.

"Susan." All three said her name at the same time.

Isabel looked from Daniel to Marcelino and back again. "Did something happen with Susan?"

"Listen, the contractor that I work for is doing a project at her house. Susan and her husband hired him to build a nursery in their house."

"A nursery?"

"A nursery, you know, a baby room. A room for a baby."

"Is Susan going to have a baby?"

Daniel looked at Marcelino. Isabel looked from one to the other.

"They're making the room for *your* baby, Isabel." Marcelino looked at her softly.

"No, that can't be. Why would she do that?" Isabel spoke to the shushing river and explained slowly, "Gabriela won't be with Susan much longer. I am going to the court. Me and Sister Bridget, and the lawyer." Tears blurred her vision, and her voice cracked.

No one spoke.

Daniel broke the silence. "Listen. I heard them talking. I think because I was speaking Spanish to the guys doing the drywall." Isabel didn't know what drywall was, but she didn't ask. "I guess because those guys don't know no English, Susan and her husband thought I didn't understand either."

"What?" Isabel contorted her face, struggling to

stop the tears. Why did Daniel keep saying *listen*? Of course, she was listening. "Just tell me what you know."

"I heard the husband, he's a lawyer, talking to Susan about you. Like if you would be deported or not."

Isabel wasn't hearing Daniel's words any longer. A light came on in her thoughts, distracting her. "Wait. You've been in Susan's house? Have you seen my baby? Is she okay? What does she look like?" She felt as if she'd happened upon a treasure. Daniel had been in the same house as her baby.

"Uh, yeah. Um…your baby is…a baby, a regular baby, I guess, like Benjamin was when he was first born. Except she doesn't cry as much as Ben did. Man, Benjamin cried way more. I only saw your baby a couple of times. Susan was holding her, wrapped in pink blankets."

"Pink?" Isabel smiled, imagining Gabriela in pink blankets.

"Anyway," Daniel said, "I heard Susan talking loud to her husband about his friend, the Regional Agent. They were arguing."

"Regional Agent?" Isabel struggled to pronounce the unfamiliar words.

"Yeah, like a border patrol agent, but I guess he's in charge of the region. Anyway, Susan's husband went to college with the guy. He is friends with him, and Susan kept arguing with her husband, telling him that the guy should do them a favor, but the husband kept saying no. She started crying because she couldn't have a baby herself. After a while, the husband said okay."

"Favor?"

"Yeah. That's the reason ICE came to get you this morning."

"But why?"

"Because you came here illegal, and you ran away from the detention place. They're going to deport you, so you can't go to family court, because Susan wants to keep your baby. Also, they said you abandoned your baby." He said that last part very softly, like he didn't want Isabel to hear it.

"Wait. What are you talking about?" Isabel rose from the water's edge. Her foot had gone numb. She stumbled and limped a few steps, trying to get the feeling back. "Does the nun know? She knows I didn't abandon my baby. She told me I could go to court and get Gabriela back. Did she lie to me?"

"She doesn't know, I don't think. I'm almost certain. Because Susan and her husband were trying to be all secret about the whole thing, but then they started yelling. You know, arguing. But, yeah, they didn't know that I could understand English."

Isabel tossed the remnants of her peach and carrot into the river. "Then let's go tell Sister Bridget…and Amanda, the lawyer lady. They won't let Susan take my baby away." She turned and walked fast in the direction from which she and Marcelino had come.

Marcelino and Daniel caught up to her. "Wait," Marcelino said.

"We have a better idea." Daniel glanced at Marcelino. "The only way you're going to get your baby back is if you take her back yourself."

Chapter 11

"Ten o'clock," Daniel said, "that's when Susan puts the baby down for her nap, and then she goes to the other side of the house to work out in the exercise room. That's when you go in to get your baby. She calls your baby *Maria*."

"What? Why? Her name is Gabriela."

"I guess she likes the name *Maria*. I don't know. I'm just telling you, so you know. Anyway, listen, hey, do you ever watch *NCIS* or *Blue Bloods* or anything like that? *Forensic Files*?" Daniel looked from Isabel to Marcelino.

"What?" she said. Marcelino didn't say anything.

"On TV, you know, police shows."

Why was Daniel talking about TV shows? Some of the families in her neighborhood had TVs, but her family didn't. "What?" She wished Daniel would just get back to the part about stealing her baby back. Though it wasn't really stealing. Gabriela was *her* baby.

"Anyway, the police are always questioning people. The *suspects*. They look for fingerprints for evidence. That's why you need to wear these." He handed Isabel and Marcelino each a pair of work gloves. "I'm going to take you in my van, so don't touch anything unless you're wearing gloves, that way if the police suspect me, and they search the van for fingerprints, they won't find any, and I won't get in trouble for helping you. Don't even touch the outside of the van, okay?

"Daniel, why are you helping me?" Isabel pulled on the dirty, stiff, too-big gloves.

"I don't know." He shrugged. "I guess a baby should be with her mother. I see Benjamin with MaryAnn, and I think, what if he was taken away from us? I mean, yeah, you made some mistakes, but taking away your baby is not right."

Isabel glanced at Daniel's forearm, at the little "B" in a blue heart. The "B" must stand for Benjamin, MaryAnn and Daniel's baby.

"How come MaryAnn didn't say anything? Why didn't she tell me you would come here?"

"She doesn't know, and I'm not ever going to tell her. She would blab everything to that nun, and that…well, that wouldn't work. It's like, I don't know…MaryAnn…she can't help it. She always tells the truth. So, MaryAnn can never find out. Well, anyway, maybe I'll tell her after you guys make it back to Mexico."

Isabel wouldn't tell on Daniel. She'll probably never see MaryAnn again anyway.

"Okay, listen, she does the same thing every day." Daniel looked to Isabel and Marcelino. "The lady, Susan, she puts the baby in the little bed in the husband's room, his office, the extra room on the other side of the house, away from the noise and dust we are making. That's the time to go in and get your baby. Susan won't be able to hear."

He opened the double doors at the rear of the plain, white van. "You'll have to sit on the floor. I made some room for you."

There were no seats in the back of the van, only paint-splattered planks of wood and cloths, cans, paint thinner, brushes, rollers, metal extension rods, and various clutter. They settled in and Daniel started up the van, pulled out of the parking lot, and merged with the morning traffic. Isabel's heart raced. *Could* she go into Susan's house and steal her baby back? She sat, cross-legged, her feet and elbows tucked in, knees up. Fright surged throughout her body, sending vibrations to her fingers and toes. Marcelino sat two feet away, his arms wrapped around his bent legs.

"Listen, the alarm company will be working at Susan's house today. They're putting security in the baby's room. They're the only ones working there today. We are the painters." Daniel pointed to himself. "We are taking the day off from her house to work at another site. I need to go to work over there at the other site today, so nobody will suspect me of helping you take your baby." He glanced back at his two passengers. "Alibi, you know." They didn't answer. "*Forensic Files*? The TV show?" Isabel still didn't know what Daniel was talking about. Marcelino's expression was blank.

Daniel let it go. "Listen, the lady, Susan, she already quit her job at the hospital. I heard her on the phone. She told all her friends and her sister and mother and everybody that she was going to stay home with Maria." Isabel's face burned at hearing her baby referred to as *Maria*. All those days since she had left home, all those days scared when El Gigante wouldn't let her go, when the baby was growing inside her, she had always called her baby *Gabriela*. Anger spread inside her, replacing the fear.

"So here." Grinning, Daniel passed back a schematic drawn on the back of a shop invoice. "Yeah, look at that and memorize it. It's the layout of Susan's house. Then give it back to me because I have to burn it or something, so no one sees the evidence." It occurred to Isabel that Daniel was having fun. It was like he was acting out a television soap opera or a police drama of some sort.

Isabel held the paper in the clumsy work gloves. The little map was drawn on yellow paper with chalk pencil.

Marcelino looked on. "Turn it around the other way. See?" Marcelino pointed. "There is the front of the house."

Isabel saw that the front of the house had a space in front of the door, like an entryway. Daniel had labeled the rooms. To one side of the entry was the living room. *Sala*, Daniel had written. On the other side lay the dining room, *comedor*. Connected to that, was a kitchen, and another living room, and then four bedrooms and five bathrooms.

Daniel corrected them. "No, no, it's better the other way. Turn the map around. Because you're going to go into the house from the back."

Isabel turned the little map back around. She counted the bedrooms twice. "Why do they have to build another room for the baby if they already have four bedrooms? They only sleep in one, right?"

"Well, if you'll believe it, the lady talks a lot on the phone. She tells her friends that she can't give up her exercise room, and her husband uses one bedroom for his home office."

"But still there is one more bedroom."

"That's the guestroom for when Maria's grandparents come to visit."

Again, Isabel's face grew hot. "Her name is Gabriela." In her head, she felt as if she had screamed the words.

"Sorry. The lady talks a lot on the phone."

Daniel turned into a luxurious neighborhood and looked at his watch. "It's nine twenty. Susan puts Mari—er, I mean, the baby down for a nap at ten o'clock. That's when she said she wanted the alarm company workers out of the house."

Isabel's heart jumped. Things were happening fast. "Maybe we should wait until tomorrow."

"Can't. We'll be finishing up the paint job in Susan's house tomorrow, and if you don't mind, I don't want to be nowhere around when you take the baby."

Marcelino spoke to her for the second time since they'd entered the van. "I can help you get Gabriela." When Marcelino spoke, he meant what he said, she knew that. And it was nice to hear Gabriela called by her real name.

"Okay, usually, when the house doors open, the alarm system makes a beeping noise, but the system is turned off right now because of the alarm company— see?" He drove by a sprawling one-story house in front of which was parked a van similar in size to Daniel's van. The blue van was covered with logos and pictures of windows, doors, and locks. It had ladders strapped to its roof. On the side, it said Keep Safe Security. Daniel went by the house and the van without slowing down. He continued out of the neighborhood through an exit different from the one through which he had entered.

****

At 9:35, Daniel dropped Isabel and Marcelino off in a wooded area at the backside of Susan's neighborhood. He got out to give them last minute instructions.

"Each house is on a large property. So, you will have to go fast to get to Susan's house in time. It's the twenty-second house. I counted them." He looked at his watch. "You have to go in the house at ten o'clock when the workers leave. The workers will set the alarm when they leave, and it will activate after six minutes. So, you have to go in and get your baby and get out by 10:06. Understand? Go in through the back door by the p—"

"No," Isabel said.

"What?"

"No, I don't understand."

"The alarm guys. I know them. I've watched them before. They put on the alarm when they finish, then they go out the back door and leave, but it takes six minutes for the alarm to activate. So that means you have from the time they set it until it activates to get in and out of the house, or the alarm will go off when you open a door or window. Remember, go in and out the back door before 10:06, and the alarm won't make a sound."

Isabel was glad she only had six minutes to get her baby. The quicker, the better.

"You don't have phones or anything, right?" Daniel asked.

Isabel shook her head. "I don't have a phone." She knew Marcelino didn't have one either.

"Here, you're going to need this." He removed his wristwatch and offered it to her.

"I can't take that." Isabel stepped back.

"Yes, you can. Here." He held it out farther.

"But I can't give it back to you. After I get Gabriela, I'm taking her home. To Mexico."

"I know. Wish I could help you more, but—"

"You've done enough."

"Just this one last thing. Take the watch. Don't worry, it's not expensive or anything." He offered it with an outstretched arm.

Marcelino grabbed the watch and passed it to Isabel. "Let's go."

Isabel looked at the time, hastily kissed Daniel's cheek, and turned to go.

"Wait. I almost forgot. Here." Daniel reached behind the seat of the van, pulled out a beat-up backpack, and handed it to Marcelino. "Stuff for the baby, like diapers and things." He picked up a glove that had fallen off Isabel's hand. "Wear the gloves when you go in the house. Fingerprints."

Isabel took the glove, Marcelino slipped the backpack on, and they turned and entered the darkness of the dense woods that surrounded Susan's neighborhood. She let Marcelino take the lead. They ran along a deer trail that edged expansive lawns.

Junipers, oaks, mountain laurels and prickly holly hid them from residents. But through the dense foliage, Isabel caught fleeting glimpses of immense properties with lush landscapes, swimming pools, and unbelievably beautiful houses. She had counted nine houses so far. Thirteen more to go. She held up Daniel's watch—9:55.

She picked up her pace. "Go faster." She prodded Marcelino with a hand on his back. He turned and without a word, grabbed her arm and pulled her off the trail and into a thick stand of junipers.

"What are you doing?" She slapped his hand and pushed him away.

"Shh." He pulled her to the ground. Silently, he pointed down the trail and held a finger to his lips. Then she heard scuffling steps in the underbrush. Isabel kept the side of her face to the ground and covered her head with both arms. Her hair spread like a carpet upon the fallen leaves, her heart pounded against the forest floor. Something cold and wet moved along her fingers and her arm. Snuffling noises up close to her ear. She opened her eyes and looked up into the mouth of a giant, white *something* that couldn't be anything but a dog. She'd never seen one that big or that white. It was huge and fluffy. It barked, like the blare of a train, into her ear. She buried her face down under her arms.

A man called in a slow, gravelly voice from the property they had just passed. Isabel hoped it was the dog's owner calling him back to his yard. "*Vete!*" she told the huge animal. The dog raised his head away from Isabel. He sniffed Marcelino and licked his face. Then he resumed his clamoring bark.

The man called again and whistled sharply. His voice sounded close. The barking was nonstop. Footsteps rustled the underbrush. Marcelino tensed up and took Isabel's arm.

The man stood above them, clutching the dog's collar. He angrily scolded them, though Isabel didn't know what he was saying.

Marcelino rose with Isabel in tow, knocking the tall, elderly man to the ground.

The man hollered and frowned, his bushy, gray

brows drawn low over his startled blue stare. His silver hair mussed.

"Are you okay?" Isabel reached to help the man to his feet, but Marcelino tugged at her. "I'm sorry." Isabel was pretty sure the man didn't understand her language.

"Run." Marcelino took Isabel in tow. The dog chased them to the next property, but then returned to its fallen owner.

"It's 9:57." Isabel forced the words out between breaths, her face hot, her whole body was wet with perspiration. She'd lost track of the number of houses they had passed. How would they know which house was Susan's?

Isabel spied a man working on a breaker box at the rear of a house. She and Marcelino watched from the woods as the man flipped a switch and spoke into a cell phone. Isabel didn't understand what he said.

"That box has electricity," Marcelino whispered.

"This must be Susan's house," Isabel said. "Gabriela is in there." The worker placed his phone in his pocket and walked around to the front of the house. Isabel looked at the watch—10:00. *I have six minutes*, she told herself. "Time to go."

"I'll go," Marcelino said.

"No, she's my baby. I'll go by myself." She figured one person would be quieter than two. Marcelino didn't argue. She looked down at her gloved hands, remembering the fingerprints. But wouldn't they know it had to be Isabel taking her own baby whether she left prints from her fingers or not?

"Here," she handed the gloves to Marcelino. "Gabriela won't like these. She'll probably cry."

Isabel heard the alarm company van start up and pull away as she slipped through the back door by the swimming pool. She found herself in an area with a shiny round table and chairs, cheerful yellow and pink flowers on its center. Sun streamed through shimmering curtains. To the right was a large, glistening kitchen. The house was silent. Not even the silvery kitchen appliances made a noise. Frosty air cooled her hot face, and it smelled like cinnamon cookies. Somewhere in her mind, Isabel thought it would be a nice home for Gabriela, but she dashed the idea.

She pictured the map that Daniel had drawn. Farther to the right beyond the kitchen were two bedrooms and the new baby's room that Daniel had been working on. Susan was over there on that side exercising. To the left beyond the large living room with its overstuffed leather furniture, fireplace, and plush blue rug, lay the big bedroom, the master, Daniel called it, and a big bathroom. Gabriela would be sleeping in the husband's office on the other side of the bathroom. Isabel panicked for a second. Would the husband be in there too? No, Daniel said the husband leaves the house every day to go to his other office.

Isabel took a step toward the left side of the house, but she stopped and cringed. Her flip-flops made a loud squeak on the shiny tile. She looked in the direction where Susan would be, but saw nothing, so she took off her shoes and left them by the door. She'd get them on her way out, *after* she had Gabriela. She made her way down the hallway, barefoot on cool tiles. She noticed there was a song playing over and over in her mind ever since leaving Daniel's van, something that they played a lot on the radio in Mexico; it was a fast *reggaeton* beat. She passed a room with a gigantic bed, and then the fancy bathroom. Gabriela would be in the next room. Isabel's heart beat fast to the rhythm of the *reggaeton*. She opened the door and was met with the unmistakable scents of a baby—powder, baby soap, diaper wipes—clean smells. And there sleeping peacefully in a white crib with pink bedding lay Gabriela. Isabel had never held her baby before, but she had helped when her little brother was born. She could do this.

But was this the right baby? She was so perfect. Smooth skin the color of caramel candy. Wispy strands of shiny, black hair combed sweetly into place. Tiny pink lips smiling in her sleep.

"Is that you? Are you my sweet Gabriela?" Isabel whispered. Static noise emanated from a baby monitor on the desk. It blinked blue and green. Suddenly there were doors slamming and sounds of running steps on the tile floor.

Isabel grabbed Gabriela and clutched her to her chest. Susan was in the hallway. Isabel slammed the door and locked it, looking around. The wall shook. Susan must have slammed her body against the door. The woman screamed and pounded at the door. There was banging on the window glass too. It was Marcelino pulling off the window screen and gesturing for the baby.

Isabel unlocked the window and raised the glass. The security alarm blared, and the baby wailed. "Oh, Gabriela. I'm sorry. Don't cry." Should she put her back? Her mind, filled with *reggaeton*. She felt as if someone else was doing her actions. As if she was detached from her body, just watching.

"*Dámela*." Marcelino held out his arms.

Isabel passed the crying infant out the window and followed. She ran for the woods close behind Marcelino. The blare of the alarm and Susan's shouts faded behind.

Chapter 12

"So, Sister, tell me, how is it you have no idea where Isabel is?" Detective Estevez's six-three frame made Sister Bridget's kitchen table look small. "You *are* her sponsor." She evaded eye contact. "Right?" When she didn't answer, he added, "She's in your charge?"

She brought the coffee pot over. "Cream and sugar, Detective?"

He looked at her side eyed. "Milk, if you have it. If not, no worries. Black is fine. I brought her backpack and the note with your name and address on it."

"Ah, yes, good idea. Maybe seeing those items will arouse more memories. You can leave them here, and I will show them to her when she returns."

"No. I can't do that…so where *is* Isabel?"

"Oh, just out for a turn about the neighborhood. Ah, *café con leche*." She changed the subject. "We have the same tradition in Mexico." She warmed milk on the stove, poured it into a small, cow-shaped pitcher and placed it and a spoon next to the detective's cup. He poured in the frothy, steaming milk first, then the coffee. He offered the milk to Sister Bridget, and she did the same.

"I haven't had my breakfast yet. Join me, Detective?" She opened and closed the refrigerator and pantry, collecting the ingredients for *migas*.

117

"I wouldn't say no to a little something."

Sister Bridget rummaged through the pantry.

"Ah, good. That's a good thing to hear."

"What can I do to help?" Estevez joined Sister Bridget in the small, close kitchen as she bustled ingredients onto the countertop.

"You may chop, or you may whisk the eggs."

He surveyed the onion, tomato, jalapeño, and corn tortillas that Sister Bridget had gathered. "I'll whisk the eggs."

"Top shelf on the left." Sister Bridget wasted no time chopping the other ingredients.

"I'd say you're making *tortilla Española*." He reached into the refrigerator for the eggs. "But I don't see potatoes."

"Ah, but I'm making a close relative to your Puerto Rican *tortilla Española*."

"Oh, a Mexican cousin, huh?" Estevez found a bowl, cracked the eggs, and whisked them smooth.

"Not really a Mexican dish, no. I believe *migas* are more *Tex-Mex*. Only in Texas can such a delicious concoction be conceived." She cut the corn tortillas into inch-long strips, fried them in a pan of hot oil, and drained them on paper towels. "I love my *migas* crunchy." She then sautéed the onion, tomato, and jalapeño. "I'll take those eggs now, Detective." Estevez added the eggs to the vegetables and stirred until they were cooked through. Lastly, Sister Bridget folded in the crispy tortilla strips.

They sat down for their *migas* and coffee. Sister Bridget made the sign of the cross and bowed her head to pray silently. Her prayers were more about Isabel and Juana and the baby than the food on the table. She added Marcelino too. She opened her eyes, sure that Estevez was about to ask about the whereabouts of Isabel again. "Detective—"

He held up a hand to stop her. "Just tell me, Sister, did Isabel run away?"

"No, of course not."

He stared at her.

"I would tell you if she did." She said this in all seriousness. For goodness' sake, Isabel was just around the corner at MaryAnn's house, but she kept that information to herself.

"Okay, I believe you. Your reputation precedes you."

She had had several dealings with the police department—finding missing persons, calming domestic disturbances, and such.

"Good. Now, Detective, I wanted to ask *you* a question…"

"*Ooo-kay.*" Estevez seemed to anticipate her question. "About this morning…I heard you had a little visit from Immigration and Customs Enforcement." He rolled his eyes. "Damn it…" he paused shamefaced. "I mean…sorry for the language. But sometimes it pis—I mean, it makes me angry. I just don't like law enforcement agencies acting without informing those of us already involved in the case.

"In other words, I would have liked a heads up before they barged in on you like that. ICE did a sweep all over Austin. They didn't bother to tell any of us, not even the police chief, the mayor, nobody. The chief is pretty pissed off too—I mean upset. Sorry."

Sister Bridget suppressed a smile, remembering the little priest's rumpled appearance that morning. "To tell the truth, ICE did not enter my residence. Father Bartosh was the one that got barged in on." Her little house at the edge of the parish grounds looked to be just another house in the neighborhood, so they must have overlooked it. "But Detective? Why did they come for Isabel? I signed an affidavit to be her citizen sponsor. I *am* a legal U.S. citizen. Naturalized. I was told that she could stay with me while she awaited her trial."

He rubbed the back of his neck, "They called it Operation Cross Check. Like cross checking illegals with people that have criminal records, and then rounding them up."

"Isabel is not a criminal."

"Well, she did escape from the detention center in Pearsall, remember? The girl isn't blameless." He grimaced, held back, but went ahead and said, "She abandoned her baby. That's a crime too. It's child endangerment."

"Isabel still can't remember what happened that morning. But I have learned…" How could she tell him what really happened without getting Marcelino in trouble?

"You've learned what?"

"I don't think she meant to abandon her baby. She was in very bad shape herself. She's been through so much. She almost died, for goodness' sake."

"I know, I know. You have a soft spot for her. I don't blame you." He waved his hands as if to surrender. "But. She *did* break the law. She ran away from the detention center, and by all appearances, she *did* abandon her baby."

It may have appeared that way, but Isabel had *not*

abandoned her baby, Sister Bridget was more sure of it than ever. She just had to figure out how to get the truth out without Marcelino and Isabel getting arrested.

"Detective…"

"Call me Joaquin…or Jack, that's what the guys call me." Estevez spoke without looking up. He was busy digging into his *migas*.

"Ah. Joaquin." Sister Bridget smiled. "Jesus' grandfather was a Joaquin. You're in good company…I want to ask you about this morning."

"Is that so?" he said.

"Excuse me? Oh, Jesus' grandfather…yes, on his mother's side."

Estevez smiled, amused. Those smiling eyes. "That's a coincidence. I get *my* name from my grandfather. And I followed him into law enforcement. He was my hero growing up. These *migas* are delicious, by the way. Really hit the spot." He'd cleaned his plate, and she'd barely touched hers.

"Thank you," Sister Bridget said. "I was very close to my grandfather too." She smiled at the memory of her fun and kind grandfather. "We called him—"

"Abuelo," they both said together. Estevez's deep, resounding laughter eclipsed Sister Bridget's. It was like he was shouting. Happy shouting.

"It seems we have something in common, Detective."

"Call me Joaquin." His smile lingered.

Sister Bridget checked her watch. Isabel was probably waiting nearby for the detective to go away. *Smart girl*, she thought.

"Joaquin, like Jesus' grandfather. Katie will like that story." He chuckled.

"Katie?" Sister Bridget said.

"My daughter. She's twelve."

"Oh? Twelve? What a wonderful age." Sister Bridget thought of the giggly middle school girls at the parish school.

"Ha! The words of someone with no children." He laughed again, that glad shout that rang out and filled the house. He leaned back in his chair and looked away. "A twelve-year-old girl is…the spawn of…a killer prosecutor, always pointing out my faults and, believe me, there is nothing I can say in my own defense…aanndd…a guardian angel…always there, always there, she's never *not* there…to save me from…my faults."

Sister Bridget could never have imagined such a relationship between herself and her father. As a child, she had been devoted to her father. She never would she have pointed out a fault. Come to think of it, she adored her father so much she never thought he had faults.

"Despite what you say, or *because* of what you say, your daughter *does* sound wonderful."

"Yeah, she's great." Estevez glanced at his watch, then looked at the ring on Sister Bridget's finger.

She smiled and held up her left hand. "Third finger, left hand." Her thin, silver band was dull and scratched up.

"Wife of God, huh?"

"Something like that." Sister Bridget laughed. "I like to think of God as more like a best friend, a soul mate. But there *is* quite a lot of bridal imagery in the bible. It's beautiful. I feel loved. I'm God's *beloved*. But then, we all are." There was that amused smile again. "Something funny, Detec—er, Joaquin?"

"No, nothing, nothing." He suppressed a smile.

"Go ahead. What are you laughing at?"

"I'm thinking it must be a lot easier dealing with an invisible spouse than a real one."

"I can assure you, that isn't the case. God has high expectations that are sometimes difficult to live up to."

He chuckled. "Yes, my wife, Janet, held me to a high standard too." She heard melancholy in his voice.

"*Held*? You have a daughter, but you have no ring." She said it gently. She had assumed he was divorced.

"Yeah, I stopped wearing it after I lost her." The sparkle disappeared from his eyes; his mouth became a straight line. "I miss the ring sometimes." He frowned, nodding toward Sister Bridget's ring.

"I'm so sorry, Joaquin." She felt his loss. "How difficult it must be to lose your wife. And so young to be a widower."

"Yup, pretty sad all right. It's been six years, almost, but it's still hard. She died October 12, almost six years ago. You're lucky. You married an invisible guy." He glanced at her ring again. "You'll never have to watch him waste away from cancer. And die."

Sister Bridget was used to people seeking her out to answer the common human question—*why would a good and loving God allow human suffering and death?*

"My dear Detective, I don't blame you for your bitterness. We can't help but fight against the human condition—the disease, the disappointment, loss, death—the challenges that make life so difficult." She took his hand from across the table. "You're right. I'll never feel the pain of losing a spouse."

"So that's the answer, huh? Too bad, that's life? I was expecting something deeper." His smile finally returned, and he shook his head as if to shake off the thought. "By the way, I turned fifty yesterday. *Not* such a young widower, as you say."

"Ah, fifty. Welcome to the club. Happy birthday." She raised her coffee cup. "And I'm happy that I've provided a bit of information for Katie. You can tell your daughter that her father's name is the same as that of Mary's father."

"Katie will get a kick out of that. She's been bugging me. Wants me to take her to church. She says she's curious and wants to see what it's all about."

Sister Bridget nodded and smiled. "Is that right?"

"I told her she's not missing out on anything. She'll get over it. It's just a phase she's going through."

"It must be difficult raising a child alone."

He blew air through pursed lips. "It has its ups and downs. And speaking of young girls..." He left the unfinished sentence hanging in the air.

Sister Bridget caught her breath and stood to gather their plates, hoping Estevez would not repeat the question: *where is Isabel?*

"So, Sister, where is Isabel? Still on that walk?"

Sister Bridget didn't want to break God's commandment. She didn't want to lie, but also, she wanted to protect Isabel.

"Maybe I'm wrong, but how can I allow a mother to be separated from her baby? Without even a day in court?" She felt heat rising in her chest and neck.

"I'm not trying to separate Isabel from her baby." Estevez rose and gathered utensils too.

"Then why are you here?"

124

"Remember, my job is in human trafficking. I just want to talk to Isabel. I'd like to get more information from her, see if she remembers anything more about Alejandro Maldonado, the guy she calls *El Gigante*. He might still have her friend, Juana San Miguel. Or at least he knows where she is. And don't forget, we think he's also trafficking drugs to the U.S."

Should she tell the detective the truth? But the truth was getting so complicated. Now there were two illegal immigrants. Would he detain Marcelino? She wanted to trust the detective, but the ICE raid shook her.

She glanced at her watch. An hour had passed. She needed the detective to leave so she could call MaryAnn.

"Oh dear. It's getting late. I really must go. Thank you for your concern, Detective. Let me give you my phone number..."

"I have it."

"Oh yes, of course." She walked him to the door. "Well. Such a nice visit. Call me another time, and we will arrange a time to go over the..." The phone on the kitchen wall began to ring. She raised her voice above the loud ringing. "Call me anytime. We will arrange..." She was practically shouting over the noise. When the ringing finally stopped, her cell phone began to buzz.

"You going to get that?" Estevez stood inside the door, not budging.

"Yes, of course." She had to answer it. It could be one of her mothers going into labor.

"Sister Bridget!" It was MaryAnn. "Where did you go?" The girl sounded panicked.

"My dear..."

"Are Isabel and Marcelino with you? I mean, I've

been over here wondering where everyone went. You left with that policeman guy, and then I got busy feeding the baby and stuff, and the baby is asleep finally, and everyone is gone. Okay, I fell asleep with the baby." The young woman spoke fast, not even stopping to breathe. "He was up all night, so…I mean I was so tired; I fell asleep too. I didn't know if I should wake up the baby and go look for them? I didn't—"

"MaryAnn." Sister Bridget tried to interrupt. Estevez pretended to read the bible that sat open on the low coffee table.

"I mean, I've been so worried…" MaryAnn continued.

"My dear," Sister Bridget interjected, looking at her watch. "I'm sure they're fine. How long have they been gone?"

"I don't know. I mean, I went to take care of the baby around nine o'clock, maybe? I mean, I nursed the baby and all and changed him and stuff…I mean, so they're not there?"

"No, they're not." Sister Bridget glanced at Estevez and lowered her voice. He was talking on *his* phone too. "Not to worry, my dear, I'm sure everything will be fine." She clicked off the call and checked the time. It was ten twenty-five.

"Detective, I really must go." She grabbed up her satchel and keys. She must find Isabel.

Chapter 13

The soles of Isabel's feet slipped over rocky terrain, leaving gritty streaks of blood on stones. Dense, low oaks and junipers grew prolific on the craggy, jagged slope. The heavy woodland shielded the runaways from view, but the barbed terrain punished Isabel's bare feet. *What happened to my shoes?* She must have left them in the house when she took her baby. She didn't know what it felt like to step on fire, but the thought consumed her that she was running on a smoldering campfire, pain with every step. She followed Marcelino at a slant, down the hill, toward the murmuring sound of the river below. She kept her focus on Marcelino's lower back, below the backpack that Daniel had given them. She looked down at her bloody feet, then returned her gaze to that stable place on Marcelino's back, quiet and calm, his legs in fluid motion, his upper body cradling the baby, *her* baby, with a rhythmic motion. But that one spot was steady and calm. Miraculously, the baby had stopped crying. She asked God, *is this real or is it a dream?* The answer came quickly—*this is real*. Her next questions—*How did I get here? Where were Juana and El Gigante?* There were no more answers, and no time for more questions. She need only follow Marcelino. They descended, slipping on rocks and crashing through bramble.

She stepped onto a sharp stone, her foot already mangled. The pain turned flesh to fire and sent a shock up her leg to her hip. She screamed, lost her footing, and fell downward past Marcelino.

Marcelino grabbed the edge of her shirt, but she slipped away and tumbled downhill. She skidded across the pebbly shore on the sides of her shins, shouted, and plummeted into the deep, dark river. At first, she gained a foothold, but the river bottom shifted beneath her feet. She floundered, trying to resurface, but unable to swim, her feet glided along the bottom, taking her deeper and deeper. Below the water, twilight turned to night in the blink of an eye. But it was only morning, wasn't it?

Underneath the water, Isabel, desperate for air, her brain, deficient of oxygen, remembered the broken-face man.

The darkness that had blocked her memory, turned to light, and she remembered. She imagined she saw Broken-Face there immersed in the river with her. She put her hand to his neck, felt the sharp wire, looked into his desolate eye.

She remembered the frightful journey on the road in Mexico, Isabel bound with Juana in the backseat. El Gigante had pulled over. He told the broken-face man, "Go, get the money."

Broken-Face had returned with forty-six hundred pesos.

"You took four hundred." El Gigante was enraged.

Now submerged in the river, Broken-Face's ghost spoke to Isabel. "I didn't take nothing." His eye was resigned to his fate though.

She remembered Broken-Face had grasped for the car door handle, panicked, ready to flee. But El

Gigante, with one smooth motion, so smooth, lassoed him around the neck with a wire and tugged, ever so elegantly severing the man's head from his body.

Isabel opened her mouth to scream. River water rushed in. As she blacked out, she recalled Detective Estevez's words, "Your mother sent *almost* five thousand pesos."

Poor, pitiful Broken-Face hadn't stolen any of the ransom money, but El Gigante killed the wretched man, nonetheless.

****

She awoke in the mud on the river's edge. Strong arms forced her onto her side, and she coughed up what seemed like buckets full of river water onto the dirt and pebbles. The big, white dog, soppy and dripping, peered with concern into her face. It was daylight again. She didn't know where she was, but she sensed Mamá and her little brother close by cooling their feet in the river.

Someone turned her onto her back, and she looked into the crinkly, blue eyes of the old man whom she had seen earlier on the trail, the dog's owner. Concern in his eyes, the man spoke, but she didn't know what he was saying.

"Are you okay?" Was it the voice of her little brother? She turned to look and thought she saw her mother holding a baby.

The elderly man lifted Isabel high off the ground. He was tall. They were both dripping wet. Was she a baby too? The man was cradling her like one. He turned his face to a house high on the hill by the radiant sun. He said some words, but Isabel only understood the word *telephone*.

The next time she awoke, a silver-haired woman

was fussing sympathetically in English, trying to wrap a towel over her even as the man struggled up the hill.

"Here, you take the baby." Marcelino handed the screaming child to the gray-haired lady and took Isabel from the man.

"Déjame!" Isabel resisted being carried, so Marcelino set her down, but the lacerations on the bottoms of her feet sent shocks throughout her body and brought tears to her eyes. Her knees buckled and she caught herself on a large rock. There were sirens in the distance as Marcelino picked her up without a word and carried her the rest of the way up the hill to the big house. She caught a glimpse of the huge dog, no longer white and fluffy, leading the way.

The elderly man hurried into the house, and the others followed. The woman rebuked the dog. "Boomer, no." The dog turned back and plopped down by the swimming pool. Still perched in Marcelino's arms, Isabel took in the posh interior of the home. Coming in from a hundred-degree heat to cool, air-conditioning felt like a second chance, like hope. The baby sucked hungrily on the old woman's pinky finger. The man returned with an armful of blankets and spread them on a leather couch. He spoke to Marcelino, gesturing for him to lay Isabel onto the blankets.

Marcelino propped Isabel on the couch and looked at her feet, wincing. Isabel didn't know what the old couple was saying, but she didn't care much. The house was a respite. It was so clean, and it smelled like flowers. She wasn't entirely sure she wasn't dreaming.

"Can I have my baby?" She stretched out her arms for Gabriela.

The woman said something, but Isabel didn't

understand. Then pinching the fabric of her own shirt, the lady pointed to Isabel's shirt and said, "wet."

"Oh yeah." Isabel wanted her baby, but she didn't want to get her all wet.

The lady said some words to her husband, and he dragged a plush chair close to where Isabel lay. The woman laid Gabriela snug on the chair and positioned two throw pillows so the baby wouldn't roll off. Then, fussing, she hurried out of the room. The man was dialing the phone.

A television droned from somewhere in the house, and the woman shouted.

The old man put down the phone receiver and hollered back.

Rushing back into the room, the woman opened a cabinet to reveal another TV. She pressed buttons on the remote, and there on the television screen, appeared a picture of Isabel.

Isabel sat up. "*Que?*"

"*No se.*" Marcelino was confused too.

The elderly couple stared at the television screen. They looked to each other, and then to Isabel. Distant sirens rose louder until it seemed like they were inside the house. From above, came the slow chopping sound of a low-flying helicopter.

On the TV screen was Susan crying hysterically and pleading to the camera. She held up a picture of a baby, *Isabel's* baby. The old couple looked to the sleeping child.

The man went back to the phone and picked up the receiver.

His wife told him something and gestured for him to wait. The husband put down the receiver and looked to the television screen. A young reporter, a woman with long, wavy, blond hair, was talking into the camera, and then there was a split screen. The reporter talked on one side of the screen, while a picture of Isabel appeared on the other side. It was the picture that had been taken at the detention center before she ran away.

The old man said something to her, but she didn't understand. He nodded and pointed at Gabriela, to Isabel, and then back to Gabriela. Isabel couldn't understand what he was saying.

"Let's go." Marcelino picked up the backpack, and reached for the baby, but the woman tamped her hands downward and said something in a soft voice.

Isabel rose despite the pain. She wished she didn't have to dirty up the couple's floor with her cut-up feet. Dizzy, she pitched to and fro as she picked up Gabriela. She pressed the baby against her body, and headed for the glass doors, the same ones through which they had entered. She would take Gabriela and hide in the woods.

The house was so high on the hill, Isabel could see the top of the helicopter as it flew past the river and low over the canyon. The old man used two fingers to indicate *looking*, and he pointed at Isabel and the baby.

Isabel hurried to the front of the house. She pulled back the drapery and peered out the window. Police cars glutted the street. She wouldn't be able to escape in that direction either.

The wife said reassuring words and used her hands to convey calm. She was tall and thin like her husband. Her grey hair was cropped short; her eyes were a different shade of blue than his. Hers were blue like deep water. His were like the sky. She put her arm around Isabel's shoulders and coaxed her away from the window.

Isabel wished she could make the couple understand that the baby was hers. These people seemed nice. Maybe they would help.

"Spanish?" Isabel asked.

The two elderly people shook their heads. "No." and "No, sorry, no Spanish." Then the man pointed to Isabel and Marcelino and said, "English?"

They both said no. Isabel remembered the app MaryAnn showed her.

"*Teléfono*?" Isabel asked.

The old woman picked up the phone's receiver and offered it to Isabel.

"No." Isabel handed the baby, whose clothing was now damp, to Marcelino. "*Teléfono*." She mimicked tapping on a cell phone.

The woman's eyes went wide, and she nodded. She said something to her husband, but he patted the damp, empty pockets of his black jogging pants and pointed at the river.

The wife fussed at the husband and rummaged through her purse. She finally produced a cell phone and handed it to Isabel. The lady nodded and indicated *go ahead* with a wave of her hand.

Isabel took the phone. She pretended to type on it and pointed to herself.

The lady bobbed her head.

Isabel searched the phone for the app that MaryAnn had used. She had to click on the App Store to find it. What was it called? *Speak and Translate?* Yes, there it was. She pointed to the app. "Is okay?"

The old woman looked at the app. Her husband looked over her shoulder.

The man took the phone and scrolled through the instructions. "English to Spanish. Spanish to English."

The woman nodded and clicked on the app, and the man walked down the hallway and disappeared.

Once the app downloaded, the woman clicked an icon and spoke into the phone. "My name is Mabel." She pointed to the hallway. "That's my husband, Walter." What are your names?" She smiled at Isabel and Marcelino.

The app translated her words to Spanish in a stilted, robotic voice.

Mabel heard the translation and clapped. She laughed out loud. "Well, what do you know!" The app translated those words too, and Isabel didn't know how to answer.

"*Sé que es mi bebé. No la robé.*" She pointed to Gabriela.

The app translated. "I know she's my baby. I didn't steal her."

"Oh, honey, I know it. That's what they were saying on the news." Mabel pointed at the television screen. "They said you are supposed to be deported, but your baby must stay here."

Isabel waited for the translation. "Why?"

"Well, honey, they said it's because your baby was born here in this country, so your baby is an American citizen."

Isabel looked to Gabriela who contentedly sucked on a bottle of formula that Marcelino had somehow produced from Daniel's backpack.

Marcelino had dumped out a pile of diapers,

clothing, and baby blankets onto the couch. He had changed Gabriela into dry clothes too.

Isabel didn't care about citizenship. Gabriela was hers, not Susan's.

"Thank you, Marcelino." She hadn't even thought to feed her baby; Marcelino had taken it upon himself. When the bottle was empty, the baby gurgled and fussed.

Mabel showed Marcelino how to burp the infant, and baby Gabriela quieted down. Then Mable wrapped the baby snug in a receiving blanket, placed her onto the soft chair, and she fell into a peaceful sleep.

Isabel gazed upon the infant's face, so smooth and soft, not a line of worry. She finally had her baby, and she wasn't ever going to give her up.

When Walter appeared in dry clothes, Mabel gave him instructions, and the app translated. "Go on out to the front of the house, Walt. I bet all the neighbors are out on the street what with all the sirens and everything. We don't want to be conspicuously absent. If they ask, just tell them I have a headache."

"Honey, you missed your calling." Walter was tying the laces of his sneakers.

"How so, dear?"

"You could have written crime novels."

"Well, I certainly have read enough of them. Now go on out, and don't slip up. Not a word about our guests." She pretended to zip her lips together.

Her husband responded in kind and added a locking motion.

Walter left the house through the front door, and Mabel fetched Band-Aids, rolls of gauze and a tube of ointment. "Now let's get you cleaned up and into some

135

dry clothes." Isabel followed Mabel to a bathroom where the woman ran a warm shower and handed Isabel a set of clean, dry clothes. "These are from...oh, the seventies, but I think they'll do. They were my daughter's."

Isabel showered, changed, and returned to the living area, with bandaged feet, limping, and wearing Mabel and Walter's daughter's jeans that had been cut into shorts and a faded green Rolling Stones t-shirt. Her long hair was washed and brushed.

"Oh, but don't you remind me of my daughter." Mabel set a pair of soft, pink slippers on the floor in front of Isabel. "Now you slip those poor feet in these. Hope they help."

Walter returned. "They've got the whole neighborhood blocked off."

"The whole neighborhood? So, no one can come in or go out?" Mabel spoke softly so not to wake the baby, but loudly enough for the translation app.

They had gotten into the routine of pausing for the app to catch up.

"That's right. Well, no, they're letting people through, but they're searching cars and checking the I.D. of each person to make sure they are residents. They're looking for the baby kidnapper."

To Isabel, the words were sharp barbs. "I'm not a kidnapper. Gabriela is mine."

"Of course, she is, hon. We know that. We'll figure this out." Mabel looked at her watch. "I bet you kids are hungry."

Walter used the griddle on the stove to grill up buttery cheese sandwiches on white bread. They ate and watched the news while the baby slept on the plush chair, tucked in on one side with soft throw pillows.

"They make no mention of you, Marcelino," Walter observed. "I don't think they know about you."

Isabel turned to Marcelino. "Susan didn't see you."

Chapter 14

Sister Bridget hung up the phone with MaryAnn, grabbed her satchel, and swung it over her shoulder. She couldn't sit around and wait for Isabel any longer.

"Detective, I must go." She would borrow Father Bartosh's car. He hid a key in the fender.

Estevez was talking on his cell phone. He stashed the phone in his jacket pocket. "Isabel kidnapped the baby." And he headed out the door too.

"What in heaven's name? Wait. I'm coming with you."

Estevez stopped and turned. "Did you have anything to do with this?" Sister Bridget almost ran into him.

She was offended that the detective asked that question.

"Detective Estevez." She was angry, but she held her tongue. *Patience and humility,* she told herself. She took a breath and started again. "Detective Estevez, you don't know me, so I can understand how you might think—"

"Come on, let's talk about it on the way to the foster family." He hurried out the door. Sister Bridget looked about for her key, snatched it up, and stashed it in the big, loose pocket of her tunic. Milagro was at her heels, eager and panting.

"Sorry, boy. You'll have to stay home and watch

the house. There's a good boy." She closed and locked the door. Heat blasted her face.

"Aren't you hot in that thing?" Estevez opened the passenger side door of his bronze-colored sedan. He waited while she settled her tunic, scapular, rosary beads, and computer bag.

"I'm fine." She had grown accustomed to Austin's summers.

He started up the car. "And why do you carry that computer everywhere?"

"I never know when I may need it, Detective. You, know, world at my fingertips." When he said nothing, she continued. "To be honest, I value the connection that my computer gives me. It connects me to people and information when I need it."

"I guess. But a smart phone does the same thing, and it fits in your pocket."

"True, but I don't have a smartphone; I have a flip phone." Smartphones were expensive, and she had taken a vow of poverty after all. She resisted possessions that duplicated the same function. "Are you sure Isabel took the baby? I can't believe it." But then with ICE visiting the parish, maybe the girl had gotten scared. But she didn't seem scared that morning at MaryAnn's house.

"Are you sure you can't believe it? When was the last time you saw the girl?"

"So, Detective, you're allowing me to accompany you because you want to interrogate me? Okay, when was the last time I saw Isabel?" In most cases honesty *was* the best policy. "This morning when you went looking for me at MaryAnn and Daniel's house. She was inside the house."

"What? You mean she was *right* there? You could have stopped her before she kidnapped the baby?"

"Is it technically kidnapping when the baby is actually her own?"

"Yes. The child had been placed in foster care, so yes, legally, it's kidnapping." She thought so.

"Detective Estevez. Joaquin, how could I have stopped her if I didn't know she was planning to take the baby? And remember, the reason she left my house was to avoid being taken by ICE."

"Now, wait a minute, I told you I didn't know anything about the ICE raid."

"And I'm telling you I didn't know Isabel was going to take her baby."

"Okay, fine, fair enough. But you knew I was looking for the girl, and you lied to me."

"I must correct you, Detective. I didn't lie. I merely didn't answer the question." Or was she telling another lie now? That's the problem with lies; they're hard to keep track of.

He let out an exasperated breath. "Uh huh, is that some kind of technicality? Not lying by not telling the truth?"

Probably.

"I keep strict account of my lies, so I can confess them once a week. Well, to be honest, sometimes I must visit the confessional twice a week. Anyway, turn here." She pointed to the right. "Let's have a quick word with MaryAnn. She might know more than she's saying."

Estevez gave her a look, wide-eyed and open-mouthed, like he couldn't believe her nerve. "No, we're going to the Johnson's, the foster family." But he turned right anyway. "Yeah, let's have a talk with MaryAnn. That's a good idea."

MaryAnn opened the door with her screaming little boy in her arms. "Oh my gosh—Sister Bridget, what is happening?"

"My dear, give me that boy." Sister Bridget took MaryAnn's raucous child off her hands. "Come on, sweetie, come to *Tia* Bridget." Sister Bridget lifted the toddler in the air, jostled him gently, and made a funny face. Her "wooga, wooga, wooga" made the boy laugh.

"Thanks, Sister." MaryAnn's face was pinched. She was on the verge of tears.

"Is something wrong?" Estevez said to MaryAnn.

MaryAnn looked to Sister Bridget.

"This is Detective Estevez. He wants to ask some questions about Isabel."

MaryAnn turned red, and when she tried to speak, words wouldn't come out. She coughed and cleared her throat.

"Do you need some water, miss?" Estevez said. Sister Bridget patted her on the back.

"I'm…fine." She cleared her throat again. "I just can't believe…people have been calling me. My phone is blowing up. And like Twitter, Instagram, Facebook, the TV *news,* everything. About the baby being kidnapped."

"We know, *mija.* We know." Sister Bridget shook her head and bounced MaryAnn's little boy on her hip.

"It was Isabel and Marcelino!" MaryAnn put her hands on her hips, paced a few steps and back again. Then she threw her hands to her side. "They took Isabel's baby from the foster mother. Oh my gosh, they're going to be in so much trouble, aren't they?

Will they get arrested?"

"Right now, let's just worry about making sure they're safe." Sister Bridget wished MaryAnn hadn't mentioned Marcelino.

"Who's Marcelino?" Estevez's question was met with silence.

"Yeah, I don't think the police know about Marcelino." MaryAnn looked like she wished she'd kept her mouth shut. "I've been glued to the TV and social media. Nobody has mentioned anything about him." She looked to the television screen, which showed a news reporter talking into a microphone in front of a police barricade.

"Who's Marcelino?" Estevez directed the pointed question to Sister Bridget.

Sister Bridget told him as much as she knew which wasn't much. She had only met the young man that very morning. It was up to MaryAnn to admit that Marcelino had followed Isabel from Mexico. He had been with Isabel when her baby was born, but Isabel just learned that information that very morning as well.

"Are Marcelino and Isabel going to be arrested?" MaryAnn looked nauseous.

"Oh, yes." Estevez took down a description of Marcelino.

"Do you know where we can find Isabel and Marcelino, dear?" Sister Bridget thought she might be able to ditch the detective and get to them before the police.

"Sister, I promise you, I had no idea they were going to do this." MaryAnn's voice cracked. Big tears slipped from her eyes to her cheeks. "And I just don't know where they went. If I knew, I'd tell you."

"Okay, dear. I know. I know." Sister Bridget had quieted the child, and she handed him back to MaryAnn. "Try not to worry." She kissed the girl's cheek and the toddler's head. "Everything will be fine. You'll see."

****

Two APD cars with lights flashing blocked the entrance to Susan's neighborhood. Estevez showed his badge to a uniformed police officer. "You have a description of the girl?"

"Yes sir, fifteen-year-old Hispanic female, five four, 115 pounds. Long black hair, brown eyes." The officer read from his notes. "She's wearing shorts and a t-shirt."

"Well, listen. Keep an eye out for a Hispanic male too. Mexican national. Short, cropped hair, brown eyes, he's thin, probably 130, 135 pounds. Five seven, five eight. Black pants, black hoodie."

The officer jotted down the description.

"Okay, yeah, let me through, will you." Estevez put his car in drive.

The officer gestured to Sister Bridget. "Should I take down her information?"

"Hello, Officer. I'm Sister Bridget Ann Rincón-Keller." She rummaged through her bag for her I.D. "Sorry, one moment. I know it's here."

"She's with me." Estevez drove into the neighborhood.

"Thank you, Detective." Sister Bridget gave up looking for her driver's license. "Susan's house is just ahead. Take the next left, and I'm sure you'll see media and onlookers."

He gave her a look—one she hadn't noticed before.

143

He lowered his chin toward his chest, as though peering over the top of eyeglasses, though he didn't wear any.

"I've been to Susan's house." She shrugged.

"Why?"

"Visiting Isabel's baby. But I wasn't allowed to see her."

"Really? Why not?"

"Her husband said the baby was sleeping and Susan was too tired for visitors."

"That's understandable. Babies can be a handful."

"True. Except, Susan has a very large mirror in her formal dining room. In its reflection, I observed her holding a wide-awake baby in the sunroom at the back of the house."

"Is that right?" Estevez turned left and parked outside another police barricade.

****

A uniformed police officer opened the door at Susan's house. Estevez showed his ID. "Detective Estevez. I'm Lieutenant Monica Dale, Officer in Charge of the crime scene. Good to meet you." They shook hands. She gave him a run down—a canine unit and search boats were on the way. A helicopter had already been dispatched.

"I understand there was an alarm company working here today?" Estevez looked at his notes.

"That's right, Keep Safe Security." Lieutenant Dale read from her own notes.

"Send a couple of officers to question them. They may have noticed something."

"On it." Lieutenant Dale held the phone to her ear and gave Estevez a *what's-with-the-nun* look.

"Oh. This is Sister Bridget. She's Isabel Ortiz's

sponsor."

"Hello, Sister." Lieutenant Dale shook her hand.

"She found Isabel and her baby. She—"

"What do you mean 'Isabel and *her* baby'?" Susan charged from the kitchen to the entry. "That girl abandoned that poor baby. Maria is *my* baby." She was still wearing her workout clothes; her skin was blotchy yet pale. Eyes puffy and bloodshot.

Sister Bridget tried to calm Susan. "Yes, my dear. I'm sorry to upset you. You must be terribly worried."

"We'll get the baby back," Estevez said. "They couldn't have gotten very far, not with such a small baby. We'll get her back."

Lieutenant Dale hung up her phone and held up a clear plastic evidence bag with Isabel's flip-flops inside. "Especially not without these, she won't get very far."

"Do you think she drowned the baby in the river?" Susan's voice was jittery, scared.

"Now why would she do that?" Sister Bridget said. "Not to worry dear. Of course not."

"What about fingerprints?" Estevez asked Lieutenant Dale.

"We know that girl took the baby. Why on earth do you need fingerprints? Just go find her." Susan's voice was harsh, not quite shouting.

"It's to place—" both Estevez and Sister Bridget said at the same time. The detective gave her that peering over the nonexistent eyeglasses look.

"Sorry, you go ahead." She looked over his shoulder to the hallway.

"It's to place the girl at the scene of the kidnapping for later when we bring charges." Estevez gave Sister

Bridget a sidelong glance.

"Sorry. I'll just take a look at the nursery." Sister Bridget moved toward the hallway.

Estevez put his hand on her shoulder, stopping her. "Oh no, you won't. I can't have people disturbing evidence."

"I completely understand. Do you mind if I ask Susan a question?"

Estevez took a deep breath. "Fine. One question. Then I need to get on with this."

"I'll make it quick." She turned to Susan. "My dear, your home is lovely."

Susan let out a demoralized breath.

Estevez looked at his watch.

"What I wanted to ask is, why did you put an addition on your home?"

"What...why?" Susan stammered.

"I'm sorry, I just noticed the lines on your tile." She pointed to the hallway. "There are remnants of the blue tape that held down the plastic that contractors use to protect the floor."

"Is it really—" Susan objected.

"Is it a nursery? Is that what the addition is?" Sister Bridget asked. "Is it for Isabel's baby?"

Susan became even more agitated. "That has nothing to do with anything. We've been planning to adopt a baby for a year and a half. We—"

Susan's husband rushed through the front door. "Honey, don't say any more." He tossed his briefcase onto a leather bench. "I got here as soon as I could. They're blocking the whole street." He hugged his wife, and she broke down sobbing. "Excuse us. Come on, sweetheart, let's go sit down." The couple went through the kitchen to the breakfast table.

"Interesting," Lieutenant Dale said.

"Yeah, I wonder how she knew Isabel would be deported, and that she would get to keep the baby?" Estevez wrote something in his notes.

Sister Bridget held on to that thought. *Maybe the court would have sympathy for Isabel, the victim of back door shenanigans.* "I won't hold you up. You go about your business. I'll wait outside."

Estevez gave her a suspicious look. "Stay out of trouble."

"Yes, of course." She exited out the front door. Now where would Isabel have taken her baby? The detective was right. They couldn't have gone very far. Not with the canine unit, helicopters, and police boats. No indeed, the young people were still in this neighborhood. Of course, the police needed a search warrant to enter a house. But she didn't.

It was twelve oh-five, and the sun was blazing. The fragrance of sage blossoms and sweet rosemary filled the air. The temperature would probably peak over one hundred degrees later in the afternoon. Sister Bridget walked around to the back of the house. Police tape and evidence tags made it obvious—the screen had been removed, and the kids had taken the baby out the window. Police officers moved about, collecting evidence, measuring, and taking photos. She knew and greeted a few. An air of confidence, she found, went a long way. No one questioned her presence there. She examined the crushed grass by the window. Probably where Marcelino paced for several minutes waiting for Isabel. She must have handed him the baby, and then they probably ran for the woods. Susan must have discovered them; that's why Isabel left her shoes behind.

Sister Bridget took the closest path to the woods—across Susan's lush, manicured lawn. *This part must have felt nice on Isabel's bare feet*, she thought.

Then she entered the dense woods where the ground sloped and became jagged and rocky. The farther into the thick cedars, oaks, and mountain laurels, the quicker the ground dropped off. She imagined making the trek bare footed. It couldn't have been pleasant. Gravity caused Sister Bridget to increase her pace, snagging and ripping her tunic in the brambles. She grabbed hold of branches and tree trunks as she descended. Did Isabel and Marcelino follow this same path? If she had not been going down the hill so fast, certainly she would have spotted a blood trail from what was sure to be Isabel's damaged feet. She feared she might plunge right into the river. Finally, she grabbed a hold of a cedar elm near the river's edge. Soaked in sweat and breathing hard, her shoes skidded on the gravelly shore. She clasped the crucifix that she wore around her neck and wondered if it was possible that Isabel and the baby might have fallen into the river? And Marcelino? Maybe he went in after them. Could either of them swim?

Blessed Mother Mary, pray for those children.

Sister Bridget looked back up the hill. Thick foliage blocked any view of Susan's house. To the right, the hill ascended higher to a cliff, the highest point in the neighborhood. At the apex of the cliff stood a regal home with a wall of glass through which someone spied on her with binoculars.

She knew exactly who lived in that house—Walt

and Mabel Morrissey from Mobile Loaves and Fishes.

Chapter 15

With police cars all over the neighborhood, Walter and Mabel convinced Isabel and Marcelino to hide out in their house for the time being.

There were constant updates on the local cable news about the *kidnapped* baby. Isabel wished she could understand what the reporters were saying. The app was no good at translating the TV.

"I have an idea." Walter called his daughter in Colorado who instructed him how to put closed captions on the TV.

He pressed buttons on the TV remote control and Spanish captions appeared along the bottom of the screen.

"It's Spanish," Isabel told Marcelino. "Look."

"Spanish." Marcelino squinted at the TV. Isabel wondered if he could read. Or maybe he needed glasses? Just in case, she read the captions in a loud whisper between bites of grilled cheese, trying not to wake the baby.

"The child's been missing for two hours," the reporter said. "The Travis County Sherriff's office has brought in their canine unit to search the woods behind the foster family's house. I'm told by a source who wishes to remain anonymous that the girl dropped something or left something behind. The source telling me that item, whatever it may be, its scent is being used by the canine unit to search for the girl and the baby."

Her shoes. Isabel and Marcelino looked to the glass doors at the back of house, beyond which lay the woods and the river.

Mabel looked to Walter. "Canine unit." She too looked to the dense trees beyond the glass doors. They all four approached the back of the house and looked out. At first, nothing looked different, the helicopter had moved on to a more distant location. But then Isabel saw the fluid movements of a black German shepherd in the underbrush. Its police handler followed, holding the dog's leash. She stepped aside, behind the wall, afraid of being spotted, her heart hammering. Would the dog sniff her all the way up here to the house on top of the hill?

She went back and sat cross-legged on the floor next to the chair where her baby slept. She read the captions on the news. The young blond with the wavy hair reported the same news again and again. Missing baby, undocumented unaccompanied minor, searching the woods with dogs. Isabel stopped reading. Instead, she watched her baby sleep. Gabriela looked perfect— her eyes, nose, ears, and mouth. All her parts were normal, but to Isabel, the little, tiny features were extraordinary. She didn't know why, it just seemed amazing to think that this was the baby that she carried for all those months. Horrible months.

"Gabriela." She didn't want to wake her; she just wanted to say her baby's name.

"*Gabriela* is a beautiful name." Mabel stood close. She carried the phone to translate her words.

Isabel didn't feel like talking. She'd abandoned her sandwich on the side table next to the couch, not hungry anymore. She thought about dogs sniffing her shoes and searching for her in the woods. "Will the dogs find me here?" She reached up and took Mabel's hand.

"No, dear, of course not." Mabel squeezed her hand, but Isabel wasn't so sure.

"Thank you for being so nice to us."

"Of course, dear. You are easy to be nice to." Mabel enclosed Isabel's hand in both of hers. "Here, let's go sit on the couch and talk so we don't wake up Gabriela. You can watch her from there."

Mable sat close to Isabel on the couch, so close their arms touched. Tears welled up in her eyes. "Can I tell you a secret?" She sniffed and took a tissue from a box on the coffee table.

Isabel glanced at Walter who had gone to the other side of the glass doors and was washing Boomer with bubbly soap and the water hose. Marcelino stayed inside the doors, scrutinizing the woods with binoculars that Walter had produced from a drawer by the bookcase.

Mabel looked to Walter and smiled. "Oh, Walt knows all my secrets."

Isabel nodded and wiped her own damp eyes with her fingers.

"You see, darling, I can't help it." Mabel shook her head and handed Isabel a tissue from the box. "My heart feels for you." The old woman closed her eyes and crossed her hands over her heart. After a short silence, she opened her eyes and looked at Isabel. "When I was your age, I had a baby too. My baby was taken away from me, and there was nothing I could do to get it back."

"But your husband was just talking on the phone with your daughter."

Mabel smiled. "Oh yes, I had another baby with Walt later. She's in her fifties now." She looked through the glass door where Walter persisted in the arduous task of returning Boomer to his fluffy whiteness. "Walt knows I had a baby when I was fifteen. It was 1958. That child, my *first* child, is now sixty-two years old, and I'm seventy-seven." She shook her head. "Not one day has gone by that I haven't thought of my first-born child."

"What happened to your baby? Was it a boy or a girl?"

"I never found out. You see, back then, they just took your child away and gave it to the adoptive parents. It was what my momma and daddy wanted. Mostly Momma. It didn't matter what *I* wanted. They wouldn't even let me see my baby. Oh, I screamed. I cried. I threw a tantrum. Nothing worked."

"That's not fair." Isabel looked to her sleeping baby. Somehow, she loved that baby so much even though she had just met her that very same day.

"I didn't think it was fair either." Mabel gazed at Gabriela too. "And I don't think it's fair that they are trying to separate you from your baby."

"Can you find your baby now that you're a grown up?"

"Oh, I tried, but that time is passed. I missed my baby's life." Mabel blew her nose and took another tissue. "I just hope and pray that he…or she…has had a good and happy life."

"I don't want to miss my baby's life." Isabel's voice cracked.

153

"Well, we're going to help you." Mabel patted Isabel's knee. "Isn't that right, honey?" Walter was hurrying by with two huge towels and a large, bristly brush.

"What's that, Mabel?"

"We're going to help Isabel keep her baby," Mabel said.

Walter stopped and stood stock-still. He scratched the back of his neck. "Yes, Mabel, yes, I guess that's right." Then he continued out the glass doors and vigorously rubbed and brushed Boomer until the big dog looked like a white cloud again.

"I love that man," Mabel said.

"But will you and Walter get in trouble if you help me?"

"Only if we get caught. But who cares? It's good trouble." Mabel smiled at Isabel and hugged her tight. "Now why don't you rest, dear? Here." She positioned a pink throw pillow. "Lay down and rest your poor feet. I need to charge this phone so we can keep talking to each other."

She turned back and told Isabel, "It's taken me all these years, but I've forgiven my mother." She looked down and shook her head. "Momma thought a baby would hold me back from accomplishing my potential. She wanted me to go to college, and I don't blame her for that." Mabel caught her breath and wiped a tear while the app translated her words. "And I did, I became a professional like my mother wanted. You can see some of my writing there." She indicated a bookshelf with neat rows of books, magazines and scrapbooks filled with newspaper articles. "I became a writer, and then an editor. I was a teacher too. People all over the world have read my stories in magazines and newspapers. I wrote about important matters, even met important people, famous people. I've had a wonderful life." She swallowed hard and cleared her throat. "But still, I wonder, did my baby have a good life too?"

Isabel didn't understand most of Mabel's words even though she heard them with the translation app. She did feel the old woman's sadness though. She couldn't help but feel a sadness that lasted a whole lifetime like Mabel's did.

****

Isabel dozed off reading the captions on the local news.

She awoke frightened. *The dogs had found her. They were at the door.* She bolted to her feet, and sharp pain shot like electricity to all parts of her body, making her fingers tingle.

"It's okay. It's just the baby." Marcelino was still looking at the woods through the binoculars.

The baby cried in rhythmic little screams. She had wriggled out of her blanket, her arms and legs lurching with each yelp. Her little round face scrunched red.

"Are you going to pick her up?" Marcelino asked. How could he be so calm?

Isabel's heart raced. Her baby's distress frightened her more than the imagined dogs at the door.

Mable hurried from the kitchen and swept the baby up into her arms. Walter entered from another direction, cooing, "There, there, pooh-bear."

"You warm the formula," Mabel told Walter, "and I'll change this little munchkin's diaper." She cupped her hand under the baby's diaper. "It's a full one."

Walter hurried off, and Mabel admonished him. "Not too warm now, remember how we used to test it on our wrists?"

"Yes, yes." Walter waved his hand above his head without turning around.

Isabel followed Mabel to a bedroom, walking tenderly in the soft slippers. The elderly woman had put layers of soft blankets on top of her daughter's old desk, so it could be used as a changing table. She placed Gabriela on the blankets and showed Isabel how to clean and change her.

Then Isabel sat on a pink swivel chair and fed the baby, while Walter fashioned a crib from a bureau drawer. She guessed Marcelino was still scrutinizing the woods through Walter's binoculars.

Mabel arranged the few diapers, onesies, and receiving blankets that had been in the backpack. "We'll need to go out and get more baby supplies," she said to Walter. And she settled onto her daughter's old bed to watch Isabel feed her baby.

"Uh-huh." Walter busied himself with the makeshift crib.

After a few minutes, Mabel spoke. "Not to pry, dear, but why did you come to the United States? It couldn't have been a safe trip, especially for a young, pregnant girl." She waited for the phone app to translate.

"It was because of the Rarámuri," Isabel said. "I couldn't remember a lot of stuff. I didn't even know why I came here, but when I saw my baby, I remembered something. It's about the Rarámuri, the people that live by Creel in Mexico."

"I've never heard of them," Walter said.

"I have," Mable said. "I read an article about them. They are the *running people*, right?"

"That's right," Isabel said. "They are really fast, and they can run a really long way, like a hundred miles. I'm serious."

"Yes, she is serious, Walter," Mabel said. "Men, women, children, they all like to run. It's a way of life."

"I see." Walter placed the dresser drawer on the floor and tested its stability. He then lined the inside with soft, well-used baby blankets, folding their fringes and ruffles over the sides for a charming effect.

The baby made sucking sounds as she drained the formula from the bottle. "Now I burp her, right?"

"That's right, hon." Mable placed a cloth on Isabel's shoulder and patiently instructed her. The baby burbled and fell asleep. Isabel put her in Walter's crib and covered her with a small, thin blanket.

"It works." Isabel gazed at her baby. "She looks cozy. Thank you."

"My pleasure." Walter beamed and took a bow.

"Okay, continue your story. What did the Rarámuri have to do with you coming here?" Mabel kept her voice low.

Isabel told about the Copper Canyons, *las barrancas*, of the Sierra Madre. "They're these really deep canyons. The rock walls of the canyons are like copper-colored and greenish and sometimes they look blue when the sun is setting."

"Sounds pretty," Mabel said. "Is that where you're from?"

"No. I'm from Ecatepec. It's by Mexico City."

Walter reached for his daughter's old World Book Encyclopedias. He plucked out the M. Taking a seat on the bed next to Mabel, he turned to a map of Mexico. He let out a low whistle. "My goodness, that's got to be, what, a thousand miles."

"Almost." Mabel used the map key to measure with her thumb and forefinger. "How on earth did you come all that way?"

"Not on purpose." Isabel's mind flashed to El Gigante and the broken-face man. She really didn't want to talk about it or feel it anymore. Not now that she had her baby.

She shook her head. "The man—we called him *El Gigante*—he took me from Mexico City and left me by the Copper Canyons where the Rarámuri live."

"Oh my God. You were kidnapped?" Mabel's face collapsed upon itself, her wrinkles drawing together and tears welling up in her eyes. "Oh, my Lord, I imagine you've been through hell, my dear." She hugged Isabel tight.

"Marcelino found me where the man threw me out of the car. He took me to his Rarámuri family."

Mabel had gone pale; she and Walter stared at each other. Walter shook his head. "What this child has been through."

"The Rarámuri took care of me for a long time. My shoulder and ankle were hurt, but I got better. And my belly grew big." Isabel sat cross-legged on the floor next to the crib.

"I remember now why I left the Rarámuri to come here." In Isabel's mind, darkness gave way to light, and her eyes filled with tears. "I made a Rarámuri friend. Her name was Bimón. She was pregnant too."

Isabel remembered bright, sunny days in the Copper Canyons. She and Bimón had walked the trails every day. One day she had clung to her friend as they ascended to the canyon's rim. The foliage was much prettier there at the top of the canyon—fragrant pine forests, not the scraggly junipers and madrona trees of the lower canyon. There amongst the beauty of the lush trees and the view of the Sierra Madre, Bimón showed Isabel the graves of her first two babies.

"My friend was going to lose her third baby too. The midwife in the village said the baby was upside down."

"Breech?" Mabel seemed to cling to Isabel's every word.

"Yes. The midwife's son-in-law drove my friend to the clinic in Creel to Sister Bridget. They let me go with her, but I had to wait while they took Bimón in to have her baby. Sister Bridget turned the baby around in Bimón's womb, and the baby was born okay. I was scared that I would have to bury my baby on the canyon rim too. So, a few weeks later, I went looking for Sister Bridget at the clinic to ask her if she would help me when my baby came. But the nuns there said that Sister Bridget had already returned to the United States. I told them I wanted to write her a letter. They let me take down her address. But really, I wanted to find her. Sister Bridget lives here in Austin. That's why I came here."

"You came here by foot?" Walter asked.

"No, the Rarámuri are close to Texas. My friend's relative that lives in the village has a car. He drove me to the place where I crossed the border. It wasn't far. I snuck across at a shallow part of the river, but then I got caught by the border patrol. They took me to a detention center. But then I was crying and very upset because some of the ladies were talking about the border patrol taking away their babies. So, then they took me to a hospital because they didn't want me to have the baby in the detention place."

"But you didn't have your baby in a hospital." The wrinkles on Walter's forehead were drawn low.

"No, there was a church lady there at the hospital. She listened to me. I told her I didn't want ICE to take my baby away from me. I told her about El Gigante and the Rarámuri. She gave me different clothes and pretended like I worked with her. We walked out when nobody was watching."

"What?" Mabel stared wide-eyed at Walter. "That's an amazing story."

"Is that even possible?" Walter said.

"I guess so." Isabel shrugged. "I showed her the address, and she bought me to this city and left me at Sister Bridget's church. It was because I wanted my baby. I didn't want them to take her away."

"But why did you abandon her?" Walter asked.

"I didn't mean to," she said. "After the lady left me at Sister Bridget's church, I don't remember anything after that. All I know is that I woke up in the hospital."

Marcelino entered the quiet room, and said, "Isabel wouldn't abandon her baby. I helped her have her baby. I seen ladies in the village do it." He shrugged, looking at the floor.

Isabel turned to Marcelino. "I know you said you were there. But I don't understand. How did you get there? The lady *drove* me to Sister Bridget's house."

"I got Sister Bridget's address from the clinic too." He shrugged. "I ran some of the way and got rides with truck drivers.

"Marcelino was going back for the baby," Isabel explained, "but the nun had already taken the baby to her house. Right, Marcelino?"

He nodded, looking down at the floor.

"Well. My goodness, young man." Walter squeezed Marcelino's shoulder and patted him on the back.

"There're police boats on the river now," Marcelino said. They left the room to look at the boats, but Isabel stayed behind. She stared at her sleeping infant and tried to imagine Marcelino helping her give birth. As her memory of other events began to return, that one last memory eluded her, the birth of her baby. Numbly, she joined the others in the big sunny room with the wall of windows.

A white boat labeled *Police* moved slowly in the water. Officers on a second boat, labeled *Travis County Sheriff,* were dredging the water.

Walter scratched the back of his neck. "They're looking for you in the river, young lady."

"Did the dogs sniff her all the way to the river, and then no more?" Marcelino asked.

"I guess so. They must have a reason to think she's in there," Walter said.

"But thank goodness you're not in the water." Mabel hugged Isabel. "You're here with us."

"I heard you fall in the water." Walter rubbed his chin. "Marcelino showed me where you went in. I couldn't find you at first; you had drifted from where you went in, and you sank pretty deep.

"Boomer here—" The big, white dog looked up and woofed when he heard his name. He was keeping watch out the window, too. "Boomer was the one that

161

swam to where you were. It was deep, maybe ten feet, but I managed to dive down and pull you out." He gently squeezed Isabel's shoulder. "I set you on the edge of the river and did CPR. After that, me and Marcelino carried you up the hill to the house."

Isabel scruffed Boomer's head and ran her hand down his soft back. She bent down and gave him a hug.

"So, the police dogs couldn't smell her no more? Because she fell in the water, and because we carried her?" Marcelino asked.

"I guess that's right," Walter said.

They all went silent.

"Wait," Mabel said. "Remember, ya'll were almost all the way up the hill when Isabel wanted to walk. She stood just for a moment. There's probably a little bit of blood there from her hurt feet."

Isabel had forgotten about that. She imagined blood-smeared rocks halfway up the hill leading to Mabel and Walter's house.

Marcelino watched through Walter's binoculars. Suddenly, he ducked behind the wall, away from the window. "The nun."

"May I use those?" Walter took the binoculars from Marcelino and looked out. "My goodness, Mable. When Isabel said *Sister Bridget*, I didn't realize she was talking about *our* Sister Bridget."

"Well, what do you know." Mabel looked too. "That's our Sister Bridget all right."

Chapter 16

Sister Bridget glanced up at Mabel and Walter's big glass window. Whoever had been observing her, ducked behind the wall. She knew the home well. Besides attending various charity events at the beautiful hilltop residence, she'd visited as a personal friend to the couple. She wiped her brow and sat upon a large rock. Waving to the officers in the search boats, she opened her flip phone and called Mabel.

"Sister Bridget. I knew that was you down there. Marcelino spotted you." Mabel sounded excited.

"So, they're with you? What a relief. Thank you, Jesus." Sister Bridget made the sign of the cross. "Are they all okay?" She lowered her voice. "Is the baby all right?"

"Oh, Sister, the baby is just fine…it's just Isabel's feet. They're in terrible shape. But the bleeding has stopped. I don't think she needs stitches."

"Thank God for that." Sister Bridget meant it.

"Sister, they're saying on the news that Isabel abandoned her baby, but she didn't."

"I know, my dear. Just keep them there, won't you?"

"Yes, of course," Mabel said.

"I'll come to you, but I mustn't be seen. I'll need to be careful. I don't want to lead the police to them."

"Sister, what should we do? I just can't let them

take this girl's baby away from her," Mabel said. "It's *her* baby."

"With God's help, we will straighten this all out. Oh, and, Mabel, keep the kids away from that window." Sister Bridget didn't know how she would get Isabel and Marcelino out of trouble, but she trusted God to find a way.

Back up the hill, Sister Bridget hiked, tolerating the upward journey infinitely better than the descent. In her whole being, she knew God's presence right then. God quelled her anxiety, and the *Knowing* enveloped her. She felt at peace. Everything *would* be fine.

She hadn't quite reached the top when she encountered the young, redheaded police officer again. He was collecting evidence on the slope. With gloved hands, he used a sharp tool to dislodge a four-inch stone from the soil. He placed it in a clear evidence bag. The stone was roughly pyramid-shaped, its tip was covered in dry blood. *Oh, that poor girl's feet*, Sister Bridget thought. She pictured Isabel's shoes in the evidence bag.

Sister Bridget watched quietly while the officer sealed and labeled another bloody stone. The evidence against the girl was certainly mounting.

"Hello, Patrick." She rarely forgot a name, and never a saint's name. Saint Patrick was one of her favorites.

"Hi, Sister Bridget." Sweat beaded up on his red face. "What are you doing here?"

"Oh, I'm Isabel Ortiz's legally appointed sponsor. It's her child that is missing."

"Okay. But what are you doing here?"

Patrick was a good police officer.

"I came with Detective Estevez. Just out here looking about while he's investigating inside the house. Trying to stay out of his way." Really, she was looking for her own evidence, and she had already found what she was looking for—Isabel herself. She just didn't want to throw suspicion on herself. She hoped she sounded casual enough.

Next, Sister Bridget located Detective Estevez who was addressing a team of six uniformed officers by Susan's pool. She listened in. With thumb and forefinger, Estevez enlarged a Google satellite map on a tablet. It was a map of the neighborhood.

"The river is deep. They couldn't have crossed to the other side, not with a baby." Estevez pointed to the enlarged area. "Here, to the north, that way," he pointed to his left, "there are seventeen houses. They could be hiding out in or near any one of them. Lots of people are at work right now, so many of those homes are empty. No one to notice if the kids are hiding out." He adjusted the map back to its full size. "Now at the end of those seventeen houses, the neighborhood ends, here at Capital of Texas Highway. There's a church right there. St. Andrews Episcopal, but they won't make it that far."

"Why not?" Lieutenant Dale asked, looking at her watch. She was the Officer in Charge of the Crime Scene. "It's been two and a half hours since they took the baby. They could have made it to the church."

"One, we already have officers there. They're just not there, and two, do you have kids?" One of the officers blew out a breath and laughed. Another said, "I wouldn't want to walk that far with a screaming baby."

"Tend to agree," Lieutenant Dale said. "As long as

we keep an eye on that church in case they do make it there."

"Now in the other direction." Estevez enlarged the south side of the map. "There are twenty-one houses. That side of the neighborhood abuts Bee Cave Road. There's a gas station there. Again, I don't think they'll leave the neighborhood. But just in case, we have patrol cars on that end. Take your teams and search the woods around each property. They're either in or around a home, or they're hiding out in the woods. If you see anything suspicious in or around a residence, call it in. We'll get a search warrant asap."

Sister Bridget would need to warn Mabel and Walter that the search teams were coming their way.

"Okay, take your teams. Six teams. Two canine officers. Let's go find that baby."

When Estevez turned to go, he saw Sister Bridget.

"Don't worry. We'll find them." Estevez closed the tablet and stashed it in a black duffle.

"You are a very good detective. I'm sure you'll find them." She meant what she said, which was why Isabel and Marcelino needed to escape the neighborhood.

They regarded one another silently. Sister Bridget regretted deceiving him. She knew when he found out, he'd probably think ill of her. But it was a chance she was willing to take.

"Well." She looked away. "I'm no help here. I'll just go back home."

They each turned to leave, but Estevez turned back. "Say, Sister."

"Yes, Detective?"

"Thanks for breakfast. I'll return the favor some

time. You can meet my daughter, Katie."

"That would be lovely." She turned to go.

"Wait. How're you getting home? I can get a patrol car to take…"

"No, no," she said. "You officers are much too busy here. I already called for a taxi."

****

Sister Bridget called Mabel from the taxi. "Mabel, the police are searching around the houses. Please keep the young people out of sight. I'll be there in," she looked at her watch, "oh, give me thirty minutes. Open the garage please. I'll park inside."

The taxi driver dropped her off at the parish. Milagro, beside himself with excitement, whined, jumped, and twirled in circles when she opened the door. "Oh dear. Okay, Milagro, you good boy, come on, let's go." She picked him up and took him with her.

She took the key from inside the bumper of Father Bartosh's car. Better to ask forgiveness than permission, she told herself. Besides she didn't want to mix the priest up in all this.

She headed back to Susan's neighborhood, which was still barricaded. This time, she was ready with her driver's license.

"Here you go, Officer." She handed the patrolman her license. "You can see my name is already on your list."

The officer paged through his log notes.

"I'm with Detective Estevez."

"Bridget Ann Rincón-Keller, yeah here it is." The officer took down her license plate number and let her through.

Once past the barricade, she turned and took a

roundabout way to Mabel and Walter's house, bypassing the blockades on either side of Susan's house.

Walter waited in the garage. He motioned her in and closed the noisy overhead door.

Sister Bridget embraced him. "They didn't fall into the river, did they?" She recalled almost falling in herself.

"No, no, well, yes, one did, but they're all fine." Walter filled her in on what had unfolded that morning. "All three are safe and resting. You know Mabel. She's feeding them and fussing—"

Sister Bridget interrupted him. "Walt, we don't have much time. They're coming." She opened the back door of the car, and Milagro leapt out. She reached in for her bag.

"What? Well, hello, Milagro." Walter bent down and petted the little dog. "Who's coming?"

Milagro scampered to the door. He knew his way around Mabel and Walter's house.

"The police are searching the area around all the houses in the neighborhood, especially the ones here along the woods." She wondered how much progress they'd made so far.

Walter gestured for Sister Bridget to enter the house ahead of him. He followed her into a gleaming utility room with shiny appliances and neatly organized white shelving. Boomer greeted Milagro. The two dogs sniffed and nipped at one another, then Boomer led Milagro to Isabel. Sister Bridget smiled when she heard Isabel squeal with delight.

"Yes, I figured they'd be getting closer to the house." Walter's wrinkles plunged low on his forehead;

his mouth was a grim line. "Mable and I, we've been thinking."

"I've been thinking too." Sister Bridget followed Walter into their towering gourmet kitchen. There were two large skylights, one on each slope of the vaulted ceiling. Mabel stood at the oversized gas stove stirring a pot of tallerini. Normally Sister Bridget would relish the aroma of beef, pork, tomato, pasta, and spices, but she couldn't think about food just then.

She hugged Mabel tight. Walter interrupted them. "Ladies, we don't have a lot of time."

"What's happened?" Mabel asked.

"I was at Susan's house about a half hour ago. The police started searching up close to the houses along the river. They think the kids might be hiding in or near a home." And of course, they were.

"But they won't come *in* the house, surely?" Mabel said.

"Only if they have a good reason," Sister Bridget said. "Even then, they'll need a search warrant."

"They might come in without one claiming exigent circumstances." Walter rubbed his chin. He was a retired lawyer. "They may claim they are entering for the sake of preventing harm to the baby."

"Oh, dear Guardian Angels, help us." Sister Bridget clutched the crucifix she wore around her neck. "And the kids? The baby?"

Mabel put a lid on the tallerini and wiped her hands on a dishcloth. "They're just over here." She turned off the stove. "Come."

Sister Bridget followed Mabel through the formal dining room with its flawless mahogany dining set and linen draperies, and into the family room where she found Isabel reclining on a plush, mauve-colored chaise lounge, her bandaged feet propped on a yellow cushion. She cradled Milagro. Boomer was stretched out on the white tile beside Isabel's chair.

"Sister Bridget. I hope you're not mad at me." Isabel put Milagro on the floor. "I took my baby back." Her voice wavered, and her eyes filled with tears.

She looked like a typical teenager, smooth-faced, bright-eyed, hair flowing,

"No, *mi amor*." Sister Bridget sat on the edge of the lounge chair and enveloped Isabel in her arms. The girl seemed so small. "I'm just so happy you're safe." And she couldn't help it. She cried too. "And you, Marcelino?" She looked up and held out her hand to the boy. He had no choice but to go and take her hand. Sister Bridget gave it a squeeze. He looked embarrassed. His hair was mussed, and he was dirty. He looked tired, worn out.

"And my friends, what a blessing you are." Sister Bridget looked to Mabel and Walter. "Thank God the young people have found refuge in your home."

"It was Walter…" Mable brought her phone close so the app could translate.

"And Boomer," Walter interjected.

"Yes…*and* Boomer, that found them." Mabel beamed at her husband and her dog.

"Praise be to God for Walter and Boomer," Sister Bridget said. "I thought for a moment that you two, you *three* had fallen into the river." Sister Bridget switched back and forth from English to Spanish and back again, not waiting for the app.

Isabel sat up straight. "Sister Bridget, you want to see my baby?"

"Of course, I do."

"Let me show you. She's so cute." Isabel swung her feet down and slipped them into Mabel's fluffy, pink slippers, but when she tried to take a step, her knee buckled, and she sat back down.

"Your feet are healing, *mi amor*. They are swollen. Here, sit, sit." Sister Bridget raised the girl's feet back onto the cushion and took a look under the bandages. "You'll be fine, *mija*, but it's better to keep weight off. Keep them up, just rest, and before you know it, they'll be all better."

"Sister Bridget, I remembered something." Isabel repeated the story of Bimón's two dead babies buried at the top of the canyon. Isabel had been afraid that she, too, would have to dig a grave for her baby. "Do you remember Bimón? She's Rarámuri. Her baby was upside down, and you turned it in her womb. And then her baby was born good, and she didn't have to make another grave."

Sister Bridget did remember Bimón. Of course, she did.

"I wrote down your address and found you here in Austin. I wanted my baby to be born okay like Bimón's baby."

"Well that certainly solves that little mystery, doesn't it? I'm happy you found me, *mi amor*." Sister Bridget gave Isabel another hug. And she couldn't help thinking of Detective Estevez. She was eager to tell him there was no nefarious reason for Isabel to have her address in her backpack.

"You rest now, hon. I'll take Sister Bridget to see Gabriela." Mabel placed Milagro back on Isabel's lap.

Sister Bridget entered the bedroom where the

infant slept. Baby scents permeated the room—formula, diaper wipes, powder. She smiled at the makeshift crib.

"Walter," Mabel silently mouthed.

Yes of course, kind Walter would transform a dresser drawer into a cozy baby bed for a complete stranger.

The baby slept peacefully. Sister Bridget once again found herself struck with awe at the wonder of new life. She thought back to the helpless, screaming babe by the Virgin Mary statue. Now, helpless no more. The child was well-fed, cared for, and loved.

And once again, the words of the Psalmist came to mind—*Be still and know that I am God.* Yes, Sister Bridget *knew,* and it was that *Knowing* that sustained her. She was certain that everything would work out fine.

"Isn't she beautiful?" Mabel hooked her arm through Bridget's, and they gazed at the sleeping infant.

"Oh yes. She looks healthy too. Thanks be to God."

The two ladies left the baby sleeping and went to another of Mabel and Walter's unused bedrooms.

As soon as they were alone, Mabel spoke frankly. "We're not turning Isabel and Marcelino in. That child belongs to Isabel, and we are going to help her keep her baby."

"I know, I know, dear." Sister Bridget rubbed Mabel's arm. "Unfortunately, I don't think it will be easy…legally that is. It seems the girl has all the cards stacked against her, as they say."

"I agree. But Walt has an idea. We are going to drive them to the border, so they can go home."

Sister Bridget hadn't thought of that. What a good

idea.

"Let me do it. I wouldn't want you and Walter to be charged with obstruction or some such thing." Sister Bridget took out her computer and looked at maps of Texas. "Look here." She enlarged the map. The Rio Grande River is just a stream right here." She pointed. "Presidio. No fence. At least the map doesn't show a fence. And it crosses right over into Chihuahua. Isabel and Marcelino can easily cross back to Mexico there."

She opened another map. It showed little red icons marking the Border Patrol Check Stations along the roads in South Texas. There were many. Sister Bridget and Mabel mapped a route to Presidio that would avoid the check stations.

Walter found the two ladies huddled together. "I wondered where you all went."

"Sister Bridget found a place where the kids can cross the border," Mabel said. "She wants to take them."

"What? No, I'm taking them. It was my idea. Besides, I've always wanted to make a run for the border like in the old westerns."

"I'm coming with you. Sister, send that map to my phone, would you?" Sister Bridget did so, and Mabel's phone dinged "Ah, got it."

Mabel and Walter studied the map on her phone.

Walter looked up. "We can handle this, Sister."

"I accept your decision." She saw that Walt and Mabel were determined to see it through. "The greatest obstacle will be getting the kids out of this neighborhood. The police have the area in lockdown. Both entrances are barricaded. They're checking passengers in every car."

Marcelino came into the room holding the binoculars. "The police are getting closer. Remember the blood on the rock? I think the dogs will smell it."

Walter told Sister Bridget that Isabel had stood for a moment on the path to their house. After he had pulled her out of the river. Her feet had been bleeding.

They returned to the sunny room with the wall of windows. Sister Bridget looked out at the woods but didn't see any police officers.

"You have to look out the side window." Marcelino watched the woods through a smaller window at the far end of the room.

Mabel and Walter's house perched so high on the hill, Sister Bridget was able to get a bird's eye view of the neighbors' properties. Indeed, the police were getting closer. They seemed to be searching thoroughly though, not rushing. The officers were eight houses away.

Was that Detective Estevez at the edge of the river? He was crouched, studying the shore. "May I please borrow the binoculars, Marcelino?" Through the lens, she saw Estevez up close. He had removed his suit coat, and his sleeves were rolled up. His face glistened with perspiration. He looked like he was concentrating and appeared to be talking to himself as he pointed out markings in the gravel. She wished she could call his cell phone and tell him the truth, but no, she couldn't take a chance.

"We can drive out of the neighborhood with the kids hiding in the back of the car. On the floor." Mabel paced, thinking out loud, it seemed. "Maybe under a blanket or a tarp or something?"

"There's not room on the floor of the car for all

three of them. "But…" Walter thought for a moment. "They don't know about Marcelino, remember? He could sit in full sight. I could say he's our grandson." He smiled, eyes wide, nodding.

Sister Bridget could see that her friend was proud of his idea, so she hated to break the news to him. "Good idea, Walt, but the police *do* know about Marcelino."

"What? The news never…" Mable looked to the TV.

Sister Bridget explained that MaryAnn had let it slip that morning. "But maybe we could smuggle them out in *two* cars."

"Doesn't matter. They're searching all the cars." Walter took over Mabel's pacing. "If we hid the kids on the floor in the back, they'd be found out."

Sister Bridget remembered that even in the taxi, the officer at the barricade looked in the backseat.

"Do they look in the trunk too?" Marcelino asked.

Nobody said anything.

"But oh no, we couldn't possibly put a baby in the trunk of a car." Sister Bridget fretted. They couldn't do that. Could they?

"Marcelino, no. My baby can't go in the trunk." Isabel brought her brows together and shook her head from where she sat on the chaise lounge with her feet propped up. "It would be scary for her. She wouldn't like it."

"No, no, of course not dear. You're right. We couldn't put Gabriela in the trunk of the car." *What else? What else, dear Lord?* Sister Bridget looked out the side window. The officers and canine had come one property closer.

Walter watched the woods out another side window in the opposite direction. "Well, would you look who's pulling up to his dock in a brand-new boat. Our good neighbors, Dr. Espinoza and his wife, Dr. Espinoza." Sister Bridget would not quite describe Walter's smile as wicked, but it was close.

Mabel joined Walter at the window. "You going to ask them? Or just steal their boat?"

Chapter 17

"Is hotwiring a boat the same as a car?" The app translated Marcelino's words. "Because I can do that."

Isabel wondered if Marcelino was the type of guy that stole cars. She hoped not.

"Afraid not, son. You got to have the key fob with a computer chip for these new boats." Walter rubbed his chin.

Mabel raised an eyebrow. "And you know this because…?"

"Never mind about that, Mabel." Walter rubbed his hands together. "I know where the good doctors keep their key fob. Now let's get packed up and go before the police get here. We're going to need extra clothes for the kids. They might be a little big, but I think Marcelino can wear some of my workout clothes."

"I'll pack some. And Isabel, I'll get you more of my daughter's clothes." Mabel hurried out of the room.

"I'll get my baby." Isabel swung her feet to the floor.

"No, *mija*, the baby is still sleeping. Better to stay where you are," Sister Bridget said. "Rest your feet while you can. You might have to use them to run soon."

Isabel turned and caught Marcelino looking at her. "Are you going to be okay?" he asked.

"I think so." She watched Walter hurry about and

disappear down the hallway. Could she do this? She had no choice; she had to escape with her baby.

"Sister Bridget, you pack some food, would you? I'll get some first aid supplies together." Walter spoke loudly from the hallway. Sister Bridget hurried to the kitchen to follow Walter's instructions.

Marcelino disappeared into the baby's room and returned with the backpack that Daniel had given to them. "I put all the baby's stuff back in here. There's only one bottle of formula left."

Sister Bridget hurried back into the room carrying a clear plastic tote filled with fruit, vegetables, bread, and other staples from the pantry. "Okay, time for the baby." Setting down the bag, she grabbed a thin, woven throw from the arm of the sofa. She shook out the small blanket. "This will work fine as a sling to carry your baby." She demonstrated. "See, place it under one arm and over the other shoulder, then bring it together in front and tie a knot to one side. Baby goes snug right here." Sister Bridget smiled at Isabel, showing her the pouch she'd created for the baby. She untied it and handed it to Isabel.

"Like a *rebozo*." Isabel had seen ladies in Mexico carry their babies that way. She set Milagro down and took the thin blanket. She followed the nun's directions. Sister Bridget left the room and returned with the baby who made small mewling noises and flailed her arms.

"Is she hungry?" Isabel worried about Gabriela.

"No time now, hon. You can feed her later." Mabel reappeared with an old backpack strapped to her back. She carried socks and snow boots. "These were my daughters." Mabel kneeled on the floor, removed Isabel's slippers, put two pairs of socks on her, and eased her feet into the snow boots, which were about two sizes too big. "My daughter's tall like me. She has big feet."

"That's okay." Isabel stood unsteadily. Her feet felt squishy and swollen. The pain wasn't too bad though. She could handle it. Smiling, she held her arms out to Sister Bridget for her baby.

"I can carry the baby. Here, I'll put the sling on." Mabel reached for the blanket.

"I want to carry my baby. I can do it."

Sister Bridget snuggled the baby into the sling and made a few adjustments, so the baby was settled and secure. Isabel protectively crossed both arms over the baby. "She won't fall, will she?"

"No, *mija. Mamás* have been carrying their babies this way for hundreds of years. More." Sister Bridget tied the knot a little tighter.

Marcelino turned from the window. "They're getting closer."

"Let's go." Walter also had a backpack strapped to his back, as did Marcelino. "Mabel, do you have your phone?"

Mabel grabbed her phone off the coffee table and put it in her pants pocket.

"Let's go out the side of the garage." Walter led the way. "You have your phone charger, Mabel?" She went back for the charger. They waited for her in the garage.

"Sister Bridget, do you know that little restaurant on the lake? Ski Shores? Can you meet us there?" Walter asked. "Bring Mabel's Land Rover. We'll leave from there and head to the border."

"Ski Shores. I can find it." Sister Bridget put the tote filled with food in the light blue Land Rover for the second leg of their journey.

"But how will you get back home after we take the car?" Mabel rejoined them, charger in hand.

"Not to worry, my friend. With God, there is always a way." Milagro and Boomer followed them into the garage. "You two watch the house. I'll come back for you." Sister Bridget said it in English and Spanish, as if the dogs understood different languages. Isabel laughed at that.

Isabel followed Walter out the garage's side door. Marcelino followed behind her, then Mabel, and at the end of the line, Sister Bridget.

The expanse between Mabel and Walter's house and that of their neighbor was densely wooded. Oaks, cedars, buckeyes, mountain laurels, and hollies screened the residents from each other.

Walter led them down the slope and through the woods at a slanting angle. "The boat key is in the pool house. It's where they always keep it. Follow me."

"Oh no, no, no." Isabel clutched her baby to her body as her feet slipped on the slanting ground. "I'm going to fall again." Her feet were throbbing in her boots.

Marcelino held her arm. "It's fine. I won't let you fall."

"I won't let you fall either." Mable took her other arm. Sister Bridget translated from behind.

They wove their way through thick foliage. A quarter of the way down the hill, the ground leveled out and Walter parted a thick stand of cypress trees to reveal a secluded swimming pool with a volleyball net and a basketball hoop.

"This way." Walter led them through the door of a

small poolside house. "I'll just get the k—"

"What the…" Identical twin boys spoke at the same time. The boys were the doctors' teenage sons, Matt and Drew. They were handsome boys with thick black hair and intense dark eyes. Walter introduced them, and Sister Bridget translated.

The boys had the TV on and were playing foosball in the air-conditioned cabana.

Mabel came forward. "Hello, boys. Sorry to interrupt. Your parents said that we…" Sister Bridget interpreted, but Mabel trailed off because the boys weren't listening. They were staring at Isabel.

"Aren't you…" Matt began.

"The one the cops are looking for?" Drew finished. Sister Bridget translated.

Isabel guessed the boys knew all about her and Gabriela. The cabana's TV was on the local cable channel, showing her picture at that very moment. She turned to run out the door. Marcelino followed.

Drew said something and ran past the adults. He stood in front of Isabel, blocking her path. "O-kay," he said slowly, drawing out the word and tamping his hands down. He pointed to the baby and said, "*Su bebé.*"

Matt went to the door and said, "Drew, tell them to come back in. Mom and Dad are going to see them." To the others, he said, "Drew's taking Spanish." Sister Bridget translated for Isabel and Marcelino's benefit.

"*Vuelven,*" Drew said with exaggerated hand gestures. He beckoned them back into the cabana, glancing over his shoulder at the house. Isabel heard a dog bark, a big, deep, angry bark. Was it the police dog? She couldn't tell how far away the dog was because of the thick woods.

"It's all right," Sister Bridget said in Spanish. "Come back in before somebody sees you."

Fearing the police dog, Isabel returned to the cabana. Marcelino followed. Walter closed the door.

"Okay, boys, so you know who this is." Walter pointed to Isabel. Sister Bridget translated.

"Yeah. They're saying the baby's hers." Matt gestured toward the TV.

"Then you know...here's the thing..." Walter rubbed the back of his neck.

Mabel interrupted. She spoke hurriedly. "We need your dad's boat to get them out of here."

"If the police catch her, her baby will be taken away," Sister Bridget added.

The twins stared at Sister Bridget and glanced at each other. The dog barked again. Matt shrugged. "Yeah. Okay."

The teenager took the key from a wall hook and handed it to Walter. "Bring it back though, okay?"

"It's my dad's new boat," Drew said.

"No problem." Walter took the key and gestured to the others. "Let's go."

"*Gracias*," Isabel said to the twins on her way out. Drew turned red. Matt nudged and teased him.

The group—led by Walter and then Isabel, Marcelo, Mabel, and Sister Bridget continued their trek down the hill to the river. Unlike other properties though, the owners had installed rock steps leading to their boat dock. Isabel was thankful for the steps, but there were many—at least forty steps to get down to the dock. She pitched forward with the weight of the baby. Marcelino steadied her. "Almost there," he said. But

Isabel looked to the dock. They weren't even halfway. She kept her eyes on each step in front of her.

The baby started to squirm and cry. "Just keep going, *mija*. Don't stop," Sister Bridget said. "The baby will be fine." Isabel's t-shirt was soaking wet, sweaty where the baby clung to her. Her feet felt wet too. Probably blood. *Just get to the boat.*

By the time they reached the shiny, red and white boat, the baby was screaming, and the police dog was barking just a few properties over.

"Get in, get in, get in." Walter held each person's hand as they climbed into the boat. His words echoed on the translation app. "Under the seats, there should be life jackets. Get them on." He started up the boat while Sister Bridget untied its line. He took off as soon as she tossed the rope into the boat.

Isabel tried to wave good-bye to Sister Bridget, but Mabel was putting the lifejacket on her and nudging her to the deck of the boat. Marcelino took her hand and pulled her down onto the deck. "So, they won't see us," he said. There hadn't even been time for hugs and thank-you's. Would she ever see the nun again? The baby screamed and the boat's motor roared. The wind blew her long hair in all directions, including onto her face. What should she do with the baby? She was all wet.

"Why is Walter driving the boat so slow?" She shouted in Marcelino's ear so he could hear her.

"I think so the police don't notice." He buckled the straps of his lifejacket.

"My baby is all wet," she shouted and struggled with her long hair in the wind.

With Marcelino's help, she placed the screaming,

squirming baby on a blanket and changed her diaper and onesie. Then Marcelino turned his back, so she could change out of her wet t-shirt. Mabel handed her a dry shirt, and Isabel handed Mabel the soaked one.

Mabel sniffed the wet shirt and said something that Isabel didn't understand. Noise was happening all around her—the wind, the boat motor, the baby. It was all so confusing. Mabel opened Isabel's lifejacket. She positioned the wailing infant in Isabel's arms to breastfeed, Isabel's hair blowing all around. The baby sucked hungrily, and when Isabel pushed her hair away, she saw Gabriela was looking into her eyes. She gasped and smiled, amazed at such a simple way to feed her baby. She had seen ladies in her neighborhood feed their babies this way.

Mabel sat cross-legged on the deck facing Isabel. The old woman was smiling and crying at the same time.

"What's wrong, Mabel?" Isabel asked, reaching to her face, and wiping a tear away even though she knew Mabel couldn't understand her words.

"Oh, hon, I'm just thinking about my own baby so long ago," she said, wiping her tears away. "Look at you and your baby. So beautiful." Mabel spoke the words into her phone and placed the phone to Isabel's ear, so she could hear the translation. Isabel really liked the kind, elderly woman. How could someone be so nice to a stranger? She hoped she'd grow up to be like Mabel.

Marcelino crouched low at the boat's stern, keeping lookout. "There's a boat coming." He saw that Isabel was nursing her baby. "Like the ladies in my village." He turned back to watch the advancing boat.

Walter looked over his shoulder. "It's probably nothing, but let's look for a place to pull in.

Mabel stood and looked around. "Walt, there aren't any places to pull in."

From where she sat on the boat's deck, all Isabel could see were tops of trees and once in a while, the roof of a house. She carefully moved her baby to the other side, like she'd seen her Rarámuri friend do.

"Look there." Mabel pointed, and her phone translated. "It's somebody's private dock, but it's empty. Pull in, pull in there, Walt. We can make like it's our place and let the other boat pass by." It was a covered dock with a little boathouse.

"They're getting closer." Walter glanced to his left as he backed the boat into the slip. Mabel lifted the cushion off one of the benches and threw all the gear out of its storage bin.

"Honey, you're going to have to hide." Mabel pointed to the large now-empty bin. She held her lips pressed together, the wrinkles to the side of her eyes looked deeper.

Marcelino took off his lifejacket, emptied the other storage bench, and climbed in. Mabel put the cushion back on the top of the bin. Good thing Marcelino was not a big guy.

Walter dumped all the contents of the bins into a storage hatch in the deck of the boat's bow.

Holding her baby tight, Isabel climbed into the opposite bin. She didn't want the police to take her baby away. She lay on her side and nestled the baby in the crook of her arm. Maybe with the sound of the boat motors, they wouldn't hear anything if she cried.

The baby fussed and cried, kicking her legs. Isabel

tried to shush her and then remembered to turn her and pat her back until she burped. With a full tummy, the baby settled down and fell asleep to the hum and vibration of the boat. Light shone into the secret hiding place, just a sliver, and voices carried through. Isabel couldn't understand what the people were saying. The other boat finally rumbled off, but she dared not move. She'd wait until Mabel said it was okay.

Mabel removed the cushions from the two benches and lifted open the tops. Marcelino climbed out. Sunlight poured onto Isabel and her baby as Mabel looked down upon them. With her silver hair shining in the sun, the elderly woman looked like an angel with a halo of green leaves from the tree above.

Mabel used the translation app on her phone. "It was just the Lake Patrol."

"Were they looking for me?" Isabel felt scared, pursued.

"No, no." Walter started up the motor. "They were checking to make sure we were using life jackets and such, not looking for babies."

"Wait a minute, Walt," Mabel said. "Maybe they were looking for Isabel, and just not telling us."

"Well, that could be, Mabel." Walter pulled the boat out of the slip. "We're almost to our rendezvous with Sister Bridget. Let's just keep going."

"I'm not so sure about this." Mabel fretted and shook her head, her eye crinkles deeper than ever.

****

Walter rounded the river bend and there waiting in the reeds was the police Lake Patrol.

A patrolman waved his arms and flashed his lights. He gave a quick blast of his siren.

"You mind if I come on board and have a look around?" The patrolmen had already pulled alongside and one was boarding the boat. Another patrolman stayed behind.

"Is there a problem, Officer?" Mabel sat serenely on the side bench.

"No problem. Just checking boats." The patrolman climbed aboard.

"Sure. Come on aboard." Walter idled the motor.

The officer boarded and looked around. He opened the two hatch doors on the bow's deck. They were empty.

"Okay, sorry to bother you." The officer made his way to the stern, stopped at one of the cushioned benches, lifted the cushion off, and looked inside. There were life jackets stored there. He rummaged through and looked underneath. Mabel was sitting on the other bench.

"May I, ma'am?" The patrolman nodded at the bench on which Mabel sat.

Both storage benches held boating supplies.

"All right, have a good day, folks." The patrolman returned to his own boat, and the two officers sped off in the direction from which they'd come.

Walter returned to the private boat dock and picked up Isabel, Marcelino, and the baby. They were sitting on the cement slab behind the little boathouse.

****

When they reached the meeting place, Sister Bridget was waiting with an infant car seat, formula, and more supplies.

The rendezvous was an old beer and hamburger joint with a dock for boats and a caliche lot for cars. Its steady lunch crowd was starting to drift away.

"Thank God and the Blessed Mother." Sister Bridget had been waiting for them on the dock. "I expected you thirty minutes ago."

"Sister Bridget? Are those my clothes?" Walter squinted at her clothing. She was wearing khaki pants, a blue plaid shirt, a windbreaker, and a Longhorns baseball cap.

"I found the clothes in your laundry room. Hope you don't mind. I didn't want to stand out too much." The clothing fit her perfectly, if not a bit tight around her bosom. The windbreaker covered her though.

Mabel whistled. "Looking good, Mister Sister."

"You wear them well. We're late because we had to double back to throw off the Lake Patrol." Walter tossed the line to Sister Bridget. She caught it and tied the boat to the dock, detecting a bit of pride in Walter's voice.

They transferred their supplies to Mabel's Land Rover. Sister Bridget had already installed the baby seat.

"For Gabriela?" Isabel asked.

"Yes, for your sweet Gabriela." Sister Bridget took the baby from Isabel. "To keep her safe. May God bless you and keep you." She cradled the infant and kissed her forehead. She then strapped the baby into the car seat and turned to Isabel. "You'll be a wonderful mother. You're *already* a wonderful mother. See how you fought for your baby? And you never gave up."

Isabel cried and struggled to get words out. "Guess what, Sister Bridget."

"What, *mija*?"

"Mabel showed me how to breastfeed Gabriela."

"Isn't that wonderful? See? I told you you're a wonderful mother already." Sister Bridget meant it.

"She's a pro," Mabel said.

The phone's app translated Mabel's words.

Sister Bridget beamed at Isabel. Trauma certainly could cause a delay in milk production, and that seemed to be the case here.

"Now. I've called the mission house in Creel. They will let your mother know when you arrive there."

Isabel kissed Sister Bridget's cheek. "*Gracias.*" She hugged her tight and climbed into the backseat of the SUV next to her baby.

"Walt, I love you, my brother." Sister Bridget kissed his cheek and hugged him.

"Love you too, my friend. You got Boomer?" He handed her the boat key, and she tucked it into her pocket.

"Oh, yes. Your boy tried to fight the police dog. Didn't want another dog coming on your property. Little Milagro backed him up. They're both fine. No worse for the wear. When I went back to get your car, I heard the ruckus and called them in. Don't worry, the doggie door is latched now." Sister Bridget said everything twice—once in English and then in Spanish.

"Well, for goodness' sake. We'll have to give Boomer and Milagro extra treats when we get back." Mabel embraced Sister Bridget. "Love you."

"Love you too, my dear. Don't worry about Boomer. I'll take him to the parish. Now you better get going. You have a full tank of gas. Take Interstate 10 but watch out. There's a border patrol check station at Fort Stockton, so exit before you get there. From Ozona, go south to Presidio. Here's the phone number of my dear friend, Sister Terésa." She took a slip of paper from her pocket and handed it to Mabel. "Call her when you get close. I told her to expect the kids in Progresso tonight. On the other side of the border."

"I'll give her a call." Mabel put the note in the pocket of her jeans.

Marcelino closed the hatch of the SUV and nodded to Sister Bridget, but she pulled him to herself and hugged him tightly. "You're a great friend, Marcelino. You saved the lives of Isabel and her baby."

Marcelino nodded and almost smiled.

"One question, my son." Sister Bridget lowered her voice and put her hands on Marcelino's shoulders. "Do you know anything about *El Gigante*? He might still be in Creel or nearby. He might still be keeping Isabel's friend, Juana."

Marcelino hesitated, but only for a moment. "He had drugs and was trying to force the Rarámuri to be a drug mule for him to cross the border. Maybe he is in Creel waiting for his money. That's all I know."

Marcelino risked his own life telling Sister Bridget even that much. She didn't try to get more information out of him. Drug dealers killed people who talked.

Sister Bridget watched the car pull away.

Merciful God, protect my friends, she prayed.

Chapter 18

Sister Bridget maneuvered Dr. Espinoza's boat along the river and back to the neighborhood. Police still searched the woods, but by this time, they had swept way past Walter and Mabel's house. Search teams also inspected the woods on the opposite side of the river. One of the searchers wore a sweat-soaked dress shirt, sleeves rolled up. It was Detective Estevez. Sister Bridget pulled her hat down low and waved because that's what boaters do. Surely, he wouldn't recognize her in Walter's clothing.

She pulled up to the dock where the twins waited. They looked up from their phones and stared.

"Oh, it's the nun." The boys said at the same time. They hadn't recognized her in Walter's clothes.

"Thanks for bringing the boat back. Where's the girl? Isabel? Did she get away?" Drew must have felt a camaraderie with the girl since they were about the same age.

"*Mijo*, I don't know what you're talking about." Sister Bridget thought it better to be tight-lipped about the situation. The fewer people that knew the truth, the better.

"We're not going to say anything," Matt said.

"The police even came over here with dogs," Drew added, "and we didn't tell them."

The boys sounded conspiratorial and pleased with

themselves.

"We're on her side." Matt shrugged. "It's her baby anyway."

"You're good boys. Thank you for the use of your father's boat." Sister Bridget looked up the hill to their home, but dense cedar and oak trees blocked the house from view.

She handed over the key and climbed through the woods to Mabel and Walter's house. She entered through the side door of the garage and changed back into her habit. Throughout the house, she wiped down surfaces, handles, and doorknobs. She scrubbed blood off the carpet, vacuumed, and mopped the floors. Praying the rosary the whole while. She bagged the trash and loaded it into Father Bartosh's trunk. She'd dispose of it in the parish dumpster.

She hoped she'd erased all evidence of Isabel, Marcelino, and the baby, though a good forensic team would surely find a hair or a fingerprint, perhaps traces of blood from Isabel's feet.

Then she put the dogs in the car and returned to her little house on the edge of the parish grounds. First things first. She called Isabel's lawyer, Amanda Jenkins.

"Hello, my dear," Sister Bridget said.

"Sister, what in the world is happening? I've been trying to call you. It's been all over the news. Is Isabel okay?" Amanda was distressed for her client. Sister Bridget heard it in her voice.

"Yes, yes, dear. I mean…" Should she tell Amanda the truth? She didn't have time to explore all the legal ramifications right then. "I'd just like to ask you a hypothetical question."

"I don't know if I'll be able to answer but go ahead." Amanda let out a sigh.

"If—" she began.

Amanda interrupted. "Now remember, I'm not your lawyer. I'm Isabel's lawyer. I can't share any confidential information with you."

"No, no. I know that." Sister Bridget paused, trying to think of just the right way to phrase her words. "Just hypothetically speaking, I'm not asking for Isabel. Just in general—if an undocumented immigrant took her American-born baby back to Mexico, would the United States extradite her?"

"Oh, I see." Amanda went quiet.

Sister Bridget thought that the line had gone dead. "Amanda, are you there?"

Amanda sighed. "It's doubtful the United States would prosecute or make her return the baby. And it's very likely Mexico would refuse extradition and refuse the return of the baby."

"Thank you, Amanda. You're a wonderful friend. We'll talk again soon, okay?"

Next, she got online and purchased airline tickets. She needed to get to the Sisters of Saint Paul's mission house in Creel, Chihuahua. As usual, all the flights made a connection in Mexico City. It was out of the way, and she'd have to spend a night in Mexico City, but the Mother House was there, so it would give her a chance to visit her sisters. What would be her excuse for visiting? She'd work that out later. With God, there was always a way.

Then she dialed her neighbor. "Alma, may I hire one of your boys to dog sit?"

She emailed Father Bartosh and told him she'd be

away on retreat. She'd go to confession later. It was a good thing the confessional was sealed in secrecy.

She only had three pregnant patients, but none were due any time soon. She arranged backup care for them in case she didn't make it back.

Then she packed a bag and called a taxi.

****

Meanwhile, Isabel begged Walter not to stop the car.

"Isabel, honey, we've left Austin far behind. We need to change the dressing on your feet." Mabel used the translation app on her phone.

"No, please, not yet." Isabel didn't want to push her luck. She couldn't believe she had actually escaped with her baby. She even learned how to feed her. But she had a feeling something bad was going to happen before she made it to the border.

"Okay, hon, we can go a little farther. Right, Walt? We can wait until we stop for gas." Mabel checked the map app on her phone. "Up ahead here, go right and get on Interstate 10."

"No, not Interstate 10. The nun said there is a border patrol on Interstate 10." Isabel felt the weight of fear. It was like carrying something heavy that she couldn't put down.

"Yes, dear, yes she did say that, but we are getting off the highway before we get to the Border Patrol Check Station." Mabel's words didn't make Isabel feel any better. What if the Border Patrol took her baby away?

Sitting in the backseat of Mabel's SUV, Isabel's mind flashed to another time spent in the backseat of a car. She couldn't help but think about the long nightmare spent with Juana in El Gigante's car. Terrified, with hands, feet, and mouth bound, the two girls had leaned on each other. El Gigante and the broken-face man drank from bottles of liquor, El Gigante at the wheel. In the dark hours of the morning, El Gigante had pulled up to a dark shack in Guanajuato. He and Broken-Face staggered to the house, leaving her and Juana bound in the pitch dark. After a while, the car door creaked open, and a massive figure filled the pitch-dark doorway.

"Shh," the figure said. It was El Gigante. Isabel had tried to scream, but her mouth was bound with duct tape. She sucked air through her nose. She thought she would faint. Juana bucked her body back and forth, trying to get away, but her hands, legs and ankles were bound with duct tape also.

"You have to be quiet. If my brother hears, he will kill me. And you." There was something different. This man was giant like El Gigante, but he wasn't El Gigante.

She had nodded and made a grunting noise behind the tape. Juana cried; her eyes squeezed shut.

"I have some drink and food for you, but you have to promise to be quiet." The man's voice was like El Gigante, but his tone was kind, concerned, considerate.

Isabel nodded. The man removed the tape from her mouth and tipped a bottle of Coca-Cola to her mouth. Isabel drank, the liquid flowing onto her chin and shirt.

"Is she going to be quiet if I take her tape off?" The man tipped his head toward Juana.

"Yes." But Isabel really didn't know if Juana would scream or what she would do.

"Let us go," Juana pleaded as soon as the man removed the tape.

"I can't. My brother will kill me. Not just me but my wife and kids too." Isabel knew he would.

"Can you at least let us go pee?" Juana asked.

"No," the man whispered, tipping the bottle of cola to Juana's mouth. "He's crazy. And drunk. He'll kill us all."

Isabel and Juana had taken small bites of the meat and bread the man offered. Isabel felt nauseous. They sipped more cola. The man replaced the tape on their mouths and disappeared into the darkness before his brother's liquor wore off.

Now, in Walter and Mabel's car, Isabel knew the nightmare would never end, not really. Not until she knew if Juana was all right.

Walter finally stopped for gas. Isabel reasoned that since they'd driven long enough to use up all the gas, they must be pretty far. Still, she would feel better if they would get off Interstate 10.

Walter pulled into a gas station in Ozona, a quiet ranching town with a grocery store, gas station, and a motel. Isabel looked around. The terrain had turned scrubby with rocky hillocks and high brown grasses.

While Marcelino pumped gas, Walter went in for food. Isabel stepped out onto the pavement and winced. Her feet felt raw. She'd been sitting, not walking. Why did her feet feel like big, open cuts splitting open?

"Oh sweetie, it's because your feet are swollen. Sit, sit, hon." Mabel helped her remove her boots and socks.

When Mabel peeled the bloody gauze away, Isabel asked, "is my skin coming off?"

"No, honey. It's just the bandages are sticking."

Isabel clamped her lips and closed her eyes while Mabel cleaned off her cuts and rebandaged them. The wounds sent stinging spasms up her leg. She could handle it though. Even if she had to run, she could handle it.

Walter passed out chips and sandwiches. Isabel fed her baby and ate her sandwich.

From Ozona, Walter exited the Interstate and went south to Presidio like Sister Bridget had instructed. He drove for two hours.

"Wait, Walter, did you see that sign? It said all cars pull over to the right in one mile. Stop Walt. Walter, pull over *now*." Mabel seemed frantic.

"Sister Bridget said there were no checkpoints on this route." Walter slowed and pulled the SUV onto the shoulder.

"Well, Walt, this checkpoint wasn't on the map. I know it wasn't. I looked too. It must be new."

Isabel's heart sped up. She *knew* something bad was going to happen.

"Can we just walk to the border from here?" Marcelino asked. "We can cut through the ranches."

"No, son, Presidio is still almost two hours away. By car." The phone app interpreted Walter's words.

Mable looked at the Maps app on her phone. "From here, it's one hundred and fifty miles to the border."

"We need to find a different route. We can use Google satellite maps, but we need to get off the road, so a border patrol doesn't see us," Mabel said.

Walter turned the car around and headed back to Ozona.

"Mabel, I have an idea." Walter glanced side to

197

side at the surrounding properties. Ranchland as far as the eye could see. "There are some ranches for sale around here. Take pictures of the for-sale signs, okay? We can find somewhere to settle in, somewhere we can study the satellite maps."

"Where you going with this, Walt?"

Isabel's stomach ached. Now they were going the wrong way. Her mind was a jumble. Why had Sister Bridget told them there were no border checks between Ozona and the border? What would she do if the border patrol stopped their car? She'd take her baby and run. That's what she'd do.

"We check out the ranches on the satellite maps, find a big one that extends to the border, call the agent, and say we want to see the property." The app translated what Walter said, but Isabel didn't really understand.

Mabel nodded at Walter's words as she studied her map app. "How about we break the lock on the ranch's gate and drive in." She showed him the satellite map of the ranch on their right. It was vast, sprawling ranchland that stretched to the Rio Grande River.

She handed the map to Isabel and Marcelino.

"And look at the river right there." Mabel pointed. Isabel enlarged the map of the river. It looked like it was almost dry.

"Drought conditions, not much rain. And all the dams and irrigation. The river is just a trickle in that spot." Walter smiled at Mabel like he was proud of her for thinking of a good solution.

"It's shorter to the border to just cut across the land where there're no roads." Marcelino showed Isabel on the map.

Walter pulled up to the ranch entrance. "Electric gate. I might be able to disable the motor and manually open it."

"What about cars driving by?" Isabel felt nervous. She looked up and down the road.

"I'll just have to do it really fast."

"It's desolated out here. I've only seen a few cars," Mabel said. "What do you think, Isabel and Marcelino?"

"Yes," Marcelino said.

"Yes." Isabel fidgeted with the straps of the baby's car seat. "Please hurry."

"Come on, Marcelino. You can help." Walter parked the Land Rover.

Marcelino watched as Walter took the lid off the gate's motor and turned a lever to release pressure from the drive shaft. Then Marcelino pushed open the gate. Walter drove the SUV through, and Marcelino put the lid back on the motor, restoring the gate's remote control.

"Even with this more direct route to the river, it's going to take at least an hour," Mabel said.

Walter pulled onto the dry desert ranchland. "Mabel, you were smart to choose four-wheel drive." Once he drove onto the open off-road, Isabel found that the land wasn't as flat as it looked. The dry terrain had big cracks and dips as well as rocky mounds and scrubby vegetation.

"I just remembered; it has built-in GPS too." Mabel's voice modulated every time the Land Rover pitched upward and down in dips and troughs. Despite the jolting, she managed to turn on the GPS map that was built into the dashboard. "Look here." She spoke over her shoulder to Isabel and Marcelino. She pointed to the lit-up map on the dashboard. "Here is the river."

"How far?" Isabel asked.

"About an hour," Mabel said. "We can't go too fast because there are so many ditches and mounds. It's pretty bumpy." Isabel heaved and jerked up and down with the SUV. Walter didn't speak as he appeared to concentrate on navigating the terrain. The baby awoke and wailed.

Isabel imagined it was like a rollercoaster ride but without the fun. She'd never been on one though. She fumbled with the straps on the baby's carrier.

"Maybe you should leave the baby strapped in," Marcelino said.

"But she's scared." Isabel removed her screaming baby from the car seat and held her close. She attempted to nurse her, but with all the random thumps, dips, and heaves, it was impossible. Mabel turned and gave Isabel encouraging looks, trying to smile, but the Land Rover's lurching made her face reel too. The pitching and hurling and the baby screaming was interminable. Isabel held tight to the back of Walter's seat. "It's okay, my baby, we are going home. Shh, little sweet baby, everything will be all right." She prayed the intense bouncing would come to an end. Then just when she despaired, thinking the bucking would never stop, the land leveled out, and the riverbed became visible.

"That felt like forever." Isabel looked up through the car window into the faces of massive black cattle with white faces chewing their cud and lowing. Gabriela quieted down, settling in against Isabel's skin.

"Get ready to go. We might have to run."

Marcelino sat forward and strapped on his backpack.

Isabel tried to give the sling back to Mabel.

"No, no, darling, you take that." Mabel waved it away. "You put that sling on and I'll hand Gabriela to you once you get over the fence." Isabel secured the sling the way Sister Bridget showed her. Her heart raced. Almost home. She couldn't wait to see her mother and her brother. And tell Juana everything that happened. But then a dark dread descended. What if El Gigante already killed Juana? *Please God, no.*

Walter stopped the Land Rover by the rancher's iron fence. The fence was topped with barbed wire. Beyond the fence, lay the mostly dry riverbed. Isabel wasn't so sure she could climb over the fence. The barbed wire looked sharp.

"I have my toolbox. I can cut the wire, and ya'll can climb over." It was like Walter read her mind.

"Okay, kids." He rummaged through his toolbox. "Hurry, let's get you packed up." It was getting dark. "Honey, did you call Sister Bridget's friend to pick up the kids in Progresso?"

"I tried to, but I don't have service here. I'll call when we get back to the road." The translation app still worked though.

Mabel adjusted the baby sling on Isabel. "How are your feet?"

Isabel felt like she was stepping on chunks of glass. "They feel good."

They consolidated the supplies from the backpacks. Isabel planned to toss hers over the fence. She'd pick it up on the other side. Mabel held Gabriela, but Isabel hugged the elderly woman nonetheless, snuggling the baby between their bodies. Walter, wearing thick work gloves, snipped the barbed wire and removed about three feet. He then shook Marcelino's hand and pulled him in for a bear hug.

Suddenly, the sound of tires screeched on gravel like scorched earth. The noise got louder, and Isabel heard men hollering. Approaching headlights cast beams onto the riverbed and into Mexico. Two ranchers in a pickup truck sped toward them. One hung out of the passenger seat aiming a rifle. Shouts and a single gun blast rang out. The bullet hit the SUV, shattering a side window. Isabel's instinct was to run. She grabbed her baby from Mabel and headed for the fence. Walter caught her arm and pushed her back into the car. Protecting Gabriela with both arms, she fell headlong onto the car seat.

The armed ranchers scrambled from their truck.

Walter shouted. He motioned for everyone to get back in the SUV. He started it up and took off. Mabel was half in and half out. She grunted and pulled herself in. Her door slammed with the forward motion. Marcelino's leg caught in the door; his foot dragged on the ground. Isabel screamed. He pushed the door open and pulled his leg in. The door slammed shut.

Mabel yelled, ducking her head, and motioned for everyone to get down. She shouted each one of their names and maneuvered her upper body to check on each.

Walter shouted angrily as the second shot shattered the back windshield.

He accelerated onto the rancher's fence. The passengers flew forward as the SUV came to a halt. Mabel hit the dashboard. Isabel held her baby to her chest with both arms. She landed on the floor; Gabriela wailed. Walter ripped the gear shift. He backed up at such speed, the ranchers had to dive to the ground to avoid being run over. Then he mashed on the accelerator and sped forward. He rammed the Land Rover onto the fencing, knocking it over. Then he barreled onto the riverbed and over the bank. The ranchers fired their rifles but missed as the SUV sped away, escaping into the Mexican countryside.

Chapter 19

In the high plains of central Mexico, lay a vast valley where Mexico City stretched and sprawled, restrained by surrounding mountains and volcanoes. The Aeromexico 747 made a quick descent into the metropolis and Sister Bridget's heart filled with nostalgia at the sight of her city's enormous Bosque de Chapultepec with its lake and forest at the center of the city.

She stepped off the plane and emerged into the rhythm of Mexico. Even within the confines of the international airport with its gleaming tiles, glass and metallic fixtures, the essence of clay and adobe, the people hurrying assuredly to claim their bags, conserving their words, it was all just something so Mexico. The passersby ignored her, and she loved it. And she ignored them in return. Letting people be was the Mexican way.

Outside, the air felt fresh and clean. Mexico City's summer deluges, its rainy season, had washed away the dense smog caused by the city's four million vehicles. Sister Bridget loved this time of year in her hometown. With the smog and the rainstorms behind them, the city's residents took to the streets and parks. Her connecting flight to Creel, Chihuahua wouldn't be until the next day. So, she'd spend the night at the Mother House, the headquarters of the Sisters of St. Paul. She hadn't told the sisters she was coming, so no one waited to pick her up at the airport. She made her way to the taxi stand, her tunic and veil fluttering in the breeze. Crossing the street was stop and go, dodging cars and buses. Motorcycles honked and veered through the heavy traffic.

"Hello, stranger." It was a man on a motorcycle. She hurried across to get out of his way. The man pulled up to the curb and removed his helmet.

"Detective?"

"Hello, Sister Bridget." Detective Estevez had a wide grin on his face. Was it really Joaquin Estevez?

"American Airlines. Early flight." He parked his motorcycle and got off. She stared, speechless. Seeing Joaquin Estevez in Mexico City was like seeing a ghost in the real world or a real person in a dream. But there he was with an electric blue motorcycle, hair pressed every which way, smiling with those eyes. Definitely Joaquin's eyes.

"What are you…pardon me for asking, but why are you here?" Sister Bridget shook her head.

"You didn't think I was going to let you have all the fun, did you?" He jostled his hair into place.

She stared at him.

"I'm a detective. I tracked you down."

He placed his helmet on the seat of the motorcycle. "So, what do you think?"

"What do I think about what, Detective?"

"The motorcycle." He stared at her with mock shock. He surveyed the motorbike and gave her a look that said he couldn't believe that she wasn't impressed.

"I believe it is a nice motorcycle." She managed a smile and a half laugh. His enthusiasm was starting to get to her.

"I rented it. It's electric." He furrowed his brow at the vehicle and rubbed his chin. "The guy at the rental place was pushing them, what with the environment and such."

She shook her head. "I'm confused, Detective. Exactly what are you doing here?" She had to lean toward his ear to be heard above noisy engines, car horns, people shouting at their rides, and slamming doors and trunks. A plane was taking off. One was landing too.

Up close, the detective's deep mahogany skin exuded a salty, beachy fragrance, like sun-soaked stones and warm sage. She quickly stepped back, opting to raise her voice above the din.

"Ahem...I'm sorry. What did you say?" She felt warm, embarrassed.

"I called Father Bartosh—" He paused as a car with a loud muffler passed. "The man doesn't return phone calls." He shouted as a motorcycle started up. "I had to catch him between confessions."

She smiled to herself, picturing the detective going into the confessional to get a word with the priest.

"Detective, I got an email from Isabel's lawyer. She is certain that the DHS, ICE, the FBI, nobody will pursue Isabel and her baby. The United States will not try to extradite her from Mexico."

"I know that. That's not why I'm here," he shouted back. "Can we go somewhere to talk?" He had switched to Spanish, that endearing Puerto Rican pronunciation.

"Yes, of course. I'll get a taxi." She switched to Spanish too.

"A taxi?" he said with an exaggerated hurt

expression, raking his fingers through his thick hair. "What are you talking about? There's plenty of room on the bike."

She spied a second helmet strapped to the rear of the seat. *Ah.*

"No," she said.

"You only have a small bag. It'll be fine."

She looked down at her tunic. "I'm not dressed for such a thing."

"Oh, come on. Your dress is so…uh, wide." He tipped the motorcycle upright. "Here, give it a try. We'll just go a few blocks to a coffee shop or something. If you don't like it, we'll get a taxi."

"Oh, for the love of Pete." She didn't want to stand there all day arguing. She secured the long strap of her satchel over her shoulder and across her bosom.

Estevez lifted the extra helmet and patted the back half of the long seat.

"Yes, I've ridden a motorbike before." She'd traveled by motorcycle often during her college years. Situating herself sideways on the seat, she bent her leg and carefully repositioned it over and onto the other side of the motorcycle. Estevez politely averted his eyes. He was right though; her wide tunic provided ample coverage.

"Perfect. Now this." He handed her the extra helmet. "You might want to take off your…er…" He pointed to his own head and wiggled his finger. "…scarf."

Oh dear, her veil. This was becoming too much. The passersby who would usually ignore one and all started to glance. Well, she'd gotten this far. She yanked off her veil and stashed it in her bag. She grabbed the helmet, pressed it down upon her head, secured the strap, and impatiently extended her hand to the front part of the seat, giving the detective a fixed look.

From his awkward maneuvers, it became clear that he should have mounted the bike before her. He settled onto the seat though and started up the motor. She inched back in an attempt to put space between them.

"Hold on, Sister." She held tight to the rubber-covered grips on either side of her seat.

"I am, Detective."

"Hold on to *me*."

"I'm fine." She shouted back, arching her back and gripping the handles ever tighter.

Smiling tight and toothy into the wind, she felt light and free, zipping in and out of traffic. Detective Estevez seemed at home in Mexico City's traffic. It must be the way they do it in San Juan, Puerto Rico, as well, gliding between cars here and there with little regard for distance, spacing, and signaling.

She directed him along Paseo de la Reforma Avenue to the sprawling forested park, Bosque de Chapultepec. He parked the motorcycle near an outdoor cafe at the edge of the park's lake, and she traded the helmet for her veil. They sat at a table by the water's edge under huge ahuehuete trees, their featherlike leaves trembling in the breeze. The cool gusts coming up off the lake enlivened the skin on her face with a spidery sensation.

"My face tickles from the motorcycle ride." She laughed and rubbed her cheeks. He grinned, running his hand over his face too, as if applying aftershave.

"How are you, Sister? Did you survive all right?"

He smiled at her.

"Oh yes, I quite enjoyed the ride." She leaned in with her elbows on the table. "Now tell me. What are you doing here, Detective?"

"You'd started calling me Joaquin back in Austin."

"*Joaquin*, what are you doing in Mexico City?" Though she had a good idea already.

He hesitated a moment and then determined. "Now, don't get angry with me." He waved his hands outward. "I called Father Bartosh looking for you. He said that *you* said that you were going on retreat to your Mother House in Mexico City."

They locked eyes until she looked away to the couples in paddleboats on Lake Minor, not really seeing them.

"Even Bartosh sounded skeptical. You're not really on retreat, are you?" She didn't answer. "You've come to find Juana. Am I right?"

"Detective…Joaquin, you are a law enforcement officer of the United States."

"So, you won't tell me what your business is here?"

"You said that Alejandro Maldonado, the one Isabel calls *El Gigante*, is an odd bird. That he's a loner, he gets away with hurting people, killing people. Well, I'm an odd bird too. I can't help it. I can't stand by and do nothing when I know Isabel's friend, Juana, is alone and scared. She's suffering. I need to tell what I know to the authorities." She planned to do much more, but she wasn't going to share that with the detective.

"*And* you're here to find the girl."

Sister Bridget didn't answer. The last place Isabel saw her friend was in the state of Chihuahua, by the

Copper Canyons where the Rarámuri live. Her connecting flight would take her there tomorrow. *After* her appointment.

"I'm only here to talk to the office for trafficking and violence against women." That was a lie. "I have an appointment for tomorrow." That part was true. She *did* have an appointment to talk to an employee at the Special Prosecutor's Office for Violence Against Women and Trafficking in Persons, but she had little hope that the Mexican government would help find Juana. Detective Estevez was right. She came to Mexico to find Juana, and she wasn't going to leave until she found her.

"Do you know how many traffickers are actually prosecuted in this country?"

"Very few. Believe me, I know. I'm Mexican, remember?" She fixed a steady eye at Estevez. "My government is a kleptocracy. Our leaders get rich off the people. Government officials will take bribes from anybody that has money. Including criminals. Don't think I don't know that."

"Then what do you think you're doing here?"

"I have to make an attempt." She couldn't live with herself if she didn't at least try.

"Okay then. May I come to the meeting with you?"

"That's not necessary, Detective…I mean, Joaquin. You're a law enforce—"

"But I won't be attending as a police officer. I'll be there as your friend." He reached across the table for her hand. She looked at their hands together, and she didn't pull away. She felt a connection. It felt good to have a friend, to be not so all alone.

"All right. Come to the meeting with me."

The waitress came. Sister Bridget slipped her hand from Estevez's. They ordered *café con leche* and shared a pumpkin *empanada*. Sister Bridget steered the conversation away from Juana, nudging the teenager to the back of her mind. She and Estevez watched families carrying picnics and young people in canoes and paddleboats. Children shouted and laughed. Ducks flapped, slapping the water, causing a ruckus. Sister Bridget and Estevez talked about their childhoods, shared cherished memories, and laughed together.

"Have you ever seen a castle? A real castle?" The coffee and *empanada* put her in the mood for a walk.

"I saw one at Disney World when I was a kid."

"I will show you a *real* castle. Built by the Spanish when they ruled over Mexico." She stood and offered Estevez her hand. He pretended to be too tired to get up, and she tugged at him. They both laughed.

They walked arm in arm carrying their small bags and motorcycle helmets. Bicycle riders buzzed past, kicking up gravel on the wide trail. Joggers plodded by. Families pushed strollers, their children giggling, running, and getting underfoot.

At first, the hill wasn't noticeable; the path steepened gradually.

"It's just around the bend there." And as they rounded a broad stand of cypress trees, they caught sight of the castle.

"Isn't that something." Estevez stopped and whistled at the sight. Joggers and cyclists veered around him.

"Built by the Spanish in the late 1700's." Sister Bridget was proud that her city preserved the historical structure.

The massive neoclassical castle stood regal above a thick forest. With its graceful arches, stained glass, and watchtowers, the castle was an anachronism against a backdrop of Mexico City's skyscrapers.

Sister Bridget had admired the structure all her life. She recalled visiting the castle often with her parents and brother.

And that's when she felt the first raindrop.

"Oh dear." She looked up. Thunder cracked, and the sky opened, spilling a torrent of rain. People scattered. Sister Bridget and Estevez ran for cover too. They dodged traffic to cross the Avenue Constituyentes and took shelter under the awning of a sidewalk cafe. Sister Bridget was soaked, her veil plastered to her head. Estevez tipped his motorcycle helmet over and poured forth what looked like a liter of rainwater. Their eyes met, and they laughed. They sat at one of the cafe tables and watched the downpour. The rain pummeling the awning, sidewalk, and street so loud, they didn't bother to speak. They just watched and smiled at each other now and then.

Sister Bridget set her bag on the table and checked for dry clothes. Her extra habit was just as wet as the one she wore. She started to say as much, but there was no point in shouting.

The rain slowed and quieted to a patter. "I believe it's time for me to get a taxi. Now would be an appropriate time to resume my journey to the Mother House. I so enjoyed our little adventure today, Joaquin." The rain let up completely and the sidewalks once again filled with pedestrians. A waitress came out of the café and handed them menus. "Would you like to order drinks?"

Estevez looked at the waitress, then at Sister Bridget. "Come on, Sister. Just one drink and then you can get your taxi and go to your House Mother."

"Mother House." She paused, not relishing a wet ride in a taxi. "A glass of wine *would* be nice."

Estevez ordered two glasses of red wine. After the waitress left, he looked down, shook his head, and laughed.

"What's funny?" Sister Bridget asked.

"The waitress. 'Would you like to order drinks?' It's funny. Here we are soaking wet, drenched, and everybody just carries on like normal. I just find it funny. Don't you?"

"In Mexico, we carry on and go about our business. It's just our way." She shrugged.

His hand at his chin, he thought for a moment. "Wait here. I'll be right back." He hurried off.

The wine arrived, and she was tempted to take a sip, but she waited, alone and shivering, as the sky darkened. How long had she been waiting?

Miserably, she removed her veil and wrung it out. She ran her fingers through her wet curls. For Pete's sake. This was childish. She was fifty years old and soaked to the bone. The chilled mountain air was setting in, and she would probably catch a cold. She'd have to hail a taxi after all. The detective would understand.

She stood to go as Estevez came running down the sidewalk, weaving amongst pedestrians.

"Wait, wait. Sorry, I took so long." He pulled a woolen, turquoise *rebozo* from a shopping bag and placed it around her shoulders. "Is that better? Here, come with me." He gathered their bags and helmets and tossed money on the table for the wine. He took Sister Bridget's arm and started down the walkway, but she held back.

"For goodness' sake." She lifted the two wine glasses and placed them on the table of a young couple that was holding hands. "Enjoy."

"*Muy amable.*" The young man smiled, surprised.

"Wouldn't want it to go to waste." She followed behind Estevez, dodging passersby.

Estevez spoke over his shoulder. "Only from a nun, should someone accept wine from a stranger."

He led Sister Bridget down the block to a small inn with canary yellow shutters, turquoise awnings, and colorful *talavera* tiles on the entry. Its sign read, *Reál Salamanca Hotél.*

A hotel?

"Please, Sister. Please. I needed to get a room for the night anyway, so I bought you some dry clothes." He handed her the shopping bag. "I knew you'd say no, so I went ahead." She looked inside the bag. He'd even purchased dry shoes. She caught his gaze. Was he trying to seduce her? A part of her, a long-quieted part of herself, awakened and cautioned her.

He took her arm and led her into the gleaming talavera-tiled lobby. The place was very old, colonial, and well-kept. She always thought that old buildings smelled like clean dust. That probably made no sense; it's just what came to mind.

"Listen, I promise, no hanky-panky." He raised his hands as if he were under arrest. "I just care about you. I want you to get a hot shower. Get dry and warm." He shrugged. "And I don't want our evening to be cut short before we have that glass of wine. That's all."

"And what about you? You're wet too." His soaked clothing clung to his body.

He held up his duffle bag. "Waterproof. My clothes are dry. I'll get changed. No problem." He nodded toward the men's room in the lobby.

He held out the room key. She stared at him. Those smiling eyes. It was just a shower and dry clothes. It was a nice gesture. "Which way?" She took the key and sloshed across the hotel lobby, her shoes squeaking on the tile floor.

Chapter 20

Sister Bridget took full advantage of the hotel's hot water. The best she could have hoped for at the Mother House would have been a frigid shower in a dorm-style stall with rough concrete flooring. Not that she would ever complain, but the Convento de San Pablo had been built in 1768. The convent's stone colonial architecture had withstood over two hundred years of elements and earthquakes, but its amenities did not include hot water. The closest the sisters came to a hot shower was warming pots of water on the stove and pouring it into their baths.

But here at the Reál Salamanca Hotél, plush area rugs lay upon smooth, yellow-gold terracotta. Sister Bridget hung her wet habit and its accoutrements on brass towel racks, door hooks, chair backs, and windowsills before she stepped into the shower. The hotel's shower reminded her of her childhood home. Floral *talavera* tiles in green, coral, and yellow covered the shower's walls and ceiling. Its floor was embedded with smooth, charcoal-colored river stones. Fluffy, soft washcloths hung from brass holders, and recessed shelves held soaps and shampoos. The fragrant bergamot and rosemary soap felt smooth and silky on Sister Bridget's skin. Lavender shampoo made her hair feel like silk. Aromatic steam enveloped her.

She stepped out of the shower and massaged

rosewood lotion onto her arms and legs. Then, wrapped in the hotel's fluffy robe, Sister Bridget reached into Estevez's shopping bag. She pulled out a blue and yellow dress. Stacked underneath the dress, were undergarments. She smiled at the lacy, pink underpants and the sensible brassiere. At the bottom of the bag were black flats in size eleven. *Ah, the deductive skills of a detective.*

After drying her hair, she wiped the steam from the mirror, and tussled her salt and pepper curls into place. She checked the tag on the dress. Size large. The detective wasn't wrong. The sky-blue wrap dress with little yellow tulips draped snug about her ample bosom and hips. It came with a yellow sash which she tied at her waist. The dress's deep v neckline revealed pale skin, which she covered with the turquoise *rebozo*.

When she stepped from the bathroom to the hotel suite, she noticed Estevez's duffle bag and the two motorcycle helmets. He must have come in with a second key while she was in the shower, but he wasn't there now.

She found him in the hotel lobby seated on a plush, overstuffed couch. He had changed into dark slacks and a sage green sweater. It put her in mind of lush moss against his ebony skin. He stood and took both her hands in his. He kissed her on each cheek, his lips lingering on her skin. Still holding her hands, he stepped back and moved his eyes down the length of her dress to her shoes, and back up. Their eyes met, and they laughed.

"Thank you for the clothing…and the shower." He smiled as if he were speechless, so she said, "That's a handsome sweater."

Finally, he said, "You're beautiful."

She released his hands, stepped back, and wrapped the *rebozo* tighter. She looked away to the registration desk where a family was checking in.

Let me drift not from you, Jesus.

"Never mind. Forget I said that…Sister?"

In her heart, she communed with Creation, with Love, with Forgiveness and Reconciliation, *the Knowing*. The Holy Spirit told her, *be not afraid.*

"Sister?"

She turned to him with a smile and a nod. "Thank you for the compliment, Joaquin. The clothes are comfortable, and I appreciate your thoughtfulness."

"Okay, good." There was that broad smile, those eyes. "I was afraid you were mad at me."

"Of course not." She hooked her arm in his. "Now, let's get that glass of wine." She coaxed him through the door into the chilly evening, and they joined the droves of people on the street.

They crossed Avenida de la Constituyentes, and once again stepped into the city's forest, the Bosque de Chapultepec. It smelled like rain. Steamy, pungent fragrances emanated from the thick groves of Montezuma cypress. Noble cedars and Jacaranda with purple blossoms lined both sides of the trail that cut through the forest. It was getting dark, especially in the shadows of the great trees, but the pudgy, bright moon, a waxing gibbous, illuminated their way.

"Detective—"

"Joaquin."

She smiled. "Joaquin, we will cross the park to Polanco on the other side."

"What's in Polanco?"

"Ah, now *that's* the question, isn't it? And the answer is *Agua y Sal Cebichería*. Do you like ceviche?"

"What do you not understand about, 'I'm from Puerto Rico'?" He laughed. "When I was boy, I would go with my uncle on his fishing boat. We stayed out from before light until almost dark. There's no better way to eat ceviche than catching a fish and cutting it up right there on the boat. My favorite was dorado, but we ate it all: snook, wahoo, bonefish, whatever. Lime juice and salt. That's it. *Ay que rico!*" He kissed his fingers like an Italian chef. "Sometimes my uncle brought an onion, a few *ajíes caballeros*. Red, spicy ones. He'd chop them up and add it in. We scooped up the ceviche with my aunt's *tostones*. Now *that's* the best way to eat ceviche."

Sister Bridget pictured the charming scenario. "Then you will love Agua y Sal. I cannot promise that the ceviche will match your uncle's, but I think you'll find it delicious."

Agua y Sal Cebichería stood a block from the park, across from the Hyatt Regency. It was a small, cheerful, brightly lit restaurant with natural oak tables and chairs that grated on green and white *fleur de lis* tiles. Skinny palm trees in green clay pots adorned the corners.

Sister Bridget and Estevez ordered white wine and crispy corn *tostadas* topped with sautéed shrimp. And they ordered three ceviches—shrimp with mango, dorado with avocado, and octopus with green olive.

"Now tell me, how does it feel to shed your habit? Now no one knows you're a nun. You don't have to behave like one."

She laughed and raised her wine glass. "I'll drink to that. To not behaving like a nun." Not that she planned to act crazy or anything.

They lingered after dinner; Estevez held both her hands across the table. She loved his hands, their warm skin, smooth and deeply rich coloring like Mexico's black onyx.

He gently turned the silver band on her left hand. "You forgot to take this off."

"I didn't forget."

"What about not behaving like a nun?"

"Just because I'm not behaving like a nun doesn't mean I'm not one."

He sighed. "Bridget." He paused. It was the first time he had left off the *Sister*.

"Yes, Joaquin?"

"Can you take off the ring?"

She slowly ran her thumbs and index fingers over and between his fingers. She wanted to memorize his hands. She knew she wouldn't have them forever.

His obsidian eyes were not smiling. Instead, she found a deep ocean there. His facial expression was…how to describe…open? Vulnerable?

"I don't take it off…because…without it, I would no longer be my true self. I am a person whose heart rests and trusts in God. It's just the way I am. God is my light."

"Lots of people love God. It doesn't mean they have to withdraw from life."

"I agree. I don't withdraw from life. It's just that God is the center of my life. God's my guiding light. Nothing's more important to me." The restaurant emptied. It was getting late.

"Joaquin, the girl, Juana, Isabel's friend. I know what she's feeling, and I can't bear that she's suffering."

Estevez leaned closer, his forehead a sheaf of lines. "That's what I lo—*like* about you, Bridget." He went quiet. "I think about it and really, there aren't that many people who care about others. Not the way you do. But you don't just care; you *act* on your convictions. Not to mention the way you reunited Isabel with her baby."

"I…"

"It's okay, don't bother to deny it. Wouldn't want you to have to lie."

"I'm not lying, Joaquin, not this time. This I won't have to take to the confessional. I did not help Isabel and Marcelino escape." Well, she helped a little, but Mabel and Walt were the real heroes, and she would take that secret to her grave. They were the ones that came up with the plan to simply drive Isabel, Marcelino, and the baby to the border, where the trio would cross over and be met by one of her sisters who would drive them the rest of the way. That was the plan, and by now—she looked at her watch—the young people should be back in Mexico.

Estevez paid the bill, and they walked hand in hand around the periphery of the park. It was far too late to walk through the middle of the *bosque*.

"Earlier, in the restaurant, you said you know what the kidnapped girl, Juana, is feeling. How do you?" He took her hand and looped her arm through his.

"I want to tell you so you might understand why I feel so strongly about the missing girl. I never speak of it…" Of course, her family and her oldest friends knew, but they shielded Sister Bridget. She only trusted God with the sacred memory. But she trusted Estevez too. He held her arm snug against his side.

"It happened when I was twelve. Esmeralda, my cousin, was thirteen. We were spending the summer with our grandparents in Acapulco. It was 1979, the early days of kidnappings." She shivered and wrapped her rebozo across her neck and over her shoulder. "We were innocent. My cousin and I had flown to be with our grandparents every summer starting when I was eight. My grandparents didn't take precautions like people do today. They had no reason to." She pictured Abuelo and Abuelita, gray-haired but still young and energetic then. Abuelo with his perpetual smile, clapping his hands and rubbing them together, the gesture he used when proposing adventures and practical jokes. Abuelita, pious, corralling the cousins, never allowing them to miss Sunday Mass.

Sister Bridget's voice wavered. She hadn't expected to relive the experience. Her chest felt tight, and she began to tear up at the memory. She reached for a tissue in the pocket of her habit, forgetting that she left her tunic behind in the hotel room. Estevez gave her his handkerchief.

She recounted what had started out as a perfect day on the beach in Acapulco. Abuelita had wrapped sandwiches, packs of cookies, and thermoses of cold lemonade.

Abuelo had planned an adventure.

"*Vamonos*, let's go, little chickens." Abuelo had hurried Esmeralda and Bridget along. "I have a surprise for you at the *playa*." The four of them started out before the sun came up. The drive to Playa la Angosta was long.

They arrived just as the sun rose over the mountains, casting its rays upon the little beach tucked between two rocky cliffs. Waves sparkled, whooshed, and crashed onto the shore. Twelve-year-old Bridget had blocked the sun with her hand and squinted so that only a dazzling sliver reached her eyes. The shore smelled of salt and fish.

"Abuelo, this is a bright surprise." Esmeralda shielded her eyes, both hands cupped. Abuelita smiled as she unpacked the blankets, chairs, and food.

"Come with me my little chickens. I'll show you the real surprise." Abuelo took their hands. They kicked off their sandals, and their feet sank into the soft, cold sand. They made their way to the water's edge, and there upon the wet, packed sand was their surprise.

"*Estrellitas del Mar!*" Esmeralda was so excited. Glistening on the wet sand were dozens and dozens of puffy, orange starfish. The two girls squatted, hugging their knees, admiring one of the creatures, its orange spines tinged lavender on its edges.

"Can I pick it up, Abuelo?" Bridget was already reaching.

"Yes, *mija*, it won't hurt you."

But Esmeralda blocked Bridget's hand. "Wait. It won't hurt *her*, but will she hurt *it*?" She looked up at Abuelo with big eyes.

"The *estrellita* will be fine as long as it doesn't dry out."

Esmeralda allowed Bridget to hold one of the starfish in the palm of her hand.

"It tickles." Bridget giggled. She turned the starfish over and examined its suction-cup *feet* on its underside.

"We should put them all back in the ocean, so they don't dry out," Esmeralda said. The girls hurried to return all the starfish to the water before more beachgoers arrived. When others did arrive, Esmeralda boldly scolded those that sought to keep the starfish for themselves.

Bridget had longed to take one of the creatures home to Mexico City to show her brother, but Esmeralda said, "*Prima*, how would you feel if someone took you away from your home?"

Bridget and Esmeralda dozed during the drive back to their grandparents' house, so Bridget didn't see when the two men in the blue car smashed into Abuelo's car. She and Esmeralda careened to one side of the back seat as Abuelo's car crashed into the railing at the side of the highway. The impact thrust Abuelo onto the steering wheel. His head shattered the windshield. Abuelita screamed and reached for him. He was bloodied and unconscious. One of the men from the blue car opened Esmeralda's door and pulled her out. "Don't fight and I won't have to kill you."

"No! Leave her alone." Bridget grabbed onto her cousin and held her tight around her waist as the man dragged Esmeralda along the pavement. Another man, fat and sweaty, wrenched Bridget away, opened his car door, and tried to force Bridget in. Bridget fought and screamed for Esmerelda.

"Just get in, and I won't kill you." The big man cursed at Bridget. She screamed, hitting and kicking.

Esmeralda twisted her body and cried out. The man dragged her to the other side of the car.

"Shut up! Shut up! Get in the car!" The man was relentless. He slapped Esmeralda's face, and she screamed. Abuelita screamed too and grabbed onto Bridget who was closest to her. Another car came up behind them, the driver furiously honking his horn. The fat man cursed and released Bridget who landed on the pavement in Abuelita's arms. The two men got into the blue car and sped away with Esmeralda.

Now thirty-eight years later, Esmeralda's kidnapping occupied Bridget's conscience as a sacred memory, the profound annihilation of Esmeralda's childhood. Sister Bridget kept her cousin's childhood in her heart, as though it was her responsibility and hers alone to hold on to it, to keep it safe and intact. Maybe give it back to her one day.

"What happened to Esmeralda?" Estevez wiped a tear with a thick finger.

"My aunt and uncle paid the kidnappers ten thousand dollars. *American* dollars, not pesos. They got her back, but they never really got *her* back. The old Esmeralda was gone. The kidnappers had raped her and beat her badly. They gave her a head injury, and she never regained her full brain functioning."

"Brain damage?"

Sister Bridget nodded and blew her nose.

"Damn them to hell. And I'm betting the way law enforcement is corrupt to hell here, those bast—sorry, those criminals, probably never went to jail. I'm guessing the police probably got some of that ten thousand."

Sister Bridget couldn't fault Estevez's anger. She had gone through that stage too. For a child is the most precious vessel of the soul. Is it not? And, no, as far as Sister Bridget learned, the two men were never apprehended. The scared witness refused to testify.

"Esmeralda and her family moved to Vancouver, British Columbia. In Canada. My uncle took a job there. But it was very hard for Esmeralda. She was

225

frustrated by hemiparesis on her right side."

"What's that? Was she paralyzed?"

"Not completely, no. She had weakness and partial loss of functioning on her right side. She forgot things too, sometimes even her name. She forgot *my* name. Later, when she was older, Esmeralda's depression led to drinking too much, then taking drugs. It started with prescription drugs, but then…you know." Sister Bridget paused to wipe her nose and take a breath. "She lost all hope, I think. I tried to talk to her, but…it was as though her brain had tricked her into believing she had nothing to live for."

Sister Bridget recalled a rare moment when her cousin opened up to her. "I feel like I'm living in a tomb," Esmeralda had said. "I'm dead, but my body just won't turn off." Sister Bridget had tried to convince her otherwise. Esmeralda smiled and appeared to be better, but she wasn't. Her mind continued to torment her.

"She tried to kill herself twice. My aunt and uncle took her to doctors and put her in treatment programs. But eventually she succeeded. She took her own life when she was twenty-seven."

Sister Bridget and Estevez walked on in silence. Other couples strolled past.

"You were twenty-six then, right? It must have hit you hard."

"I loved my cousin. I had nightmares about what I imagined she went through at the hands of the kidnappers. I guess I had survivor's guilt too. When she took her own life, I had just finished with medical school and was applying to residency programs. I had a boyfriend, a fiancé."

"Was he in medical school too?"

"Yes, we, the two of us, his name was Antonio, we talked about doing our residency training at the same hospital, or at least the same city, but then Esmeralda died. I went to Vancouver. She hung on to life in the hospital for a week and a half, and I stayed with her. I missed my residency interviews. And she never regained consciousness."

"You couldn't reschedule your interviews?"

"I suppose I could have, but my heart was no longer in it. My aunt and uncle took Esmeralda's ashes back to Mexico, but I stayed on in Vancouver. In a way, I felt immobilized. I called Antonio and told him to go ahead with his residency, not to wait for me."

"So, you broke up with Antonio. You became a nun, *a religious sister,* instead." Estevez's words were statements, not questions.

"That's correct."

"Sheesh."

"I didn't become a sister right away. That came later. After my aunt and uncle left, I took off north, stayed at campgrounds. I spent almost a year camping in forests, hiking, canoeing. I became a wanderer."

Sister Bridget recalled a year of roaming aimlessly in the Canadian wilderness like a lost sheep separated from its shepherd. She had promised her parents she would keep them apprised of her location. Back then, there were no cellphones and GPS; she relied on public telephones. It had still been warm when she reached the summit of Black Tusk Mountain, a remnant of an ancient volcano, but when she reached a little community called Yellowknife in the Northwest Territory, the summer began to wane, and she

227

encountered the prelude to Canada's bitter cold. She also encountered her father who brought cold weather provisions. Papi also presented himself as her traveling companion. Together, they ventured further north. They camped and canoed the Mackenzie River, guided by the Aurora Borealis. When the river froze over, they turned back.

"What about your mother? Your brother?"

"My brother was busy with his schooling. Mamá joined us a few times, but mostly she stayed in Mexico City tending to her medical practice. She knew Papi would be the one to help me mend. I think Papi thought that I never really healed from the initial trauma of the kidnapping. And then the guilt. How could I still be having nightmares about it, when it was Esmeralda that bore the brunt of the suffering? We had long talks, Papi and I, and often times we just silently communed with nature. And at the end of our journey, I decided to explore the religious life."

"And what about Antonio?"

"I think it was hard on him. He wanted to marry me, but it was better, *for me*, that I let him go. It was what was best for him too. Eventually. He has a lovely wife and children now."

"And what about you? Do you regret not getting married and having children?"

"Oh, my calling was in a different direction, and I don't regret it. I was called to the religious life just as you *and Antonio,* were called to marriage."

Estevez made no reply.

Finally, he broke the silence. "You remind me of her, you know. My wife. Janet was smart, caring, funny, a good sport, always willing to try things, always willing to do whatever it took to help people."

She squeezed his hand. "I take that as a great compliment."

"She had faith too. Faith in, you know…God…religion." He paused. "But look where it got her."

"Faith isn't an antidote for cancer, Joaquin. If it were, then it would be a commodity, no? Someone would determine a way to bottle and profit from it."

"Then what good is it?"

They had walked far from where they had started at Agua y Sal and had reached the brightly lit *Museo National de Antropología* where a jazz concert was taking place in the sculpture garden. Sister Bridget stopped and smiled. "But Joaquin, think about it, my friend." She looked into his eyes. "Are you sure you have no idea what God is good for?" Estevez didn't respond. "How have you managed to be happy and survive these six years since your wife died?"

"I've survived by my own will. Not by anything God has done for me. I've survived by loving my daughter." He went quiet, then continued. "My parents…my sisters…my friends have helped me. I've survived by focusing on my work…for my daughter's sake."

"You've answered your own question, my friend. 'What good is God?' God is love. God is hope…and trust, compassion, the charity of friends and family, and forgiveness and all those things that helped you get through your wife's death. God is the joy that you find while loving others and allowing yourself to be loved. Joy gives you perseverance. Joy makes you want more joy."

He looked at the ground, frowned, and shook his head. "No, I don't believe in God...well maybe...hell, I don't know."

They sat close on a bench in the sculpture garden. Smooth, cool saxophone and piano notes rose and fell in the chilly night like translucent, light-winged dragonflies. Couples and chatty groups of young people ambled about.

"Joaquin, you know how I told you that Esmeralda saved the lives of the starfish?" Her eyes welled up, and she used his damp handkerchief to catch the tiny rivulets. "I took one." She sniffed and paused. "I put it in the bottom of my beach bag. I wanted to show it to my brother. I found it there later. It was all dried up and cracked. That's when I remembered what Esmeralda said. 'How would you feel if someone took you away from your home?' "

Sister Bridget wept for Esmeralda. Again. Estevez took her in his arms. She wrapped her arms around his waist and laid her head on his shoulder.

When the tears faded, they watched the concert-goers come and go, Estevez's arm around her shoulder.

"Let's go for a ride." Sister Bridget anticipated the wind on her face. They held hands and retrieved the blue motorbike.

"You won't be too cold? I should have gotten you something warmer."

"I'm fine. It's a lovely dress." She tied the *rebozo* around her waist. She didn't want it to fly away. They had left the helmets in the hotel room. "Take the freeway, Viaducto Rio Piedad to Calzada de Los Misterios. I'm going to show you Our Lady of the Americas."

It was a fast ride. Sister Bridget leaned in and held tight around Estevez's waist this time. The cold wind lashed her face and whipped her hair.

They arrived at the nearly deserted Plaza Mariana where eight or ten people knelt on the cold concrete *plaza*, soundlessly moving their lips, petitioning God. Rosaries intertwined in their folded hands. One woman was accompanied by four children. She had blankets spread on the ground on which a small child lay bundled up, sleeping. The other youngsters chased each other about the *plaza*.

Sister Bridget and Estevez walked the motorcycle to a low brick barrier that encircled the *plaza*, and they sat on the wall.

"In the morning, when the priests unlock the doors to the basilica, these people will continue their journey on their knees." She pointed to the distant church across the *plaza*. It was a low, massive arena with a peak rising from its center. At the tip of the peak was a cross.

"Wow. That's a long way to go on their knees."

"Yes, this *plaza* holds fifty thousand worshippers."

"But why on their knees? What's the point? What's in the basilica?"

"They go on their knees to ask for a miracle. Some go to make reparations for sins." She paused and gazed in the same direction as the worshipers. "In the basilica is a miraculous image of Mary…the mother of God." She looked back at the petitioners who knelt on the *plaza*. "We call the image *Our Lady of Guadalupe.*"

They sat in silence for a while.

"Reparations can be helpful between humans, but I don't believe that God requires them." Sister Bridget took Estevez's hand, turned it over and traced the lines of his palm. "Like Jesus told the woman whom the people wanted to stone, 'go, and sin no more.' God would forgive me if I broke my vows tonight." She stood and stepped in front of him, looked into his eyes. "Being with you is not a bad thing. But, rather, being with you or not being with you are two good choices. I believe that either way is fine with God…as long as my faith and trust in God is not shaken. My faith is precious to me." She paused. "And I'm sor—"

"Wait. I know what you're going to say. But listen, you mean a lot to me, Bridget. And I think we could be happy together. I'm not saying jump into it all at once, but let's keep seeing each other. Let's give it a try. You're the first woman that I've even *wanted* to be around since Janet died."

"I don't want you to think that I've been leading you on, Joaquin. I've enjoyed being with you, too, but I made a vow."

She kissed him on each cheek and returned to sit beside him on the low wall. They watched the people praying.

"Perhaps it's been selfish of me to enjoy your company. You say that 'we could be happy together,' and that's true, but for me nothing on earth can equal the happiness that I have with God." She looked into the distance and shook her head. "Since that day, the day that my cousin was taken, and then later, when she took her own life, I searched for happiness. I became depressed; life seemed meaningless. Such injustice! She was only a small girl. If such a thing could happen to an innocent, then what's the point of life?"

Estevez took her hand. His warm, sturdy touch anchored and secured her.

"Every time I seemed to find a purpose in life—even before Esmeralda's suicide—medical school, my friends, my fiancé…happiness eluded me. I had access to money; remember my family was well-to-do. They tried to help me, but in my teenage years and in college, I turned to alcohol…and pills, just to numb my mind from the emptiness." She usually only spoke of those matters to her fellow sisters, her best friend, Sister Teresíta, her brother, but she wanted Estevez to know. She longed for him to understand that God was her joy. "I don't know if you know…do you remember the Bible story of the widow and the dead son?"

Estevez shook his head. He returned his gaze to the woman and the sleeping child on the concrete ground before the basilica. "I don't think so."

"It's in the Bible. The story goes, there was a widow whose only child, a son, had died."

"When you lost your cousin, you must have felt like that widow." He raised her hand and kissed it.

"No, I wasn't the widow. I was dead like the son."

She went quiet. The noise of distant traffic animated the silent lip movements of the praying lady.

"I was dead on the inside…like the son in the Bible story, but I turned to God. God was my last resort. I'd tried alcohol, drugs…other bad choices…and God had mercy on me. In the story, Jesus said to the dead son, 'I say to you, arise!' and, on my journey in Canada with my father, God spoke those same words to *me. Arise.*

"I regained my inner vitality, my optimism, my enthusiasm, and…and something brand new—joy. Joy in the risen God. I no longer regard life as a ceaseless deathbed where I wait to die." She turned toward the pilgrims kneeling before the basilica. "Now I know joy.

233

"Am I talking too much?" She smiled and released Estevez's hand. She reached for her crucifix—she had a habit of holding it tight—but there was nothing there. She only grasped a handful of the soft *rebozo*. She had left the crucifix behind at *Hotél Reál*. It hadn't matched the turquoise dress. "The life of a religious sister is my place in this world."

Estevez didn't answer.

"I'm sorry. *Did* I lead you on?" In her heart, she knew she had.

"Yeah, pretty much…I don't know. Maybe I led myself on. I used all the charm I could mobilize."

"Your charm is quite effective." She took his hands once again, brought them to her lips and kissed each one. "I have suffered in life, but you have suffered more than I, for you have lost your beloved spouse." She crossed her hands upon her chest. "I pray that you will find the consolation that I have found."

They left Plaza Mariana and returned to the hotel at two in the morning.

Sister Bridget found her black and white habit dry, as well as her nightclothes from her bag, but she didn't change just yet. Instead, she slept in the dress that Estevez had chosen for her and wrapped herself in his *rebozo*. She lay on her side on the downy bed, and he followed. Side by side, like petals in a rose, he wrapped his arms around her. "Thank you for staying for that glass of wine."

"Thank you for following me to Mexico."

She drifted off, blanketed by Estevez, the dress, and the rebozo he had gifted her. She slept, content that the silver band still encircled her finger.

Chapter 21

When she awoke, Estevez was gone. And his belongings were nowhere to be seen.

She found him waiting for her on the sidewalk in front of the office of the special prosecutor for Violence Against Women and Human Trafficking, which was in a high-rise in the *Distrito Federal*.

"Good morning, Detective." She shaded her eyes from the sun. He didn't say *call me Joaquin.*

"Sorry, I left without saying anything. I didn't want to wake y—" He stopped talking. It was obvious the three *policía federal* who stood at the entrance to the building were listening. The men in black uniforms, gold insignia, and bulletproof vests stared at them.

"What is your business here?" The young, stout police officer at the entrance looked and sounded belligerent. His hat appeared on the verge of popping off his thick, black hair. He looked Sister Bridget up and down, conveying an air of skepticism, and Sister Bridget knew that whatever she replied simply would not be taken for truth. The other two officers, also young, stood by as though waiting their turn to get something.

"I am Sister Bridget Ann Rincón-Keller, and I am here to make a report to the Special Office for Violence Against Women. I have an appointment."

The officer smirked. "Why? Has there been

violence committed against you?" Again, he looked at her habit.

"Look, just tell us which way to go." Estevez made his way past the officers.

The officer stepped in front of him. "And who are you? Did you commit the violence against her?"

Sister Bridget was used to the sarcasm. Every interaction she'd ever had with Mexican police was unhelpful. Their initial response was always one of *just go home*, and *don't cause a problem*. Now she could tell Estevez was getting irritated. She knew how to handle the situation, and it would be better if the detective would just leave her to it. She took him aside and said in English, "Why not go on to the airport, so you don't miss your flight? You'll need time to return your rental. I'll take care of this matter and then go on to the Mother House."

"I'm not going anywhere."

Inwardly, she acknowledged, *this* is why it is better to stay unattached to a man. "Then please, when it comes to the *policía federal*, it is best to cooperate and not question them. It's not like the United St—"

"What are you? Americans?" the officer asked.

"No. I am a Mexican citizen, and this is Joaquin Estevez. And yes, he is an American citizen." She had dual citizenship.

When Sister Bridget said *American citizen*, the other two officers smirked at each other with mocking admiration, pretending to be impressed.

The officer scowled at Estevez. "You don't sound like an American."

"Well, I am." Estevez spoke Spanish.

"I think these two are trying to pull one over on

us," a small, thin officer said. His black uniform hung on his frame, a size too big.

Sister Bridget tried again. "We are here to speak to an assistant in the special prosecutor's office."

The officer stared at her, and then shifted his stare to Estevez. He allowed them to enter the lobby. "Wait here." From the desk behind which three ladies sat typing at their computers and speaking on phones, he made a phone call. "Let's go. Follow me."

The officer escorted them to the fourth floor where they encountered another counter behind which three more ladies sat. The officer spoke to one of the women and told Sister Bridget and Estevez to sit and wait.

"What's wrong with that guy? He acts like *we're* the criminals." Estevez seemed out of patience.

"I'm sure there are some police officers that are not corrupt, but most of them expect some sort of compensation for providing any service whatsoever."

"Even just letting us through the door?"

"Yes."

They were left waiting for over an hour, and Sister Bridget explained to Estevez that the waiting was typical, and that in many cases, in the end, people were told that the person they were waiting for was not available.

"We're the only ones here. That's just a way of weeding out crime reports." He muttered something else Sister Bridget didn't catch, then stood, stretched, and walked to the wall of government official portraits. The ladies behind the desk followed him with their eyes, not pausing their typing and busywork.

Though Sister Bridget was praying with her eyes closed, she was well aware when Estevez returned to sit next to her.

"As I was saying before…" his voice cracked a little. "I'm sorry I left in the middle of the night." He leaned forward and gazed into her eyes. "Did you even notice that I left?"

"Of course I did, Joaquin." Though she hadn't.

"I couldn't sleep at all…with you, your body next to me…and not being able to…touch you…to *love* you."

She couldn't have both worlds—be with Estevez *and* be a religious sister. She chose the religious life. She thought she felt the receptionists' eyes on her. She looked up, but the ladies were busy at work, not looking at all.

"Joaquin, I'm so sorry—"

"No, you already said that. I know you're sorry. I'm sorry too." He looked at the floor and shook his head. "Sorry we can't be together. Just, you know, regretful. Sad."

She felt like a woman who had committed adultery. *I'm married,* is what she should have said from the very beginning, but instead she chose the excitement and companionship of a good man. She had always known she wasn't perfect. "I'm sorry I hurt you."

A door opened, footsteps echoed on the stone floor, and a small man emerged from a hallway. He made a straight line to them, and they stood. The man extended his hand to Estevez.

"Come to my office. Come. Come. I'm Rogelio Ramos. Come, and tell me why you're here." The man smiled and seemed accommodating, but Sister Bridget knew better. His small eyes shifted between her and Estevez. He had black, slicked-back hair and a neatly trimmed mustache.

"I assume you're Sister Bridget." He closed the door to his office. He bowed slightly but didn't shake her hand. "Sit, sit." He indicated two chairs across from his desk.

"Yes, I am Bridget Ann Rincón-Keller, and this is Joaquin Estevez." The two men nodded to one another.

Ramos settled into his chair behind a shiny, immaculate desk. "What can I do for you?" He addressed Estevez.

Estevez began to speak, but Sister Bridget spoke over him.

"I want to report a case of kidnapping."

"Yes, go on." Ramos nodded with an air of patience, turning his attention to Sister Bridget.

"Juana San Miguel has been missing from her home since January. I know who has her. It's a man named Alejandro Maldonado, a serial kidnapper. They call him *El Gigante*. This man must be found and arrested."

"Wait. Slow down." Ramos twisted at small tufts of his mustache. "Where is this girl? What's her name? Juana?" He spread his hands and looked about his office.

"I am telling you about the girl. She is not here because she has been kidnapped." Sister Bridget was used to law enforcement officials pretending ignorance.

"But you yourself are not a victim?"

"No, of course not. But—"

"Then how can you expect to file a report if there is no victim?" He spoke as though he were explaining the rules of a game to a child. Sister Bridget felt Estevez tense up and lean forward in his chair. She put her hand on his thigh. Ramos caught the gesture and smirked.

"Let's say there is a victim. What did you say? Juana? Was she taken by force, or did she go of her own free will? Because you know how these girls can be. They run away with men and then they complain." Ramos shrugged and pouted.

"I repeat, the girl, Juana San Miguel has been kidnapped. I would like assistance in finding her."

"When did this girl…Juana? When did she go missing? How do you know the kidnapper? What connection do you have with him?"

"I have no connection with Alejandro Maldonado. But I have done some research. He has family in Guanajuato. He's thirty-six years old. Six foot six, two hundred and eighty pounds. As a child, he was sexually molested—by his father. Then when he grew bigger, he beat his father severely, very nearly killing the man. He was sent to *little jail*, where he continued to be abused." In Mexico, youth detention centers are called *little jails;* the children have no rights, no visitors, and are regularly beaten. "Alejandro fought back. He spent twelve years in solitary confinement. Since his release, he has committed violent crimes nonstop, even murder."

"*Señora*, this girl, Juana. Why would she associate with such a man? He sounds like a maniac."

Calling a religious sister *Señora* was disrespectful, but Sister Bridget wouldn't be baited.

"Juana San Miguel is not *associating* with Alejandro Maldonado," Estevez said. "He is holding her against her will."

"What do you mean *holding*? Is he holding her or is he kidnapping her? You seem to be getting your story mixed up. And do you have any proof of any of this? And by the way, what is a nun doing going around with a man? Who are you anyway?" Ramos said to Estevez.

"That has nothing to do with it," Sister Bridget said.

"I am a detective with the Austin Police Department, Human Trafficking and Vice unit." Estevez reached into his breast pocket for his credentials.

This was exactly what Sister Bridget wanted to avoid. She turned and gave him a telling look, glancing sideways toward the door. She kept her voice low and spoke in English. "Don't take your badge out. He will confiscate it."

"Do you know that it is against the law for a foreign official, such as yourself, to present yourself to a Mexican official, such as myself, without express permission and clearance from the government? Or is Mexican law of no consequence to you people?"

Estevez whispered in English, "Bridget, what are we doing here? This man is useless."

Sister Bridget rose. "Thank you, Señor Ramos. We won't take up any more of your time." Estevez rose too. He took Sister Bridget's elbow and didn't bother to shake hands with the prosecutor's assistant.

****

Sister Bridget and Estevez left the government building. She should have listened to her instinct. Her gut had told her she wouldn't find help from her government, and she had been right. They'd accomplished nothing. She'd have to find the girl herself.

At least reporting to the prosecutor's office had

satisfied Estevez's suspicions. She told him that she had gone to Mexico to report the missing girl, and she had. Now he could go back to the U.S., and she could go about her real business.

"I best be getting along. Mother Superior will be expecting me." She tried to sound casual.

"You said you didn't tell your superiors you were coming."

She was having difficulty keeping track of her lies. And she wished she didn't have to, but she couldn't risk ruining his career. If Mexican authorities caught an American police detective investigating a crime without permission, he would be charged with conspiracy and jailed. But keeping track of lies required diligence. What was her story again? She was supposed to go to the Mother House for a retreat. In reality, she hadn't informed her superiors that she was coming. In actuality, she was going to the Sisters of St. Paul missionary house in Chihuahua next.

"I called this morning after you left." She looked away and hailed a taxi.

He gave her that look, the dubious one. "Listen, don't feel bad about last night. I lured you in with my best charms. Don't blame yourself." He smiled that smile. "I'm broken-hearted, but I get it." He shrugged and gave her a mirthless smile.

Sister Bridget waved to the driver that pulled to the curb in a yellow taxi.

"Wait. Hold on." Estevez unzipped his backpack. "I parked the bike in the garage around the corner. I'll need to return it and catch a shuttle to the airport. But I did a little shopping this morning." He tugged a yellow-wrapped box from his bag and handed it to Sister

Bridget.

She accepted the gift, embarrassed, said her goodbyes, kissed him on the cheek, and climbed into the taxi.

Chapter 22

The only flight Sister Bridget was able to book from Mexico City to Creel, Chihuahua was an eight-passenger turboprop, and she was its only passenger. It was a turbulent two-hour flight. She had ample time to pray all four mysteries of the rosary, the Chaplet of Divine Mercy, the Litany of the Saints, and various other litanies.

When the pilot announced the plane's descent into Aeropuerto International de Creel, Sister Bridget breathed a sigh of relief. *Thank you, God.* She didn't mind dying, but not before she found Isabel's friend, Juana. She remembered the gift that Estevez had given to her in Mexico City. She took the package from her duffle and ripped away the yellow wrapping to reveal a box labeled *Heavy Duty Stun Gun.* She hadn't fooled him a bit, had she? He knew she planned to find Juana. She tucked the gift back into her bag and covered it with her extra tunic and scapular.

Her best friend, Sister Terésa, met her at the airport. It had been almost a year since she'd last seen her. Just the sight of little Teresíta with her freckles and wire-rimmed glasses filled Sister Bridget's soul with peace. Some of the sisters called them *the odd couple* because of their height difference. Sister Bridget was almost six feet tall, and Sister Terésa barely reached five feet. No matter. They were soul mates, drawn to one another during novitiate in their mid-thirties, comparatively late for taking the veil. They were both risk takers, *doers*. The Sisters of St. Paul sent Sister Terésa, who had been a nurse before taking the veil, to medical school. They sent Sister Bridget to the United States to teach, and then later, she became a certified mid-wife.

What made them best friends was that Terésa knew everything about her, even her worse faults, and she still loved her. When Sister Bridget embraced the small sister at the airport, all her troubles melted away. She was home in the arms of the only person in the world that made her feel *in the present*. She was in the presence of her dear Teresíta. All was well in the world.

"My sister, I wish for all mankind to have a lovely soul mate, a confidant, a best friend like you." Sister Bridget breathed deep and easy, taking in the fragrant spruces that garnished the rocky landscape. "And the young people? How are they?"

"They haven't arrived yet, my sister. I've kept my phone by my side. I haven't heard from them yet." Sister Terésa climbed into the driver's seat of the old beat-up truck that belonged to their religious community.

"But they should have arrived by now." Sister Bridget tossed her bag into the bed of the truck and settled into the passenger seat.

"Let's not panic. We're sure to hear soon." Sister Terésa pulled away from the curb.

"Yes, my sister. You're right. Let's not panic." Sister Bridget's heart raced, panicked.

"Oh but, my sister, why are you not wearing your pink habit today?" Teresíta was trying to distract her from her worries; Sister Bridget knew that.

Sister Bridget smiled at the memory of the pink habits. Sister Terésa's laughter was soft and pleasant. She swerved momentarily onto the gravel at the side of the road.

The *pink habits,* as they referred to the incident, occurred after Sister Bridget had *taken the veil* and entered upon her novitiate. She remembered it felt so right—receiving her veil. Not only did the novitiates wear white veils, but also white tunics. She had felt like a real sister.

Novices were assigned chores. Occasionally, she and Terésa were assigned to the same chore, and as it happened, she and her newfound friend were assigned to wash and iron the novices' white tunics and veils.

"We would have done a fine job, had it not been for my errant red sock." Sister Bridget shook her head and smiled.

"The novices in their pink tunics and veils!" Sister Terésa laughed.

Sister Bridget remembered the pink-clad novices lined up on the kneeler for morning prayers. "Dear, dear sisters. Too sweet to even complain."

"And Mother Superior talking to us privately. What a kind soul…" Sister Terésa said.

"'I believe bleach is in order!'" Both sisters recalled the words of Mother Superior and delivered the punch line simultaneously.

When their laughter died down, Sister Terésa cleared her throat. "So, tell me, dear one, did you come in person to check on the travelers? Or do other matters bring you to Creel?"

Sister Bridget was in Creel because the kidnapper,

El Gigante, had abandoned Isabel nearby. Should she tell Terésa that she had come to find Isabel's friend, Juana? El Gigante might still have methamphetamine. She must keep that in mind. El Gigante was trouble enough, but if *narcotraficantes* were involved, she would be putting her sisters in peril. She'd never lied to Sister Terésa before, but she must do so in order to keep her friend safe.

"I came to check on the travelers."

Sister Bridget knew that the Rarámuri's foot race had been canceled the previous week because a drug gang had kidnapped the village of Urique's two police officers and executed the police chief. Sister Bridget didn't want to do anything to draw the attention of drug gangs. She just wanted to get Juana away from El Gigante. The fewer people involved, the better.

She hadn't called Juana's father, not yet. She'd try to find the girl on her own. Less conspicuous that way. Just a regular sister going about her business.

She'd keep her eyes and ears open about town. Visiting bars and brothels was out of the question of course, but maybe someone would let some information slip. A man the size and character of El Gigante would not go unnoticed. But no, she couldn't tell Sister Terésa the real reason for her visit.

Instead, Sister Bridget opened up about another matter. She recounted her tryst with Joaquin Estevez. For to be honest, a tryst was what it was.

"Do you love him, Bridget?"

She didn't answer for a long while. "Love is God." That much she knew, and she didn't think she would ever waver from that truth. "Yes, I love Joaquin. As a friend. As a dear friend."

"But do you *love* him? Are you *in* love with him?" Sister Terésa had always spoken openly. And she was persistent.

"You mean do I wish to be his life partner? No. The answer is no. Not that kind of love. I have had that kind of love. The kind you fall in and out of."

Sister Bridget smiled at the thought of love appearing and disappearing at the whim of men and women. God doesn't fall in and out, appear and disappear. God was permanent and eternal.

"Do you ever miss the man you were engaged to marry so long ago?" Sister Terésa kept her eye on the road. "Do you ever wish you would have married him and had children?"

"I accept my life. I am happy. No, I wouldn't trade it for a different life. And you, my sister? Are you happy? Do I find you here in this out-of-the-way place practicing medicine…*happy*?"

"I'm satisfied here. And yes, happy. My soul…" and Sister Bridget added her voice, "proclaims the greatness of the Lord. My spirit rejoices in God, my savior." The words of the Virgin Mary from the bible.

****

The Sisters of St. Paul mission house in Creel, Chihuahua was tucked into a lively neighborhood filled with families. The home was a boxy light green stucco, with white-framed windows and a red tiled roof. Its lawn was packed dirt. Sister Bridget didn't recognize the Land Rover parked in front. She couldn't even tell what color it was. The vehicle was covered in dust and sludge. The mud-caked license plate dangled by one loose bolt. Its windows were shattered, and the bumper was missing. And was that a bullet hole?

Isabel ran out of the house, limping, to greet her.

"What in the world?" Sister Bridget stood shocked as Isabel hugged her tight around her neck.

"We made it. We're here in Mexico." Isabel's smile lit up her face. She was fresh out of the shower, smelling like soap and apple-scented shampoo. "I didn't know you were coming here."

"Is this…" Sister Bridget looked more closely at the Land Rover. "Is this Mabel's car? Are Mabel and Walter all right?"

"Yeah, they're fine. They're inside."

Sister Bridget rushed into the house. Sister Terésa followed with her bag.

Mabel was in the kitchen having coffee with elderly Sister Maria Inmaculada. Mabel was also newly scrubbed. Her short, wet hair brushed back neatly. She wore clothes and shoes from the box of hand-me-downs the sisters kept for the needy.

Sister Bridget and Mabel hugged tight.

"What are you doing here?" Mabel looked tired but she seemed energized.

"Oh, I belong to the Sisters of St. Paul. This is our mission house. What are *you* doing here? Where's Walter?" Sister Bridget looked to Isabel. "And the baby and Marcelino?"

"Oh, everyone's fine. We're all fine now," Mabel said.

"Gabriela's asleep." Isabel glanced toward the hallway. "In Sister Esperanza's room. Sister loves her so much. Sister Esperanza is a nurse. She said Gabriela is happy and healthy." Isabel beamed.

"Good, *mija*. I…mean to say…that's…wonderful." What was going on? Sister Terésa was supposed to pick up Isabel, Marcelino, and the baby from the border and bring them to Creel. Mabel and Walter were supposed to turn back at the border and go back to Austin. But here they all were. How did they get here? Why? "*Disculpame*, sorry." Sister Bridget, distracted and confused, introduced Sister Terésa to the others. She remembered to say everything twice for Mabel's benefit. She bent and kissed elderly Sister Maria Inmaculada hastily on the cheek.

"I'm sure you have quite the story to tell." Sister Terésa looked to Mabel and Isabel. "Judging from the appearance of your vehicle." All the sisters spoke perfect English, but Mabel insisted they speak Spanish for Isabel's benefit. She used the translation app to follow along.

"Yes, Sister." Mabel glanced at Isabel. "We barely escaped Texas."

"Ranchers tried to shoot us," Isabel said.

Sister Bridget, her hand over her mouth, looked from Isabel to Mabel. Mabel nodded, confirming Isabel's statement.

"We'll tell you the whole story later," Mabel said. "You just got in. You must be tired."

"And Marcelino?"

"Marcelino went to his family in the barrancas," Isabel said. "To tell his mother that he's all right."

"Good boy. I'm sorry I missed him. And you, *mija*? Have you called your mother?"

"Yes, Mamá is going to send me money for the bus. As soon as she can get some."

"You tell your momma don't worry a bit about that. Walt and I can get you a bus ticket."

"Thank you, dear friend." Sister Bridget stroked

Mabel's arm. "Speaking of Walt, where has he gone?"

"Come with me." Mabel gestured for Sister Bridget to follow. They walked through the kitchen, past Sister Maria Inmaculada who had fallen asleep in her chair, through the sun porch, and outside to a walled courtyard. Bulging tomato plants, peppers, wild onions, and squash thrived alongside bright red geraniums and tall sunflowers. Bees and butterflies flitted about. The garden was like a tropical mirage in the middle of a desert. And there in the center of the refuge, amid chirping birds and sweet-smelling honeysuckle lay Walter, fast asleep on a hammock that hung between two papaya trees. Her dear old friend could use a washing. "He drove all night," Mabel whispered.

Sister Bridget and Mabel returned to the kitchen table where Sister Maria Inmaculada still dozed. The hundred-year-old's day consisted of more sleeping than waking.

"Should we move her to her bed, so she's more comfortable?" Mabel asked.

"No. Sister likes to wake up where she falls asleep. She usually picks up the conversation right where she left off."

****

Dinner at the missionary house consisted of *enchiladas coloniales*, black beans, and lettuces from the garden. The sisters kept the food warm while they waited on Walter. He soon appeared in hand-me-down clothing and *huaraches*. Bleary-eyed after sleeping in the hammock all day, he presented himself freshly shaved, neatly combed, and smelling of peppery after-shave.

"Oh good. You found the razors." Sister Esperanza

251

was in her thirties, stocky and energetic. She was one of three nurses that lived in the missionary house with Sister Terésa, who was a doctor. And, of course, Sister Inmaculada.

The sisters and their guests served their own plates and found places at the long, wooden kitchen table.

"Yes, thank you very much, Sister." Walter took a seat next to Mabel. "I wasn't expecting to find men's toiletries in a house filled with nuns."

They all laughed. "Sister Esperanza fetched the items for you. She is very considerate like that," Sister Terésa said.

"Yes. Esperanza is the heart of our house." Sister Bridget smiled and nodded at Sister Esperanza.

"Well, thank you, Sister Esperanza." Walter smiled and bowed his head to her.

"I've never had enchiladas like these." Mabel inspected the folded over fried tortillas after prayers. Inside were shredded chicken and a sauce of tomatoes, onions, and peppers. The enchiladas were topped with shredded cheese and sour cream. "Delicious." She closed her eyes and savored the flavors.

"So, three nurses and a doctor, huh?" Walter said. "Are you a healthcare professional too, Sister Maria Inmaculada?"

"No, I'm just very old." Sister Maria Inmaculada's voice was low and gravelly. "I would rather die here in this little missionary house, than in the big convent in Mexico City."

"Sister Inmaculada works in the gardens," Sister Esperanza said. "She has a green thumb, and she is the soul of our little house."

"So," Isabel said, "Sister Esperanza is the heart,

and Sister Inmaculada is the soul? Does every house have a heart and soul?"

"Yes, *mija*, by the grace of God, every home has a heart and soul," Sister Terésa said.

In the course of dinner, Walter, Mable, and Isabel recounted their harrowing escape from Texas and their off-road search for a roadway to Creel.

"We finally found a road, but then *banditos* tried to stop us outside of Ojinaga," Isabel said, wide-eyed.

"Walt stepped on the gas," Mabel said. "And we lost them in La Perla."

"Then we ran out of gas," Walter said, "and Marcelino siphoned some from a tractor at a farmhouse in the pitch dark."

"God bless Marcelino," Sister Bridget said.

"Here's to Marcelino." Sister Inmaculada raised her thick goblet of red wine.

And they toasted to Marcelino stealing gasoline.

Then they made plans to drive Walter and Mabel to the airport and Isabel and her baby to the bus terminal in the morning. Marcelino would be the recipient of the Land Rover. It had gotten the travelers far, and it still had life in it.

The next day, after dropping off Mabel, Walter, Isabel, and her baby, Sister Bridget returned to the missionary house and found Marcelino there. He was picking up the Land Rover.

He had been doing some scouting, and he told Sister Bridget where El Gigante was.

"But you're not going there, are you? He's too dangerous," Marcelino said.

"Do not worry about me, my son."

Chapter 23

At midnight that night, Sister Bridget's heart pounded as she made her way through the dark kitchen of the missionary house. Deep down, her soul murmured St. Paul's words—*walk as children of the light, walk as children of the light, walk as children of the light*—over and over as she embarked into the dark night to rescue Juana. The words reminded her that as a child of Light, God was with her. The internal scripture throbbed in her chest like ocean waves.

She'd found men's jeans and a black sweatshirt in the storehouse of second-hand clothing that the sisters collected for charity. She wore the sweatshirt inside out since a depiction of a voluptuous woman on a motorcycle adorned the outside. It wasn't so much the content of the illustration, but rather the reflective material from which it was made. She hoped to go unseen in the night. She hadn't thought to bring her running sneakers. Her everyday black, lace-up shoes would have to do. Without a sound, except for her heartbeat and the internal strumming of St. Paul, she slipped out of the house and through the garden to the back alley.

She held the courtyard's gate handle, noiselessly released the latch, and locked its padlock. It was cold and misty. The night smelled of burn piles and garbage. Rustling movement at the trash cans to her left triggered prickles at the back of her neck and goose bumps. Probably an alley cat chasing a rat. She rubbed the back of her neck, longing for the warmth of her veil, but she dared not reenter the house to get a scarf at risk of waking the sisters. Looking up at the starless sky, shrouded by a curtain of clouds, she was comforted by the words God spoke to Isaiah—*I will turn the dark places into light before them and make the rough places smooth.* And she called upon the Holy Spirit for courage and strength. As she turned to go, a hand reached out from the darkness and grabbed her, taking a firm grasp of her arm, and squeezing hard. She jumped back, raised her other arm high above her head and brought it down hammer-like on the man's wrist, breaking his grasp. He hollered and cursed.

She only ran four or five strides before the man tackled her from behind and bear hugged her to the ground. A second person placed a cloth bag over her head as she screamed. Dirt stuck to her mouth; grit irritated her eyes. "Let me go!" She yelled, twisted her body, and kicked at the man on top of her. A blunt metal object was jabbed into her side. Was it a gun?

"*Callate!*" the man hissed.

Her mind searched for a way out. She flashed back to her thirteen-year-old cousin's return after being kidnapped from her family. She had been beaten and raped. Sister Bridget's aunt and uncle had paid the ransom, and the kidnappers left their daughter on a dark dirt road. Forever fearful, silent, and withdrawn. To young Bridget, her cousin seemed tattered on the inside. Sister Bridget had always feared that one day she would be the victim of kidnapping. Back then, only wealthy families, families like hers, feared the voracity of criminals, but now the scourge had spread to the middle class and really to anyone whose family might produce a ransom. The ruthless preyed upon family devotion. Kidnappers banked on that love.

Now, *her* time had come. She didn't think about herself, or who might pay a ransom for her life. Instead, she thought about Juana San Miguel. How could she ever save the girl now? *Saint Jude, patron saint of desperate cases, pray for me,* she inwardly pleaded. Breathing hard and sucking in dirt and the cloth of the hood that covered her face, she kicked and fought. Two pairs of strong hands gripped her arms harder. She screamed. Maybe a neighbor would hear and come to her aid. The sisters? Couldn't they hear her? A hand reached into the hood and stuffed a rag into her mouth. Gagging, she inhaled dirt through her nose, attempting to twist her body, to punch and scratch her captors. She pulled one arm loose and managed to pull Estevez's stun gun from her pocket. One of the men immediately grabbed it from her. How could she be so foolish, she thought. Would the man use the stun gun on *her*? She fought, but the captors relentlessly dragged her on her back through the dirt, gravel, and weeds.

"Julio is bringing the car," one of the men said. He sat atop Sister Bridget while the other man wrapped duct tape around her wrists.

"Here he comes," the other said. She heard a car pull up and skid to a stop on the dirt road. A door opened.

"*Metela.* Stick her in the car. *Apúrate.*" Someone thrust her downward onto a car seat, got in beside her, and shoved her over. She heard three doors slam shut.

She made what noise she could with the rag in her mouth. She kicked the seat in front of her and tried to get to the door by climbing over the man beside her.

"Don't fight. It will be better for you if you don't. We are not going to hurt you." She didn't believe him. She knew what kidnappers did to their victims. She sat back against the seat and then, with a smooth motion, she turned toward the person on her left. She butted her head hard where she hoped his head was. She smashed his skull with a sick thud. Her own head recoiled, throbbing, stunning her. Nevertheless, she lunged toward where she thought the door was on the other side, feeling around with her bound hands, grabbing for the handle.

"*Ay maldito!*" The man cursed. He dove on top of her and after much grappling, cut the tape from her wrists and bound them behind her back instead. Still, she struggled, twisting her body, and attempting to kick the men. The driver pulled the car over and joined the struggle.

"Better do her ankles too." It took all three men to accomplish this. She gave up trying to get away after that, but in the struggle, she'd managed to remove the rag from her mouth.

"Don't you have any shame?" She struggled to say the words through a hacking cough, spitting out gravel and dirt. She was breathing hard and so were the three men. The one on her left cursed under his breath and grumbled about *dolor de cabeza*.

"We told you, we're not going to hurt you." The words came from the man driving the car.

"Then tell them to remove the hood from my head at least. If you're telling the truth, what do you fear?"

257

"Not yet," said the man on her right. "We'll remove it soon."

The car came to a stop. "We better use the rag again, so she doesn't scream." Over her objections, the damp rag was once again shoved into her mouth.

She was dragged from the car by her arm and then carried by three people. Twisting and thrashing, she was lifted up a step and into another vehicle of some sort, a van she guessed. She felt the bounce of the suspension and the give of the tires. Metallic creaking and clanging noises accompanied the men's movements. Drawing in breath through her nose, she smelled rubbing alcohol and antiseptic. They placed her on a seat and belted her in. *An ambulance?*

She heard the other vehicle drive away. "Ok, let's go," someone said. The vehicle she was in sped forward, maneuvering turns at a high speed. She swung from side to side, strapped to her seat.

"Take the cloth from her mouth. No one can hear her in here," the driver said.

"*We* can hear her," a man objected, but nevertheless, he reached under her hood and grabbed the rag. She considered biting his hand, but she didn't think it would do much good since her hands and feet were bound.

"And the cloth over my face? Please remove it also."

"No."

The driver said, "We're almost there."

"It's not too late to stop. Please stop and let me out here." Sister Bridget prayed for the conversion of these men's souls. "I've been praying for you, my sons. Did you know that you were once in darkness, all of mankind was, but now because God has come into the world, you are now in the light? The light of God?" She paused. The men didn't say a word. "Why? Because Jesus is divine yet took on the life of a human." She paused again, waiting for some response. "God became human. God knows exactly how you feel. God loves you. You see, now you don't have to worry about your sins. You're forgiven. You need only repent." Again, there was no response. Was she talking to deaf ears? Was there no help for her?

She thought of the words of the Psalmist, *why are you in despair, my soul? Why are you disturbed within me?* And then*, hope in God!* Yes, she told herself, *never give up hope.*

"Slow down now. Make it look like it's not an emergency." The driver slowed, turned, drove up an incline and parked.

She couldn't think of how to talk her way out of it, so she started quoting scripture. "Try to live as children of the light, for light produces every kind of goodness." Someone grabbed her by the arm and pulled her to her feet. "God knew you before you were formed in your mother's womb!" She spoke faster. "Whoever lives in love, lives in God, and God in them," and then, "love covers a multitude of sins!" Someone stuffed the rag back in her mouth. Silenced, St. Paul's words throbbed within her—*expose the unfruitful deeds committed in the darkness, expose them to the light and walk as children of the light.*

One of the men slit the duct tape from her ankles.

"What are you doing? She's going to run," another man said.

"Just hold her tight," the first man said. "She's too

heavy for just the two of us to carry."

"Walk." The first man tugged Sister Bridget forward. "Two steps down." She felt her way down the steps of the vehicle. Where was she? She felt no breeze and heard no nighttime noises, only a low, mechanical drone; the air was stifling and smelled of car exhaust. A parking garage? Should she run? With the hood over her head and her hands bound, she likely wouldn't make it very far. Her captors took her into an elevator, which descended at least two floors. *Jesus, my sweetness,* she imagined herself holding her Savior's hand, *I fear no evil, for you are with me.* If there was an elevator, there must be stairs. She began to formulate an escape. As soon as her hood was removed, she would dash to the stairs.

The elevator doors opened, and she told herself, *be not afraid, be not afraid.* The men led her forward. They stopped and someone pulled the hood off her head. One of the men removed the gag from her mouth.

She blinked and squinted in the shadowy gloom, looking about for stairs on which to ascend to the surface. But she didn't see stairs. Was she hallucinating? What she saw couldn't be real.

"Teresíta?" Sister Bridget stared at the diminutive sister, doubting what she saw. Her head hurt. Was it a concussion? Was her cognition impaired?

Sister Terésa wore her white lab coat over her habit. The petite sister, her eyes red and teary, stepped forward and reached out. Sister Bridget stepped back, shrinking from her lifelong friend.

"Teresíta?"

"Here, let me take the tape from your hands." Sister Terésa reached for her, but Sister Bridget recoiled. One of the men stepped forward and used a pocketknife to cut the tape away. "Please, get her some water," Sister Terésa told the other man. "Come sit." She tried to take Sister Bridget's hand.

"Terésa! Tell me, what is the meaning of this. What is going on here? Why are you here?" She looked around. "What is this place?" The walls were rocky and uneven; the floor was dirt and stone.

The man returned and handed Sister Terésa water in a blue plastic cup. She took it and offered it to Sister Bridget.

Sister Bridget didn't acknowledge the water. She stared at her friend. "Answer me. What is going on here?" She felt as if she had stepped into a backward world, a dream, a nightmare really.

"As you can see, we are underground." Sister Terésa glanced at the walls. "This place is an abandoned mining shaft located underneath the women's clinic."

"What? What are you saying?" Sister Bridget looked around. Against the rock-hewn walls were crates of bottled water, boxes of medication, and piles of neatly folded blankets and clothing.

"I'm sorry to put you through this whole act, pretending to kidnap you, but you see, we had to make it look real," Sister Terésa explained. The two men that *kidnapped* her stood apart, listening.

"You have come here to rescue Juana San Miguel. You did not tell me as much, but I surmised it from what Isabel told me. We know that *El Gigante* has her. His name is Alejandro Maldonado."

Sister Bridget knew as much.

"El Gigante doesn't just have Juana San Miguel,"

Sister Terésa said. "He has four *other* girls. One of the girls has become quite ill, so time is of the essence. We must get her and the others *tonight*."

"Five girls? What do you mean 'we must get them tonight'? What do you have to do with all of this? What is going on?"

"He is a very troubled man, this Alejandro Maldonado, *El Gigante,* as Isabel calls him. Yes, he extorted Isabel's mother, and he has been extorting money from Juana's family. What you don't know is that he has been extorting from four other families."

"Your plan was to free Juana San Miguel. Is that not so?" Sister Bridget recognized one of the men's voices. It was the one whose head she had pounded with her own head. She turned to him, rubbing the dull pain on her forehead. He was a small, middle-aged man, clean-shaven with short hair, a large, red lump at his right temple. "Our plan is to free *all* the girls tonight."

"This is Mateo," Sister Terésa said. "He is a pharmacist at Farmacia Bienvenido. *"*

"You have a strong head." Mateo's expression was something between a grimace and a grin. He looked away, embarrassed, rubbing his head.

"We think of ourselves as *secret policía*." The other man raked his fingers through his sandy, shoulder-length hair, brushing it back over his head. He was young and lanky.

"This is Esteban," Sister Terésa said. "He is a teacher at the primary school."

Secret policía? Sister Bridget decided to sit down after all. Sister Terésa took a seat next to her at a resin table and chairs that were positioned in the middle of the space.

Sister Bridget took a drink of water but didn't care to swallow the dirt that remained in her mouth. She turned away and spat the water back into the glass. Mateo took the cup and brought another.

"Bridget Ann, listen to me, my dear." Sister Terésa enclosed Sister Bridget's hand with both of hers, a doctor's hands, cool and smooth. "As you know, the terrible curse, the plague of kidnapping has become like an epidemic here in Chihuahua, like all of Mexico."

"Terésa, don't you think I know this? That's why I came here. But you say El Gigante has *five* girls? Could you have *told* me instead of deceiving me? And scaring me half to death?" She made a sweeping motion toward the men that stood by. "These men wrestled me to the ground and brought me here against my will. Don't you realize how frightening that is?"

"My dear, dear friend, forgive me." Sister Terésa eyes were watery. "I love you more than anyone on earth. Please, do not be frightened."

"It was for your own safety," Esteban said. "It's good that Sister Terésa found out about Juana San Miguel."

"It was Isabel that told me about her friend. And she told me about *El Gigante*," Sister Terésa said. "I was afraid that Isabel would venture to find her friend and put herself in danger. So, I was relieved when she took the bus back to Ecatepec. Then I guessed you might be planning to find Juana, and so you are."

"We have been monitoring El Gigante's movements, waiting for the right moment to go in and get the girls," Mateo said. "He keeps the girls like prisoners at that falling-down apartment building by the oil refinery."

"Things have changed here. Kidnapping has become like never before. Listen to me, Bridget Ann. As a physician, all I could ever do was try my best to repair the victims that have been beaten, raped and used as commodities." Sister Bridget saw rage emerge in her friend's words. "By the time the girls, the women got to me for medical care, and yes, boys and men too, some were without fingers, tortured, some with their eyes gouged out. Oh, I could help them physically, but mentally, spiritually, most were beyond repair."

Sister Bridget knew about such barbarity. Were horrible things happening to Juana and the other girls at that very moment?

"I finally had enough. I was disgusted. The *policía* wouldn't help. They are corrupt or scared." Sister Terésa gestured, pointed in the air, condemning the police officers. "I said I wasn't going to wait for the criminals to decide when to release the captives." She stopped to take a deep breath and went on more calmly. "I…we…" She indicated the two men. "Now *we* decide when to take the victims away from the criminals. *Before* they injure them beyond repair."

Could all this be true? Was her closest, dearest friend some kind of undercover secret *policía*? A vigilante? No, the idea was ludicrous. "How could you carry out secret activities without the other sisters knowing?"

Sister Terésa gave her a knowing look.

"They are involved also? Even Sister María Inmaculada?" The woman was a hundred years old.

"We try not to tell her too much. For her own safety, but yes."

"That's not all," Esteban said. "There are more teachers involved too."

"And others," Mateo said. "We've created an alliance. An alliance for good."

Sister Bridget let the information sink in. "But why did you kidnap *me*? You said it was for my own safety. How could it be for my own safety?" She thought about the frightening, high-speed trek and the two vehicles it took to get to their present location. And the duct tape, the hood, the gag.

"Forgive us. Forgive *me*. But you have been seen. You are known all around Creel. El Gigante would come after all the sisters." Sister Terésa paused. She struggled to hold back tears. "And God forgive me. I more than anyone know that you yourself were traumatized as a child when your cousin was kidnapped."

"But we had to make you disappear," Esteban said. "So, the sisters wouldn't bear the brunt of El Gigante's vengeance." He and Mateo took a seat at the table with Sister Bridget and Sister Terésa.

"And for the continued secrecy of our endeavors," Mateo added.

Sister Bridget began to get a clear picture. "No one can be trusted."

"That's right," Mateo said. "Oh, there are a few police officers that are not corrupt, but they can't take a chance. They can't make arrests because then their own families would be in danger. You heard about the murdered police chief in Urique."

Yes, Sister Bridget had heard.

"The neighbors, the mine workers, those that work for the railroad, the store workers. Nobody is safe from the threat of kidnapping," Esteban said. "Anybody who they think can be a source of money. They know a family will pay all they have to get their loved one back."

Sister Bridget knew. Somehow in her own lifetime, evil had taken root. Her countrymen preyed upon her countrymen.

"And it is not safe to have information either. *Los bárbaros* will get it out of you, and your family will suffer," Mateo said. "Informants don't live long around here."

"Just think, *mi amor*. If you were to rescue the girls, and I have no doubt you would have accomplished it, then El Gigante and everyone else would know that it was you that did so. He and his friends would exact revenge. Yes, you could go back to the United States, but they would come after the Sisters of St. Paul at the missionary house."

Sister Bridget pictured the scenario. *Yes*, she admitted to herself, what Sister Terésa said was true. "But that problem has been solved—I've been kidnapped and have disappeared." Sister Bridget looked down at her lap, her hands clasped. She imagined herself dead and gone. Disappeared. "What's the plan?"

"We have people listening," Esteban said. "We know that El Gigante likes to use his extortion money to get drunk and brag at the bars. It's sickening." He frowned and pinched his nose, choking back tears. These saviors were hardened, Sister Bridget could see that, but their humanity showed through. "He brags that he beats one of the girls severely." Esteban shook his head with disgust. "Each time, he takes a picture of the girl's cuts and bruises and sends them to the family. He tells the family that if they do not send money, the child will be killed. He tells them if they send money, he will release the girl. It's been two and a half months, and still, he does not release the girl."

"You see," Mateo took over the narrative, "this particular girl, the youngest one, Adriana is her name. Her family sends money every time he demands it, so he injures the girl more and more to get more money." He spoke matter-of-factly.

"Then let's go now. Let's take the girls away from that devil." Sister Bridget thought of the psalm, *they are like men coming up with axes to a clump of trees*. Well, she could carry an ax too. She felt in the pockets of her jeans for the weapon Estevez had given her.

"Looking for this?" Mateo handed Sister Bridget the stun gun. "Sorry, I didn't want you to use it on me." She stashed it in her pocket and stood to go.

"Slow down, my sister," Sister Terésa said. "You're right, we must go soon to rescue the girls. Now that we have a good idea of when El Gigante will be coming and going from the *apartamento*, we have made a plan."

"We'll go in while El Gigante is at the bar. We'll rescue the girls and disappear before he gets back," Mateo said. "He'll never see us."

Esteban looked at his watch. "We will be picked up and delivered to a location close to where the girls are being held. About thirty minutes." He indicated himself and Mateo. "Sister Terésa will return to the hospital to await the girls."

"I'm going with you to get the girls." Sister Bridget wasn't going to take *no* for an answer.

Esteban and Mateo looked to Sister Terésa.

"Yes, of course you'll go, my sister."

Sister Bridget, Mateo, and Esteban waited outside for their ride. "But why couldn't you just explain your secret society to me? Why did you have to scare me to death by pretending to kidnap me?"

"It was actually Sister Maria Inmaculada that came up with the idea of kidnapping you. At first, we dismissed such an outrageous stunt. We laughed, but then we thought, what better way to make you disappear? And have the neighbors witness it."

"This way, all the neighbors and everyone else saw already that you yourself have been kidnapped and taken away, so there is no way you could be responsible for rescuing the girls," Mateo explained.

Mateo looked at his watch. "Sister Inmaculada is reporting your disappearance to the authorities at this very moment."

"And our little secret society will go on," Esteban said.

Chapter 24

Julio, a secret society accomplice, picked up Sister Bridget, Mateo, and Esteban at the designated location a few blocks from the clinic. It was the same car in which the men had *kidnapped* Sister Bridget. Sister Terésa stayed behind in order to make her way back to the hospital to await the girls. Sister Bridget prayed that she and the men would indeed get the girls to Sister Terésa for medical care.

Rio Parral Apartamentos sat at the outskirts of the mostly deserted, outlying neighborhood of Santa Rogelia, which for three centuries was home to one of the world's most abundant silver mines. Once the silver was depleted though, the area over two hundred years or so became a *barrio* for homeless people and criminals. The French and Spanish style architecture of centuries past, left untended, crumbled away. The lack of trash collection, sewage and electricity guaranteed that those who inhabited the place would be left alone to live in squalor.

The *apartamentos*, originally an old Spanish hacienda, had later been divided into six apartments. If the secret society's informants were correct, that's where they would find Juana San Miguel. And four other girls.

In the car, Esteban filled Sister Bridget in on El Gigante's routine. "He goes out each night around midnight and returns around three." His voice was shaky. Sister Bridget reached over and squeezed his hand.

"I'm nervous too, my son." Who wouldn't be? El Gigante was colossal, a very scary character. She looked at her watch. "We have one hour and twenty-five minutes to get the girls out."

"El Gigante visits the *cantinas* at Calle Centenario," Esteban said. "We have a helper there now making sure he *is* there. She will text to confirm." Sister Bridget was impressed and grateful for the organization's members. They were like a squad of guardian angels. "Sofía is always reliable. She is a waitress at Empressa. She sees El Gigante there all the time, every night. She says he is like clockwork, never misses a night."

They arrived at the drop-off point, a back alley by an abandoned sawmill, two blocks from the *apartamentos*.

Julio shut off his lights and rolled to a stop. "This is where I'll pick you up. Be careful. God be with you." Sister Bridget, Esteban, and Mateo got out of the car, and Julio drove away. Dressed in black, the three would-be rescuers melded into the dark, thickening mist and stench of raw sewage.

"This *barrio* is nothing but trouble." A black cat screeched and dashed by, invisible in the pitch dark, punctuating Esteban's comment. Navigating the murky night, the three kept to the center of the street, avoiding the abandoned buildings and whatever lurked inside. They passed by the overgrown *plaza* where human night dwellers maintained a fire that sizzled and crackled in a metal bin. Sister Bridget felt eyes following her every step. She was thankful for Esteban and Mateo's company.

"Has Sofía texted yet?" Mateo asked.

Esteban looked at his phone. "No, nothing yet. Wait." Frustrated, he examined the bars on his screen. "Damn. I don't have service." His youthful face glowed by the light of the phone's screen.

"I don't have any bars either." Mateo clicked off his cell. "What about you Sister? Any luck?"

She didn't have a smartphone like the others did, but she flipped open her phone, hoping for the best. "No, nothing."

"We have two choices then," Esteban said. "We can go in and hope that El Gigante is not there, or we can call it off for tonight. Go back to the pickup point and wait for another opportunity."

With conditions the way they were—no water, no plumbing, the girls in total darkness—Sister Bridget couldn't bear to leave them one more night. Especially because the health of the littlest one, Adriana, was uncertain. Was she in pain? Would El Gigante injure her again tonight when he gets back? Sister Bridget longed to bring light to the girls' darkness.

Her walking became a jog, and the others followed.

"Do you believe in the works of Christ? What he did while he lived on Earth?" She breathed hard, forcing the words out. Neither man answered. She couldn't help herself. It was just how she coped. She loved scripture. "I mean to say, Christ accomplished miracles, no? And in John's gospel, Jesus says, 'he who believes in me, the works that I do, he will do also, and he will do greater works than these.' " The men made no reply. Sister Bridget had no idea what their expressions were. It was pitch dark.

They were almost to their destination. One more block.

"Wait, hold on. Stop." Mateo spoke into the darkness. They stopped in the middle of the street and huddled together. She placed her hand on his shoulder. She linked arms with Esteban and thought about Christ's words, *where two or more are gathered in my name, there I'll be in their midst.* She took comfort in the closeness of the men as she listened to Mateo's words. "Listen, we have kept this secret rescue group together by being careful and not taking too big of chances.

"We must be sure. We can't afford to have a run-in with El Gigante." Just then Mateo's phone vibrated. It was Sofía. She had sent a series of texts. The last one said

—*He has left. He is on his way.*—

"What time did she send that? The last one," Sister Bridget asked.

"Ten minutes ago."

"Then we still have time." She ran for Rio Parral Apartamentos. Mateo caught her arm. "We estimated that it would take El Gigante thirty-five minutes to get here from the bar."

"Yes, let's hurry."

"Wait." Esteban caught her arm this time. "Thirty-five minutes if he *walks*. Maybe he'll get a taxi."

"It's a chance I'm willing to take." Sister Bridget couldn't let the girls be hurt and scared for one more minute. The men looked skeptical. She took their hands. "Listen to me. In the ancient Jewish tradition, there is a saying, 'he who saves one life, saves the world entire.' You two have saved many. You have done your share. Let me go in. I'll bring the girls out."

And with that, she took off. Esteban and Mateo followed. *No more time for discussion,* Sister Bridget thought.

They reached the *apartamentos,* and Esteban shined his phone's flashlight onto the incongruously pretty *talavera* tiles that marked the dark, ominous entry. The place had been abandoned for many decades. Without waiting, Sister Bridget pulled open the heavy, intricately carved door. Black rodents scattered. The odor of trash and urine and excrement assaulted her. She raised her hand over her nose and gagged. A drunken man lying on the floor raised his head and cursed. Esteban shined his light on him. The man cursed again.

Mateo took a flashlight from his jacket and looked around. All the apartments on the first floor were blighted, walls rotted and fallen away, a brick fireplace in shambles, doors hanging off hinges.

Sister Bridget drew near to the drunken man. "Are there other people in this building?" Mateo shined his light on him. The man, gray-haired and grizzled, lay twisted in a pile of rags, his head red and scabbed up in bald places. He only mumbled and cursed again. Sister Bridget wished she could take the man away from this place, but she didn't have time.

She held her hand over her nose and mouth. "Upstairs." Mateo and Esteban followed up the creaky, narrow steps, the walls of which were covered in filth and graffiti. There were two apartments on the right and one on the left. They went to the left first and found it empty and decimated.

She led the men to the other end of the second floor, noisily stepping upon the debris that littered the hallway.

They paused while Esteban shone his phone's flashlight into an empty apartment, onto piles of trash, mattresses, decrepit furniture, and excrement. "Those poor girls."

There was only one other apartment left to check.

They got to the end of the hallway, where they found one last door.

"This must be it," Mateo said. Sister Bridget called upon the Holy Spirit and turned the knob. It was locked. She took two steps back, propelled herself forward, and with a running step, kicked the door open with the flat of her foot. A muffled scream and crying arose from behind a closed door within the apartment.

"They're in there," Esteban said. The inner door was latched with a heavy padlock. Sister Bridget and the two men tried throwing their weight onto the door and kicking at it, but the heavyweight metal lock held. Behind the door, the girls whimpered.

Sister Bridget raised her voice as high as she dared. "Juana, are you there? My dear, I am a friend of Isabel's. We are here to take you home." She doubted that the girl heard her over the cries of the other girls.

"Look around for the key," Mateo said. With their flashlights, he and Esteban searched the trashed apartment. Sister Bridget felt along the upper doorframe, but there was no key. She looked at her glowing watch. Ten minutes had passed since they had been warned that El Gigante had left the bar. They had ten minutes.

"Juana, I'm Sister Bridget." She hoped the girls

would be comforted by a woman's voice. "My dear, where does El Gigante keep the key to the door?"

No answer. "*Mija*, I am a friend of Isa—"

"He keeps it in his pocket," came a broken, childish voice from the other side of the door.

Then a small, shaky voice said, "Look in the oven."

Sister Bridget ran to the kitchen and Mateo shined his light into the decrepit oven. A putrid smell of rotted meat emanated. She looked beneath the decay to the bottom, and there was the key.

She unlocked the door and entered the room. Esteban shined his light on a teenage girl ferociously wielding a baseball bat. The tall, skinny girl with long, stringy hair held a fierce expression. Sister Bridget held up her hands, as if to surrender.

"Juana?" Sister Bridget hardly recognized the teenager. She looked nothing like the merry girl in her photo. She looked emaciated and damaged.

The girl didn't answer.

"I am a friend of Isabel's." Sister Bridget kept her voice soft and tried to be patient, but time was running out.

"We're here to help you," Mateo said.

"Do not fear, *mija*." Sister Bridget patted her hands downward. "We are here to help you. Where is Adriana? The sick one?"

"Nowhere. Get out of here and leave us alone." Juana threatened them with the bat.

"My dear, there is not much time."

"El Gigante will return soon," Esteban said. "Where is Adriana? We must get her and all of you out of here." Mateo shone his flashlight about the room.

275

Three other girls cringed in the darkness.

One of the girls cried from the darkness. "Tell them, Juana."

Sister Bridget looked into the gloom. "I'm Sister Bridget. These are my friends. We are here to help you. What is your name, *mija*?"

"I'm Josefina." One of the girls came forward into the glow of the flashlights. She was a slight teenager with the thin, reedy voice of a small child.

Two other girls slipped out of the room. Sister Bridget could hear them running through the trash in the hall.

"We won't hurt you, *mija*. We won't hurt Adriana. We are here to help." Sister Bridget looked from Josephina to Juana and then carefully approached Juana and gently took the bat from her.

"I hid her in the drawer," Juana said.

Josephina ran to a large bureau that was turned backward against the wall. She pulled at it, trying to move it forward.

"You mean she's behind there?" Mateo handed his light to Sister Bridget, and he and Esteban took hold of the heavy wooden bureau and slid it away from the wall. The bureau had no drawers. Sister Bridget shined the phone's light onto a small girl that lay curled up cradling her swollen, discolored, disfigured arm. She wasn't moving.

"The bastard broke her arm with the baseball bat. He was so drunk and high, he left the bat." Juana's stolid voice became angry. "I'm going to take his head off with it when he comes back." She took the bat from Sister Bridget.

The men shone their lights upon Adriana.

Sister Bridget knelt beside her. The girl was unconscious but still breathing. "It would be good to apply a splint, but time is running out. Let's strap her arm to her body and carry her out. Esteban, give me your jacket please."

Esteban took off his jacket. Sister Bridget placed Adriana's arm across her chest. In a way, she was glad the girl was unconscious; otherwise, the youngster wouldn't be able to withstand the pain. She secured the injured arm by wrapping the girl snugly in the jacket and tying the sleeves together. Mateo handed Sister Bridget his light and gathered Adriana up in his arms.

"Let's go, girls." Sister Bridget stashed Mateo's phone into the pocket of her jeans and hurried the girls out the door of the bedroom.

Before they got to the outer door, she heard a commotion in the hallway. Girls screaming and crying, an angry man cursing.

"He's coming back." Juana's voice trembled.

"He's got Leticia and Araceli," Josefina cried.

Sister Bridget took the bat from Juana. "Get behind me. Get with your friend. Esteban, Mateo, hide. Don't let El Gigante see your faces." The men mustn't be identified. Mateo, carrying Adriana, stood behind the wall in the kitchen. As did Esteban and Josephina. Juana refused to leave Sister Bridget's side.

El Gigante kicked the door open and dragged Leticia and Araceli in as if they were sacks of useless refuse instead of human beings. The giant man was a strange figure in the darkness. He must have slipped his flashlight into his shirt, for he glowed like a phantom. A massive, powerful phantom descended from a gigantic indigenous people that had once roamed the desert regions of Mexico and Texas. He held the girls by their arms, and they slumped to the floor whimpering and begging to be let free.

"Who the hell are you?" El Gigante towered over Sister Bridget. "How did you get in here?" He reeked of body odor, urine, and sour alcohol.

Devil, we meet. Sister Bridget stood, bat in hand, determined to hold her ground. Jesus gave his disciples power to cast out demons, and though she was certain that this man was evil incarnate, she was not confident she could cast it out. She felt emboldened by the Holy Spirit, though. "Alejandro, I know you had a difficult childhood. The horrible things that happened to you were not fair. Those abuses were not your fault, and it's not too late to turn your life around."

El Gigante threw the girls to the ground, smirked, and relished bringing his big boot down, crushing Araceli's leg. The girl screamed and sobbed. Leticia scrambled to her friend's side. The giant then turned to Sister Bridget, laughing, taking pleasure in his cruelty.

"I have come to get these girls. Give them to me without any trouble!" Sister Bridget imagined Jesus' disciples standing with her, shouting with her.

Like the photo Estevez had shown her, El Gigante embodied the DNA of the previous century's roaming Karankawa people, between six and seven feet tall. Though thick and bloated by debauchery, he exhibited the sculpted face, sharp cheekbones, and deeply ruddy skin tone of his ancestors.

Sister Bridget shouted, "God, forgive me," as she ran at him with the bat, swinging with all her strength. El Gigante laughed and drunkenly raised his hand to catch it. She heard the crunch of breaking bone as the bat hit the man's hand and made contact with his face. She then applied Estevez's stun gun to the man's chest. El Gigante dropped with a thud, convulsing. The walls of the apartment shook. Fearing that he would get back up, Sister Bridget closed her eyes and held the bat high. *Forgive me.* She brought it down mightily and struck the giant's chest.

"Let's go." Sister Bridget tossed the bat and stun gun to the floor. She stood behind to account for everyone. Mateo carried Adriana. Esteban picked up Araceli. They ran. The three girls followed. Juana spat on El Gigante and cursed him as she passed.

"Hurry, dear," Sister Bridget said to Juana, nudging her along. She brought up the rear and was almost out the door when her conscience tugged at her and forced her back to the giant. He was entitled to last rites no matter what, wasn't he?

The man's soul was questionable at best, but who was she to judge? She hadn't been there for his upbringing and the inhumane atrocities he must have lived through as a child. All people are precious to God, but something evil happened in this man's life. Something made him cold-blooded, heartless, and cruel.

She had no holy oil and technically only a priest could administer last rites, but nonetheless, she knelt alongside the man. His flashlight had fallen to the floor. She picked it up, shined the light onto his face, and gasped. His bloated, meaty face was covered in blood. His nose bent, crushed to one side. Sister Bridget closed her eyes, made the sign of the cross, and prayed, "Our Father who art in heaven, hallowed be thy name. Thy kingdom come. Thy will be d—"

"On Earth as in heaven!" El Gigante sputtered, spraying blood onto Sister Bridget's face. He sat up, groaning and cursing. *"Maldita! Puta!"* He took Sister Bridget by the neck and attempted to stand. Instead, he fell over onto his back still gripping her. She regretted what she had to do next, but when she felt swelling in her face and saw black spots before her eyes, she knew she needed to act before it was too late. She couldn't die there. She still needed to protect the girls. She gathered up strength in her legs and then with all her might, bashed her knee into El Gigante's genitals. She knelt there hard, pressing up off the floor with her hands. El Gigante bellowed, enraged. He let go of her neck and pushed her off him.

Dizzy, Sister Bridget rolled onto the floor, choking and faint. She scrambled about blindly for the stun gun, but it was nowhere to be found. By the light of the giant's fallen flashlight, she watched him rise and descend upon her. Cursing, he kicked the side of her body. The force of his boot lifted Sister Bridget from the floor and dropped her down again. The blow shocked her body. Her lungs seized; she was neither able to breathe in nor out. Desperate, she closed her eyes, and her soul cried out to God.

El Gigante wailed, animal-like. Then she heard a sickening thud. Sister Bridget opened her eyes and took a breath. There was Isabel with the stun gun and Juana with the baseball bat, both breathing hard, standing over El Gigante. Juana raised the bat high and struck him again and again. She grunted and screamed with each blow. Isabel tried to take ahold of Juana to stop her. Sister Bridget clambered to her feet. She clutched her side; sharp pain kept her stooped, unable to stand up straight. She staggered to Juana and grasped her from behind too.

Together, they all three lurched back and forth as Juana struggled to pull free and hit El Gigante more. She finally dropped the bat and sobbed in Isabel's arms.

Sister Bridget retrieved the flashlight. She shone the light on the big hulking mass that lay upon the floor. *All that is hidden in darkness shall be revealed in the light.*

Juana had struck with such force that the man's head now lay unnaturally, downward onto his shoulder. He was no longer a menace.

Sister Bridget habitually considered all people redeemable, but she couldn't muster up forgiveness for the monster. Not yet. And she couldn't help but think that the man's soul must be relieved to be set free of this world.

Chapter 25

Sister Bridget, Isabel, and Juana emerged from the *apartamentos* into a crisp, dry night. The mist had cleared, and the waxing moon shone upon dank colonial cobblestones. Clutching one another, they descended the steps onto the walkway. Sister Bridget stopped to get her bearings, holding up Juana who in turn clung to Isabel. At that moment, a cold breeze blew the rot, decay, and stench of sewage away from their faces. She resisted the urge to take a deep breath, though. Not there in that God forsaken place, not yet. She turned back to the doorway, making sure El Gigante hadn't straightened his neck and followed. No, the monster wouldn't be rising. Not in this lifetime. She was certain of that.

A taxi approached slowly, its headlights off.

Sister Bridget huddled Isabel and Juana back toward the gloom, hiding them. The taxi, a yellow van, slowed, its rear door sliding open even before it came to a stop.

"Let's go. Get in." It was Esteban, leaning out of the taxi, gesturing for them to hurry. Julio was driving. They piled in amongst the scared, weeping girls. Esteban climbed into the front passenger seat.

Juana clasped Isabel. "Thank you for coming back for me." She cried and held tight to her friend.

"I told you I would." Isabel cried into Juana's hair.

The two girls wept.

"Did you have your baby?" Juana's voice was thick and throaty. Isabel pulled back, looked Juana in the eye and nodded, her lips pressed tight, unable to speak.

"Is it good? Is the baby all right?"

Isabel nodded again with a smile this time, tears flowing. Juana smiled too. They laughed a little and embraced again.

"It's a girl." Isabel wept.

"Did you name her Gabriela?" Juana asked.

"Yes, Gabriela." Isabel held tight to Juana, not letting go.

Julio drove a block, stopped at the abandoned *plaza*, and threw something into the bonfire. Sparks flew and flames flared in the metal drum. Then he drove a few more blocks before turning on the taxi's headlights.

"Everybody, stay down!" Julio had to shout over Araceli's screaming and crying. The injured girl leaned against Leticia on the rear bench of the taxi, her leg likely broken judging by the force with which El Gigante had crushed it.

Sister Bridget clutched her side where El Gigante kicked her. She crouched on the floor of the taxi and winced. Mateo still held Adriana. "How is she?"

"The same." Mateo's voice was flat, catching in his throat. "She hasn't opened her eyes. She has a fever."

Sister Bridget felt the girl's head. She was burning up. "Poor child. She needs antibiotics and fluids. How long until we arrive at the hospital?"

"About twenty minutes," Julio said. "There's water behind the last bench." Sister Bridget clambered on her knees, painfully climbing past the girls, to get to the water. She passed out the bottles. "Try to drink a little, *mija*," she said to Araceli who whimpered in pain.

"Does anyone have a handkerchief?" Sister Bridget asked. Julio produced one from his pocket. Sister Bridget dampened it and placed it on Adriana's forehead. "Hold on, *mi amor*. It won't be long now." She smoothed the girl's cheek. She nodded at Mateo who took the water bottle and tended to the wet cloth.

Oh, but the ride seemed *so* long. Sister Bridget used the time to check on each of the girls. Araceli and Adriana would need attention first, but all the girls would need looking after. She remembered her young cousin so many years ago. To be sure, the girls would never be the same.

The taxi left the dead *barrio* behind and entered the city center where colonial light posts and bougainvillea lined the streets.

Julio slowed down and called ahead to Sister Terésa so she would be ready for the girls. The taxi pulled around to the dark service entry of the hospital where deliveries were made, where dumpsters were emptied.

Esteban jumped out and slid the back door open. Leticia and Josefina stepped off the taxi, weak and dirty, into Sister Terésa arms. She embraced each girl. "It's going to be all right. You're safe now." A female nurse in green scrubs spoke kind words too.

"Take them to exam room three," Sister Terésa told the nurse. "Let them stay together. It's bad enough, at least they won't be alone."

The nurse ushered the girls into the dark entry of the hospital, and up through a freight elevator to a locked, unused unit on the maternity floor.

Mateo carried Adriana and Sister Bridget followed, trying to stand up straight so her friend wouldn't know she had been injured. "Oh, my dear friend," Sister Bridget said to Sister Terésa.

"Was it terrible?" Sister Terésa asked as Mateo helped a male nurse place Adriana onto a wheeled stretcher.

"For the girls, yes. There is a dead body at the *Rio Parral Apartamentos*." Sister Bridget stood back to allow room for the medical staff.

"El Gigante?" Sister Terésa asked.

Sister Bridget nodded.

"We'll talk later. For now, I'll make an anonymous report to the authorities. Thank you, Bridget Ann.

"Take her to room five. Start I.V. fluids," Sister Terésa said to the nurse that pushed the stretcher on which Adriana lay.

"She'll need an x-ray," Sister Bridget said. "The man broke her arm."

Sister Terésa shook her head but didn't act surprised.

Next came Araceli. Esteban reached to the back bench of the taxi, carefully lifted the girl, and carried her to a second wheeled stretcher. The girl had quieted down, exhausted and in shock.

"Another broken bone." Sister Bridget was regretful that she hadn't been able to save Araceli before the monster crushed the girl's leg.

Isabel and Juana sat in the taxi, holding on to each other. Sister Terésa stood by, waiting. The girls said good-bye, and with a sob in her voice, Juana asked Isabel, "Can you call my *papá* and tell him to come get me?"

Isabel said she would. Sister Bridget hugged Juana, then Sister Terésa put her arm around the girl and walked with her into the hospital.

"Sir, may I borrow your phone, *por favor*." Mateo handed Isabel his phone, and she called Juana's father.

The three rescuers, Mateo, Esteban, and Julio, huddled together, whispering, and even laughing a little. Sister Bridget had to ask, "What's going on, my brothers?"

"I picked up the monster's *drogas* on my way out," Esteban said.

"Crystal meth," Mateo said.

"The fire." Sister Bridget thought back to when Julio had stopped the van and tossed a bundle into the bonfire. "I wondered what you had thrown into the barrel."

Esteban smiled and clapped Julio on the back. "Smart idea."

Sister Bridget felt so tired, but somewhere in the back of her mind, she thought she might tell Detective Estevez—someday. El Gigante's drugs did not make it to the U.S. market after all.

"Juana's *papá* is coming to get her." Isabel handed the phone back to Mateo. "He's going to take me home too."

"That's wonderful, *mija*. But I believe I saw with my own eyes that you got on the bus this morning. I thought you'd be home by now."

"When you left, I got off the bus and got the money back. Sorry. I just couldn't leave Juana behind. I went back to the Rarámuri. Bimón told me where El Gigante was. I left my baby with her while I went to find Juana. I couldn't leave Juana."

Sister Bridget hugged her tight. "I know you couldn't, *mija*."

"*Adios*, my new *amiga*." Esteban kissed Sister Bridget's cheek and bowed to Isabel. "I have work in the morning."

"Yes, don't we all." Mateo kissed Sister Bridget good-bye and patted Isabel's head. The two men walked into the darkness to their cars.

"You ladies need a lift?" Julio said.

"You go on, Julio." Sister Bridget knew Julio must have a family to go home to.

Only Sister Bridget and Isabel remained in the darkness, surrounded by the intense high-pitched drone of cicadas.

"Look." Isabel leaned her head back, scrutinizing the sky. She pointed. "See that? It looks like smoke across the sky?"

Sister Bridget was stunned by the dazzling display. Billions of flickering stars beckoned to her from a place so opposite her current locale. A place that resided within her own heart, really. She closed her eyes and prayed, *Praise Him, sun and moon! Praise Him, all you shining stars!* She tried to take that deep breath she had resisted earlier, but it was too painful to breathe deep.

"Sister Bridget? See? Right there." Isabel pointed again.

"Yes, *mija*, I see it, the milky trail across the sky."

"Do you know we can't really see the whole Milky Way because we are actually inside of it? To us, it just looks like a trail of smoke, but from way out there, like twenty thousand light-years away, it looks like a spiral."

"That's right. We can't see it because we're in it. It's very smart of you to point that out." She felt bone tired. And weary.

"Yeah, I learned it in school. Stuff like that, galaxies and solar systems and stuff. Someday Gabriela will learn too. I can't wait to teach her."

"Yes, *mija*." To Sister Bridget, nature's cycle continued. Hopefully, baby Gabriela will learn all this and more. It was good that Isabel contemplated the sky. The girl knew that there existed more than just her own harsh surroundings. She was in it, yet she saw it for what it was. She knew there existed a bigger picture. Isabel and her baby would be just fine.

"Sister Bridget? Sister Esperanza said there is a house for teenagers with babies in Mexico City. She said the house belongs to the Sisters of St. Paul, and maybe I can live there, and work and finish my school."

"Sister Esperanza is correct, *mija*. It's called *Casa de Luz*. They provide childcare, so the girls can work and go to school. Would you be interested in that?"

"I am interested, but I don't want to leave Juana. She's going to need me."

"Yes, she will need you probably all her life." Sister Bridget thought about her cousin and the starfish so many, many years ago. Juana was different though. Juana fought back.

Sister Bridget and Isabel settled onto a low wall and fell into a comfortable silence, embraced by the brisk night, and blanketed by the shimmering sky.

"You're a good mother and a good friend. You fought hard for your baby, and you never gave up on Juana. What you did tonight was very brave."

"I had to. I wouldn't get over it if Juana died. I

can't wait to show her my baby. Gabriela is so cute." Isabel's happiness was infectious. Sister Bridget felt a spark of joy too. She needed it at that moment.

Sister Esperanza pulled up in the old pickup, and Isabel got in. "Sister Bridget?" Isabel spoke through the truck's open window. "Don't think about El Gigante. I'm not going to." And they drove off.

Blessed Mother Mary, pray for Isabel. Pray for all the girls. Sometimes Sister Bridget feared that her own prayers alone were not enough.

She shook her head and sighed. So much violence, hate, and greed in this world. She felt a little depressed and demoralized, rare feelings for her to process. Though she had helped to rescue Juana and the other girls, they would all be scarred for the rest of their lives. She knew that, and tomorrow more girls would be abducted and victimized. But not by El Gigante.

Sister Bridget lifted her arms to the night sky. *I lift it all up to you, Lord.* And she entered the hospital.

The bright light of the corridor made her squint. She looked about, rubbing her temples, but there was no one in sight. The service entrance was deserted. On a metal pushcart sat her duffle bag and computer. Inside the duffle were all the articles of her habit as well as her passport and wallet. When she saw an airline ticket, she remembered—she must now *disappear*. That had been the plan, though now she need not fear retribution from El Gigante. Still, it was probably best to make herself scarce.

There was also a note with directions to the doctors' locker room and showers. It, too, was deserted. She stood motionless under the scalding shower for a few minutes, then cooled down the water and willed herself back to life.

She examined her side. It had already started to bruise. Luckily, El Gigante's boot had missed her rib cage. She didn't think she had a cracked rib. And she was neither dizzy nor nauseous, so it was unlikely she had a lacerated kidney or spleen. It certainly hurt though.

She got dressed and discarded her filthy clothing. She rubbed the grime off her shoes with wet paper towels.

Comforted by her habit and veil, her crucifix, and rosary beads, she began to feel like herself.

The freight elevator was locked, so she followed the signs up three floors to the maternity ward.

Pushing open the double doors, Sister Bridget was met by tinny, vehement screeches of newborn babies. The ward was bright and clean, smelling of baby powder, soap, and floor polish.

A nurse walked by with a stack of linens. "Hello, Sister. May I help you? Do you have permission to be here?"

Should she ask for Sister Terésa? She didn't know whom to trust. She looked to the nurses' station and recognized the male nurse that helped take the girls through the service entrance. He surreptitiously shook his head, no, and looked away.

"No, dear. I must have taken a wrong turn. Pardon me." She turned around and left through the double doors.

Now what? She'd helped rescue the girls. Isabel was on her way to her baby. Juana's father was on his way to her. The families of the other girls were being contacted. She supposed her part was done.

Once the girls were well enough to travel, they would go home with their families.

Mexico, such a beautiful homeland. So many seemingly insurmountable problems.

She rode a taxi to the airport as the sun teased the horizon. Hazy pink sunbeams pierced billowy, gray-edged clouds. And she contemplated Paul's letter to the Romans.

The night is far-gone, and the day is near.
Let's therefore throw off the works of darkness,
and let's put on the armor of Light.

Yes, Saint Paul, my comrade. Sister Bridget sat back and relaxed, comforted by fellowship. *Truly the only way to solve earthly problems is with weapons from heaven and the armor of Light.*